BRUMBACK LIBRARY

3 3045 00204 6338

D1289366

$19.95
813.0108   Anthology of short
ANT   stories by young
            Americans.

THE BRUMBACK LIBRARY
OF VAN WERT COUNTY
VAN WERT, OHIO

PRESENTED BY:

Victoria Dickman

ANTHOLOGY OF SHORT STORIES
BY
YOUNG AMERICANS®

2004 EDITION
VOLUME XXX

813.0108
ANT

Published by Anthology of Poetry, Inc.

©*Anthology of Short Stories by Young Americans*®
2004 Edition
Volume XXX

All Rights Reserved©

Printed in the United States of America

To submit short stories
for consideration in the year 2005 edition of the
Anthology of Poetry by Young Americans®,
send to: poetry@asheboro.com or

> Anthology of Poetry, Inc.
> PO Box 698
> Asheboro, NC 27204-0698

Authors responsible
for originality of poems submitted.

The Anthology of Poetry, Inc.
307 East Salisbury • P.O. Box 698
Asheboro, NC   27204-0698

Paperback ISBN: 1-883931-48-7
Hardback ISBN: 1-883931-47-9

Anthology of Poetry by Young Americans®
is a registered trademark of
Anthology of Poetry, Inc.

"We the people…"

From the moment those three words were penned in ink, on the most important document in the history of the world, the unique experience of what it means to be an American began. Those three words opened the door of hope to a world mired in oppression and tyranny, giving the opportunity of freedom to both domestic and foreign people. The remainder of the document that followed, has been defined by us, the people, as much as it has defined us.

Without question, the freedom of expression is the first of our freedoms that we employ. From an early age we begin to present ourselves to the world, to our families, to our young friends. The Constitution of the United States of America guarantees us the right to free speech via public speaking, artistic theatrical endeavors, the far-reaching and proven influential airwaves, and of course, the mighty written word.

In the pages that follow, stories are told, the freedom of expression unfolds itself before us in the form of the mighty written word. Our eyes will take it in, our brains and our imaginations will work in unison to assemble the written words into the inevitable pictures, and our ears will create voices and soundtracks necessary to move the stories along. And at last, each of the stories will culminate in a wave of rhythms and meaning, and the small warmth of satisfaction will sweep us in as we are woven together in story and we smile, quietly thank the author for sitting down and sharing with us the great freedom of expression.

"We the people…" dovetails our lives together. Though we are rugged individualists, we stand shoulder to shoulder as Americans. Together. Concertedly. Collectively. With our sights set on the future, and our minds and hearts wide open let us move forward in this unique experience that is known as the *Anthology of Short Stories by Young Americans*. Enjoy the stories as we have. These young Americans have impressed us once again in 2004.

The Editors

THE MYSTERY OF THE MISSING MATH BOOK

It all started with a girl in the fourth grade. Her name is Lindsey Dinkelacker.

Lindsey was in math class and she was getting out a piece of loose-leaf. She got out the piece of paper. When she was done, she realized that her math book was missing. She asked Madeline if she had seen it.

She said, "No."

So Lindsey looked in her book bag, to make sure she didn't put it back in, and she didn't. She looked around and she found a note and it said:

> Dear Lindsey,
>   "I have your math book."
>   "Do not tell the teacher."
> Sincerely,
> ?

Lindsey wondered who wrote the note.

As she looked around the room, the teacher asked, "Lindsey, what are you doing?"

Lindsey had no idea what to say. She asked Taylor Reilly what to do.

Taylor said, "Just say..."

Before Taylor could finish the teacher asked, "What is going on?"

Then Taylor finished, she said, "Nothing."

It was time to go home and Lindsey told her mom about the math book.

Lindsey went to her room, and there was another note on her bed. It said:

> Dear Lindsey,
>   "I'm in your math class."
> Sincerely,
> ?

Lindsey still had no idea who wrote the notes.

The next day at school Lizzie Miller said, "Here I found your math book."

Lindsey asked, "Where at?"

Lizzie answered, "I've had it since yesterday. I thought it was mine."

"Then, did you write the notes?" asked Lindsey.

Lizzie said, "No."

What had really happened was Madeline and Taylor knew about Lizzie having your book, Madeline wrote the notes to trick you. Lizzie really didn't take the book on purpose, but Madeline and Taylor were just having fun!

Sarah Shappelle
Age: 10

A WONDERFUL DAY

I could have sworn my arm was turning purple. From here, the front of the classroom seemed miles off. I didn't stand a chance reading anything on the chalkboard from here. So, here I sat, drawing inane pictures on my arm. I think my arm is purple. That's... great. Actually, my entire day was great. I wake up this morning and my frog is dead in the frog tank.

My dad's explanation: "It was the crickets. I knew they would get him someday."

My dad was always the weird type. He's about six feet and two inches, graying hair and a boisterous outlook. He always looked up in bad times, including when a screw came loose on a valve where he worked, and it screeched like a bullet through two doors and three inches of cement. See, my dad's a valve engineer, and I can't complain. It's not like he refers to valves in everyday life. Often. Anyways, my frog was eaten by crickets, and I get out of the house just in time to see the school bus drive by my street.

So, what do I do? I go inside to call my dad at work. I explain the situation, and he overreacts just a little bit. Says he going to make me go back to my old school. This is actually a really big threat, considering going back to my old school would be like going back to work in a coal mine right after you sneak past all the guards and reach the light of day. My old school was divided by popularity, wealth, and power. There was the upper class, the class that no one has anything against and cannot make fun of. Then, there's the other half. They consist of misfits, freaks and the runts. Among them was me. I couldn't stand up to the other kids. They had all the graces, they had all the jokes, they practically owned the school. We stood for the subject of jokes, hatred-infested jokes that made everyone on their side seem bigger and better than everyone else. Then, I moved here. Everything changed, and I was finally known not as the kid who was so weird and clumsy through grade school, but as a new kid who tried his best not to make too many people mad at him at one time.

Good title, I know. Anyways, I hang up the phone and go to the window to wait for my dad. After a half-hour, I decide he's not coming here too fast. I walk over to the TV, and trip over a pillow. I pick it up, put it on the couch, and trip over my cat. I just stay on the ground, knowing if I get back up, I'll just hit something else and trip.

I slowly get to my feet just as the doorbell rings and I trip over my shoelaces going to the door. It's my dad, angry face and all. I walk out in the rain to speed along the highway. It's only a few blocks away, until there's a roadblock cutting off the only fast way to school. So, I have to go the long way, along the highway and into another state and back to our state and there we are. Two hours late for school. And so here I am, in math class writing nonsense from one of my favorite songs on my arm and having a good time. Finally, the bell rings, and I write my homework on my arm along with several indistinguishable signs from songs, bands or from the back of my head. There are tons of things there. Now I have to walk ALL the way up to lunch from the third floor. It's on the most inconvenient fifth floor. Do you know why? Because this day bites. I'm going home. On my way to the cafeteria, I turn directly around and head back down the fifth staircase.

I turn the corner to my right, and go down the staircase to the third floor. I keep turning right until I'm at the second floor, and turn a left. Finally, I thought. A change. I walk calmly down the hallway to the side exit. Most people would call it an entrance, but it's only an entrance when you're looking from the outside. I open the door casually and dash outside. I hit a security officer.

"What do you think YOU'RE doing down here?!" he yelled at me as soon as he got up from the ground. I searched my mind for escapes. I only thought of one.

"Hehe, I thought today was an out day from school?" I mumbled to him. I was looking at my extremely dirty airwalks the whole time.

"Well, they announced it over the intercom. For thinking I'm an idiot, you have detention tomorrow!" he yelled at me still.

"Why? I really didn't know..." I shot, but quickly drifted off before he started again.

"Because I think you're just doing this to go do drugs with your other dropout friends in an alley because you have long hair! Ahaha!"

Despite the fact that I have long hair and have friends that are dropouts doesn't mean I smoke pot! Really! I thought this over while Mr. Security Guard walked off, muttering under his breath about dropouts and druggies. I walked back up the depressingly tall staircase from the second floor to lunch, just as the bell rang for French. I was beginning to get angry. This whole day has been blowing chunks at me since I got up this morning. Looks like just one more great day. As I reach the fourth floor, I round the staircase to go up to see a new face. She was going down the stairs with a big lunch on a tray, when... SPLAT! Everything went everywhere, the corn was on the marble floor, the pear was rolling down the stairs and the pizza was on her head. She didn't seem too pleased with her day really. I looked down and pitied her, so I decided to get on my knees and help her out. I picked up the pear at the bottom of the stairs and walked it up to her. She thanked me, and continued walking down the stairs.

I call to her, "You're not allowed outside today, it's an 'in' day!"

Immediately she wheeled around and walked back up the stairs. I walked by her and asked her name. She didn't answer at first. I could relate. Where I'm from, someone asking that would be a little too suspicious and would probably be playing a trick. She stopped walking suddenly and it caught me by surprise, and I turned back. She decided to tell me her name.

"Angela..." she said softly and with growing unassurance. I held out my hand and shook hers. I told her my name and we continued walking around the school during seventh bell. I guess French 1 could wait for someone who had just as bad a day as me. We walked over the smooth but dull tile floor for about a half an hour now. Every once in a while one of us would slip and we would laugh at each other. Always looking out for security guards, of course.

Finally, the bell rang and we walked to our classrooms. I walked her to her classroom, that is. I don't know what it is about her. She is about up to my shoulder in height, probably five feet two inches. Long, blonde hair and green eyes. Nothing particularly special, but I felt something. I just wished I would have another day like this tomorrow.

Kevin Andrew Behm
Age: 13

3

Daddy's Ghost

On a cool and foggy morning, Sarah got dropped off at her piano lesson. Sarah always had piano lessons on Saturdays instead of sleeping in, since it was the weekend and all. Her mom always dropped her off at the instructor's house while her dad went to work for a couple of hours. Then, after her lesson was over, her dad would come straight from work to pick her up, but this day was going to be a day that she would never forget, maybe.

She had her lesson from eight in the morning to noon. That is exactly what happened. Then, after her lesson was over, she sat outside on the instructor's porch and waited for her dad. For some reason, today her dad was pretty late, but she couldn't go inside because there was another lesson going on that she didn't want to interrupt.

When Sarah's dad finally picked her up, he pulled up in his Jaguar, but today something was really wrong. Her father's Jaguar was demolished, and her dad looked exceptionally insipid.

"Dad, what happened?" Sarah asked with a tear in her eye worried that her dad might be hurt.

"Oh, I just got into a little accident, no big deal," her dad said with kind of a blank stare in his eyes.

"Was there anyone hurt, are YOU hurt?" Sarah asked her dad, because he looked a little shaken up.

"No, the other car just drove away," Sarah's dad stated with the same blank stare in his eyes.

As Sarah and her dad were driving down the road, one very similar to Five Mile, Sarah noticed a lot of police cars and fire trucks, along with life squads. Trying to avoid the sight of the accident, Sarah's dad got into the other lane, but Sarah could still see.

"Oh look, that looks just like your car, Dad," Sarah said with some kind of questioning to her voice.

"Well, it's not, so let's just keep it at that!" her dad exclaimed back at her with strong conviction.

Sarah was right; it did look like her dad's car, a lot like it. As a matter of fact, it WAS her dad's car. She didn't know it at first, but there was something weird about seeing the exact same car, and with the way her dad reacted, she knew something had to have gone wrong somewhere.

As the car pulled up to Sarah's house, her dad pulled up in front of the door and told Sarah that he would come inside in a few minutes. Along with that, her dad told her that he loved her, which Sarah thought was kind of strange. Then Sarah got out of the car and went inside. When she got inside her mom ran up to her crying.

"How did you get home?" her mom asked in a panic, "I called Mrs. Gonzalez, and she said that you had already been picked up!"

"Yeah, Mom, Dad brought me home, just like always," Sarah told her mom with reassurance, "why?"

"Honey, that's impossible, because your father died on the way to coming and picking you up. He got in a horrible auto accident!" Sarah's mom exclaimed with tears in her eyes.

"Mom, what happened, because I know Dad picked me up; I just know it was him!" Sarah now cried, with tears rolling down her face.

"Oh honey, it will be okay, I promise," Sarah's mom now really confused giving her daughter comfort.

Sarah, not knowing what was really going on, but knowing that her dad had both died and picked her up all at the same time, ran outside to prove to herself that her dad's car was still in the driveway. When she ran outside, all she saw was her mom's car sitting in the driveway, and her dad or his car was nowhere to be seen. That was when Sarah got really scared and started to scream.

As she was letting out the loudest scream in her life, Sarah woke up finding herself in her own bed. She was scared and in a cold sweat. She walked into her mom and dad's room and saw her dad lying next to her mother, sleeping soundly. Sarah walked over to him and gave him a kiss on his cheek and told him that she loved him, because tomorrow was Saturday.
80831704

Matthew Steuer
Age: 17

7:36 a.m.

Drats! Forgot to set my alarm clock again. Oh well, nothing I can do about it now. I sit up in bed and gaze at the beams of sunlight flowing through the slats of my venetian blinds. I sigh, wishing I could lie back down and let the sunlight pour over my overworked body all day. But there is no time to do that, much less to even think about it. I live in the heart of the hustle and bustle of New York City. I have to get up and face the nonstop honking of cars, shouting of stock brokers and ringing telephones. I heave my tired self out of bed and shuffle across my vibrant oriental rug out to the kitchen. Lucille, my maid, is already there, making me my daily breakfast of buttered toast. In my opinion, buttered toast is not a proper breakfast for New York City's finest twenty-four-year-old defense lawyer. Well, I'm not quite a lawyer, just an intern studying to become one. I still have to deal with the violent court cases of this city's finest fugitives almost every day. I choke down my starchy breakfast and head to my room to get dressed. I already laid out my brand-new Armani suit and diamond earrings my boyfriend bought me last week. After dressing myself and running a brush through my frazzled brown hair, I grab my Gucci purse and the keys to my BMW. Lucille greets me at the front door and hands me my go-cup of French vanilla coffee. She waves good-bye as I walk down the sidewalk and into my car. I just don't know what I'd do without Lucille. I would have to do all of my laundry myself, dust the shelves, vacuum my multiple rugs and even clean up after my cat, Arturo. I shudder at the idea of scooping out his droppings myself. Ewww... thank goodness I have Lucille.

10:42 a.m.

After two hours of stop-and-go traffic, I am finally at my office. One would think that if it takes me two hours to reach my office, I must live miles and miles away. I don't. The law offices are only about five miles away. It would probably be faster if I were to walk, but then I would constantly be bombarded with hot dog and sauerkraut vendors, toothless people begging for money, and the homeless and skinny kittens that roam around. That truly is ashame. The poor animals don't have a place to live. That's why I donate much of my money to the New York City Humane Society. I drive my car into the parking garage and approach the escalators. One reaches my floor and the doors open to reveal an unshaven man in grubby clothing. I have definitely seen this man before. Our paths always seem to cross. At first I thought it was just coincidence he was always where I was at the same time, but then I realized he had to be planning our meetings. He never says anything to me, just gives me a harsh glare and some sort of a deep growl. After a few weeks of us meeting like this, I finally began to realize who he was. His name is Fredrick Wilson and he was accused of murdering some innocent woman and was taken to court. The woman's husband pressed charges and claimed that he was some sort of a mass murderer and should be locked in jail. The woman's husband hired a lawyer, Alexander Bellemini. Mr. Bellemini is also my employer. I follow him around to all of his court cases and he sometimes even lets me help out and say a few things. Somehow or another, Mr. Wilson won his court case against the widowed man and Alex. This was quite a shock, as Bellemini is one of the best lawyers in this city. Deep down in my heart I believe that Mr. Wilson did murder that poor old woman, but I have no way of proving it. There was no evidence left at the scene of the crime that led anyone to believe that Fredrick Wilson was guilty. I find that hard to believe, because of the multiple rings he wears on his right hand. It must be hard to keep them all on there at the same time. His whole body is like a grimy sponge, but his right hand always glitters like a million bucks. And from the looks of those rings he got ahold of, his right hand probably is worth a million dollars. After that court date, Fredrick never has been very fond of me, because I let on the fact that I thought he was guilty of the murder, no matter what he said. Every time we have met, he gives me that same evil stare and stiffens his upper lip, like a Rottweiler preparing to pounce on its next victim.

2:45 p.m.

Ahhh... It feels great to be back in my car. The day at the office was totally dreadful. Mr. Bellemini caught the flu and was unable to come in today. I pretty much just sat around and listened to the normal jibber-jabber of the office. I am now on my way home, anticipating the smell of the apple pie that Lucille always makes me every day after work. I round the bend of my street and immediately slam on the brakes. I hardly missed hitting a man! Grr... I hate people that don't look both ways before they cross the street. The man runs past me in a hurry, not even notifying me that he is okay. I apply pressure to the gas once more and pull into the garage. I step out of the car and I suddenly realize who that man was. Fredrick Wilson! What could he have been doing in this area of town? Oh well, it's probably not something I should fret over. I drive my car into the garage and step out. I wait a few moments before approaching the door of the house. I wonder if Lucille heard the garage door open. She usually comes out to greet me and take my coat. Maybe she is resting. I shall go in and check. The creak of the door as I open it is about loud enough to wake the dead. Surely she is awake now. I go up the stairs and check in the living room. No such luck. I walk back to her bathroom, maybe she is in the shower. Nope. I check her room. There is Lucille, laying face-down on the ground with a knife sunk deep into her back. There is dark blood splattered everywhere. I back out of the room, not quite believing what I am seeing. Oh, my goodness! Who could have done this to poor Lucille? She was nice to everyone. She is about the last person on the planet that would have a single enemy. A horrible thought crashes through my mind. What if it wasn't an enemy of Lucille's? What if it was one of my enemies? It could possibly be Fredrick Wilson. It very well could have been Mr. Wilson, but I have no way of proving that... unless... I go back into the room where poor Lucille lies dead and I check the floor for any evidence. I have no such luck. I turn to head out the door and call the police, but something catches my eye. A brilliant flash of gold and ruby peeks out from under her bed. I crouch to find out what it is. I pull out a beautiful ring... one that I do not own. This ring is much too small for my slender fingers, but I do know someone whose finger it may fit. I pick up the telephone to call the police. Fredrick Wilson, I'll get you this time.

Tracey Mulroney
Age: 15

Once upon a time in a land far away which goes by the name of Kog there lived a group of Shrodes. These Shrodes were odd-looking creatures with pudgy little noses, fur on their face, and scales on their feet. But odd as they may look, they were the kindest-hearted people you can come by.

There was a specific young fellow by the name of Moses McGee. He was a short boy that was very adventurous. He and his friends liked to act like they were great and powerful kings that roamed the land and saved all the people from the dark lords.

One day Moses and his friends wandered far from home, too far to be exact, and ran into a great wizard. He told them that evil was now about them and was coming quickly. He told them they were chosen to fight against it. He also told them they needed to go to the land of Ontario and find the crystal ball, when they all touched it, it would give them great powers.

The wizard soon left and they rested for the night and decided they would head north in the morning.

When Moses awoke he noticed his friends were gone. He hunted for them but they did not come. He continued his search for hours but still no sign. After a while he thought of what the wizard said and began his journey to Ontario to find the crystal ball.

He journeyed through wind and rain, sleet and snow, and finally came to a town where he decided to rest. This was the town of Chicago. He found himself quite relaxed here and enjoyed it well.

After about three days he met a stern-looking man by the name of Childress. Childress knew much of the crystal ball and of the dark lords. He wanted to go with Moses on his journey to save his friends and reach the ball.

After much discussing and thinking Moses made his choice to bring Childress along to help him in his journey. Childress had a great horse and carried both him and Moses. This made the journey much quicker.

They decided to stop at Mount Boa for the night, it was only fifty miles from south of Ontario. Childress started a good fire while Moses made and set out the beds. After they ate and talked awhile they went to bed. In the middle of the night Moses awoke suddenly to a crackling he did not know of. He quietly awoke Childress.

Childress drew his sword ready for battle, as well did Moses. Out of the corner came a black object heading for Moses. Childress jumped in front of him and swung his sword at the monster. It stepped back and became very cautious. This time he threw a blade. It pierced Moses, and he let out a loud screech. Childress ran to his side making sure he was OK. Then charged after the demon again. Moses could see that Childress was giving it his all, trying to destroy it. Finally he stabbed it right in the heart. It let out a cry and vanished into nothing.

Childress hurried back to Moses unharmed. He wrapped the wound and told him they need to hurry to Ontario were the Sweeds could heal him.

They traveled all night and day until finally they reached Ontario. Moses was terribly bad and couldn't remember anything.

He lay in his bed for nearly two weeks with Childress by his side the whole time. When finally he awoke.

He looked up at Childress and asked where he was at. Childress told him that they were in Ontario. Moses leaned up very fast and told him to help him up so they could go get the crystal ball. Childress sadly looked at him and replied that it was not there, it had been taken somewhere that could not be named. He also told him that when he fully recovered they were going to go find it so they could defeat the dark lords.

Moses could not believe what he was hearing. He lay back down in bed and suddenly started crying.

Childress asked what was wrong but he already knew the answer. Moses was scared that he wouldn't find his friends and sad because he did not know where the crystal ball was.

After a few days Moses and Childress began their journey again thanking and saying good-bye to their friends. They had a plan to travel through Toronto, next Canada, then across Lake Erie, and finally Ohio.

When they reached Toronto they decided to eat and have a little rest. They stopped at the VC Pub. The waiter came around and asked what they wanted to eat. After they left, they both came suspicious. They noticed the waiter had a slight evil grin on his face.

Finally he came back with their food. Childress asked the man a few questions. The waiter became very cautious of what questions he answered. He started to leave when suddenly Childress got up and drew his weapon. The waiter turned and also drew his weapon. Childress struck first and cut the man's (or thing's) arm.

The man came back with a good blow to Childress' head. But Childress shoved his knife deep in the man, and he vanished just like the one at Mount Boa.

Childress told Moses they needed to leave immediately because this place was not safe.

They hurried out of there and headed for Canada, with still no sign of the crystal ball. They traveled all through Canada but still no sign.

They finally reached Lake Erie and boated across into Ohio. They looked everywhere in Cleveland but still nothing. Onward they went for about three or four more hours when they reached a small town called Russia. They quietly snuck into town so no one would see or hear them (like anyone would, everyone was partying on about some state champs thing). They were entering a wealthy part of town when suddenly Moses saw a shining something on top of the second house to the left. He hurried up the side of the house when he saw a young boy inside. This boy was about the age of fourteen, five foot three inches, brownish-blonde hair and thin. He now took it a little slower. He reached the top and took the crystal ball and ran down to Childress. The boy heard him and scrambled outside.

He yelled to Moses to come back and give him his ball. Moses stopped, turned around, threw him one shoelace and yelled, "GOTTA GO!" and they disappeared into the night.

Childress and Moses got the powers and found Moses' friends. They stopped the dark lords and everything was OK.

Andrew Cloud
Age: 14

9

MAT CONFESSIONS

"Philpot you slacker, practicing like that will never get you to state!"

Wrestling practice was coming to an end and I was exhausted. Unfortunately, with Coach Allen, the conclusion of practice is the most intense. As I sprinted circles around the mat, I reflected my accomplishments throughout the season. I had won every tournament, and was ranked first in the city. I was definitely a contender for the State Championship. Now, the fifth of February, the state wrestling tournament was only three weeks away. I realized I only had twenty-one days to prepare for Mike Shoot, a kid from Cleveland. Shoot and I were most probably going to see each other at state.

"Bring it in," Coach Allen shouted. "Before you guys hit the showers, does anyone want to challenge the varsity wrestler for his slot on the roster?"

Jason Whalen volunteered; he is one year older than I, but I'm stronger and faster. The assistant coaches consulted the rest of the team as Jason and I stepped to the line. The whistle shrieked and we started at each other. Right off the bat I hit a fireman's carry and put Whalen on his back. He fought for a brief couple of seconds before the coach slammed his hand on the mat declaring a victory by pin. When we got to our feet, I attempted to shake Whalen's hand; he declined and stumbled off the mat cussing me out under his breath. Coach raised my arm into the air, and the team applauded my success.

While I was getting dressed, Aaron Hay, our one-hundred-and-thirty-five-pound wrestler asked me if I wanted to grab a bite to eat. I accepted his invitation, and we headed to a restaurant.

"Can I get you boys something to drink?"

Our reply was identical, "Water."

When the waitress returned, we ordered the salad bar, since each of us has to keep our weight down.

Aaron and I discussed Whalen's bitterness towards me after I defeated him earlier today.

"He's just angry because he lost his shot at state to a freshman," Aaron said.

"I concur," I replied.

After a long conversation and the waitress' rejection of Aaron's date proposal, we went our separate ways. Reason being, we each parked in separate lots.

As I was coming upon my truck, a dark, shadowy figure was rapidly approaching me. As it got closer, I recognized the figure; it was Jason Whalen. He attacked me at full sprint, knocking me to the ground before I had a chance to defend myself. He then smashed my knee with a baseball bat several times, before scampering off into the darkness. I crawled over to my truck and climbed in. I started it, and drove to the nearest hospital. When I got to the parking lot, I passed out on the account of the intense pain. Paramedics quickly rushed me inside.

"Well, there's good news and bad news; which do you want to hear first?"

"Good, I guess," I replied.

"The good news is nothing's broken; the bad news is you won't be able to wrestle."

Once I heard nothing was broken, I immediately tried to get out of bed. Revenge never entered my mind, all I could think about was wrestling in the state tournament. However, the pain was so awful, I collapsed back into my bed.

"A nurse will be back to check on you in a bit," said the doctor.

I was awoken during my nap by the wrestling team, who decided to visit. They reassured me that Whalen was kicked off the team, expelled from school, and will be facing legal charges. They eventually left, as my family arrived. My parents stayed the night with me. The next morning, the doctor said I was free to go home. I rolled myself out the door in my temporary wheelchair, which I would be using until I was able to use crutches.

The next day, I went to practice, to watch the freshman that was under me. He looked decent, but I knew he was no match for Shoot. The district tournament was that weekend, and the kid didn't even place; therefore, he didn't make it to the state tournament. Shoot ended up winning the state championship with ease. It didn't bother me though. I knew in my heart I could have defeated him, and that's all that matters to me. Also, I discovered a passion I have for coaching. During practice, I limped around the mat, trying to inspire the other wrestlers to do something great. I know when they saw me and what I could have been, they worked three times harder because they wanted to do it for me. A couple of our guys went to state, and I sat beside the coaches, dishing out moves for them to try.

By the time the banquet came around, I was perfectly healthy. On the way there, the radio announced that Jason Whalen would be tried as an adult and would be facing jail time for assault. I was glad that justice was served. When I entered the room, the team welcomed me, and I took a seat by my friends. The coach talked about every wrestler, and how bright their future looks and more. He saved me for last. He talked about my incredible success throughout the season. Then he mentioned something that had never even crossed my mind. There's always next year. I thought to myself, next year I'm going to be a champion, and no one is going tostop me.

Zach Philpot

11

MY GREEDY FATHER!

OK, this is what I remember; the sweet beanie smell of coffee in the morning, my dad's tart, yet soothing cologne and money?

Yep, that's right money! That is all my dad really cared about, money! I remember that morning like the back of my hand. The day my life was over and the beginning of a tragedy my family would have to cope with until their dying day comes. You may be wondering what is going on here, but you will find out soon enough.

OK, so here I was walking home from the grocery store. It was wet, mucky, and muddy. I had my new Justin Timberlake autographed, all white tennis shoes, my dad had gotten me for Memorial Day. We always gave gifts on holidays, no matter what the occasion. Well, anyway, I had the brown, prickly bag in my hands filled with an assortment of sweets and sugary candies. I kept hearing soft pattering footsteps behind me. They kept getting closer and faintly louder. Every once in a while I glanced over my shoulder not knowing what was going to happen to me.

I finally, got to the ol' homestead and dropped off the package of treats my mother had sent me to get. Looking up at the large structured building I realized something, my family is pretty rich and maybe that was a stalker trying to stalk me to get my very own pair of soles on my feet. Then I thought, nah no one would want to follow me, my dad is too rich and with the high security out front no one will ever break in. I WAS WRONG. That man, my enemy, my killer, my worst nightmare did get in and I was about to die.

I walked into my dad's study dropping off the Hostess Cupcake he wanted me to get him. Then all at once I heard my mother screaming. The words I have never forgotten, the last words I would ever hear her say,

"LOOK OUT BEHIND YOU A MAN, AN UGLY MAN DRESSED IN BLACK WITH A GUN GET MARIE OUT OF HERE NOW!"

I cringe every time I think of those words. The last words my mother spoke directly to me, the thought that my mother was trying to save my life, but being way too late.

The next thing I knew the money my dad had sitting on his big, round cherry wood desk was gone along with my dad.

"Marie, get out of there now and follow me into the safety den!" My father kept screaming as loud as he possibly could.

All at once I was gone. It was too late; the only thing in my eye's vision were big giant Pearly Gates and a line. I was standing in a long extensive line that seemed to keep going on for miles at a time. In this long line there were ghastly like souls and ghostly type creatures. The man would ask for your name and then tell you which gates to pass through once you entered the main gates.

Finally, after an hour seemed to pass I got up to the ghastly man. He asked me for my name, Marie Honchbuk, then told me to pass through the main part and enter through "Gate Number Four." I passed through the main gate and WOW. The streets were paved with gold; the place was packed with these extremely kind, people. That is when I realized that man, that horrible man was my killer. On a TV screen in the window of the shop they showed the murders of my area, I was in that horrible scene. My father was yelling, my mother started screaming, and there I was panicking! That man that I was for sure committed the crime really did pull the trigger and I was in HEAVEN!

I walked deeper into mystical land and found a "cloud guard" in front of an apartment building. He was snoozing, so I decided to wake him and ask where I might find a place to stay.

After about five or six shakes he finally acknowledged me and so I proceeded with my question.

His answer was exactly what I wanted to hear. He said that I could stay in the apartment structure he guarded, until I was personally invited to a condo or house. My new room number was thirty-three. Which meant I was on the third-floor, third room down.

I entered through the sliding doors, continued up the elevator and walked hastily to my room. When I opened the door a very fresh smell entered my nose. The aroma was heavenly. I sat down in the snow-white chair by the telephone and looked around at the all-white room. The phone rang and it was him, the big man, "GOD."

He told me to come and see Him immediately. I busted through the door and briskly traveled to the main cloud. It was gigantic. Everything was fluffy and soft. It reminded me of the cotton candy I used to devour when I was living, and could go to the local festival. I entered through the next set of gates to find Him sitting in a comfortable chair. He introduced Himself to me and told me to turn my picture tube on to watch for the trial.

Three months after the most important man, in my eyes talked to me, my killer's final verdict appeared. It was shown on the high-definition flat-screen located in front of my chair in my apartment room.

The evidence clearly presented, showed without reasonable doubt, that he was guilty. My parents won the case. The criminal was not only convicted in my case, but in three other murder trials. He was sentenced to the electric chair. I sluggishly picked up my controller to the television and turned it off. I was happy that the man could not continue with any more murders, but the feeling that he was going to die overwhelmed me. The criminal dressed in black, which pulled the trigger on the .357, was my...

Marci Holloway
Age: 12

THE MYSTERIOUS MISHAP

"She found another mysterious note on the floor by the girls' bathroom. Written in lipstick it said: 'Beware, I'm warning you, beware.' She gasped as she read," Lucy Shalding read aloud to her two best friends, Nancy and Netta Templeton, sisters.

"Wow," Nancy gasped.

"Mysterious," Netta said as she smiled mischievously.

Lucy, Netta and Nancy were reading a NANCY DREW book, which was written by Carolyn Keene and the girls loved them.

Just then, a shrill whistle sounded that the girls noticed as the recess bell. They jumped down from their perch on the monkey bars as Netta yelled, "Last one lined up is a rotten egg."

Nancy and Lucy looked at each other and laughed while Netta started running.

***

"Okay, class you will be writing short Christmas stories, which I will explain thoroughly tomorrow," said the teacher.

Cool, thought Lucy, and then something hit her foot. She looked down and saw a folded up piece of notepaper, and realized it was a note. She grabbed it as fast as she could.

> Hey, Lucy,
>   This sounds so cool; maybe you could come over after school and Nancy and
>   I could brainstorm with you. How 'bout it?
>   Netta

Lucy wrote a quick "sure" on the paper, wadded it back up and dropped it on the ground. Then she kicked it to Andrew and he kicked it back to Netta.

"Okay, class, now we will have free reading time."

Yes! thought Nancy, as Netta, Lucy and her all smiled at each other and brought out their NANCY DREW books.

***

"I really can't wait to start writing these Christmas stories," said Nancy as the three girls were walking home.

"We could even write about snow," said Netta.

"I know, I wish it wasn't too warm in Florida to snow, it's nothing like winter in Ohio," replied Lucy who used to live in Ohio.

***

"Mom!!!" Netta yelled as they walked inside the Templeton's house. "We brought Lucy home to play, can she call her mom?"

"Hello, girls, hi Lucy. Yes, Lucy may call her mother," Netta and Nancy's mother said calmly from the kitchen.

"Thank you, Mrs. Templeton, when should she pick me up?" asked Lucy.

"Ehh, I'd say around 5:00, since she doesn't get out of work 'til 4:00 and it's already 3:00," replied Mrs. Templeton.

While Lucy was calling her mother, Rick, Nancy and Netta's older brother who was four years older and sixteen, came downstairs and started for the television.

"Hey, Lucy," he said good-sportedly to Lucy. They knew each other pretty well.

"Hey, Rick," Lucy replied nicely to Rick, while on hold with her mom.

After Lucy had called and talked to her mom, they started brainstorming ideas, in Netta and Nancy's shared bedroom. They each came up with ideas they liked the most. So they each dug through their book bags to get their NANCY DREW books, but when Lucy went to look in her bag for her book she didn't find it, couldn't find it! It's not there, she thought, then looked again, still not there! She ran upstairs to Nancy and Netta.

"I can't find it!" exclaimed Lucy.

"Can't find what?" said Nancy calmly, tilting her head to one side.

"Her book," replied Netta.

Lucy was speechless and bewildered, so she just shook her head.

"Could you have left it at --"

"School?" Netta interrupted Nancy and asked abruptly.

"Sure, I guess. I didn't think about it. Although I thought I left it on my desk when I loaded my book bag," Lucy finished, out of breath.

"Could someone have taken it?" questioned Nancy.

"You mean like stolen it?" asked Netta, getting interested.

"That could have happened, because when I was packing my book bag my back was towards the book," Lucy said, more to herself than to Nancy and Netta.

"Now all we have to do is find out who stole it," said Nancy.

"A real mystery, one like Nancy Drew solves. We could even act like real detectives," gushed Netta.

***

"I just wish I could find it," moaned Lucy, into the phone.

"Well did you tell your mom about this fiasco?" Nancy asked.

"Yeah, she said she'll bring me in early tomorrow morning, to look for it," replied Lucy.

"If you don't find it then we could solve a mystery, just like Nancy Drew!" Netta exclaimed excitedly.

"Yeah that would be cool," said Lucy, "but I was at an exciting part and I'd like to get my book back," continued Lucy somberly.

"Thanks for dropping me off. Bye, love you," said Lucy as she jumped out of the car when they arrived at the school.

"You're welcome honey, love you too!" Lucy's mother replied as she drove away.

Here goes, thought Lucy as she walked up to the school and stepped inside. She quietly walked upstairs to her teacher, Miss Camik's room. "Miss Camik," said Lucy. "Miss Camik, hi, it's Lucy and I was wondering if I could look around the room for a book I lost?"

"Oh, sure. Feel free to peek around," said Miss Camik, kindly.

"Thank you," replied Lucy, nicely. A few minutes later Lucy still hadn't found her lost book.

"Did you find it yet?" asked Miss Camik.

"No luck, yet, thanks for asking," replied Lucy.

***

"Okay, class, let's get out our science books now," instructed Mr. Larson, Lucy's math and science teacher.

Lucy's book had been nowhere in Miss Camik's room. She had thought about looking in Mr. Larson's room, but decided against it because she had not been in Mr. Larson's room yesterday.

The rest of the day passed by quickly, and Lucy still hadn't found her book.

***

That night Lucy thought of people in her class who might want a NANCY DREW book. She thought hard and long about Leslie Smith. She was in charge of the lost and found, so if she saw something on the floor she took it. Even if it was beside a desk, she didn't ask, just took it.

Lucy would have already checked the lost and found that Leslie kept in her desk, however, Leslie had been absent since the day after Lucy lost her book. Then, the next day Leslie had come to school. So Nancy, Netta, and Lucy had all gone up to her desk to talk to her.

"Excuse me? Leslie, I lost a book that I owned, may I please look in the lost and found for it?" asked Lucy politely.

"Sure, why not? I have seven books I found in this classroom," Leslie replied.

"Thank you. Here's a NANCY DREW book, but it's not mine," Lucy said as she was rooting through the books. "Here it is!" exclaimed Lucy.

"Well, I'm glad you found what you were looking for," said Leslie, sweetly.

"Yes, we found it!" shouted Nancy.

"Finally," said Netta sarcastically.

"Phew, I'm so glad it was all just a misunderstanding, and that no one had stolen it," said Lucy, happily. "Now I can finish it!"

Danae Marie King
Age: 12

CINDERELLA BUNNY

Once upon a time there was a little bunny named Minnie. Her nickname was Minnie the Maid. She lived with her two mean stepbunnies. Their burrow was always dirty of carrot peels from her sister's carrot candy. So, Minnie was always sweeping up carrot peels. That was mostly her life carrying carrots from the garden through the burrow and into the kitchen. Today was the ball and Minnie was making carrot cakes and carrot juice. Minnie so wished she could go to the ball but she had to stay home and clean the burrow. Her little guinea pigs heard her and started to make her a fur coat. When they were finished Minnie tried it on and it was too small so now there was no way she could go to the ball. When her sisters left, she was crying.

Right before her eyes her fairy godpika appeared and said, "You want to go to the ball, Minnie?"

"Oh, yes" answered Minnie!

"Well we'll need to get you a butterfly to ride to the ball." She turned Holly, one of her little guinea pigs, into a butterfly that was pink and white. She made a beautiful fur coat for Minnie. It was pink. She had a gold tiara with pink diamonds on it.

"Oh, fairy godpika it's wonderful! Oh, and glass slippers, too," cried Minnie.

"Yes dear, but at midnight the spell will be broken and everything will be as it was before," said her fairy godpika.

"Thank you," Minnie cried, and she was off to the ball.

When Minnie arrived she was searching for Prince Jack Rabbit, but he found her first. They danced and danced all night. But Minnie forgot all about the time. The clock struck midnight and Minnie hurries up the burrow steps and loses one of her glass slippers, but she doesn't have time to go back to get it and she jumps on her butterfly.

The next day her sisters were talking about the mysterious bunny at the ball who had captured all of the prince's attention. The royal footmen were coming to their house to try the glass slipper on every bunny in the kingdom. The sisters locked Minnie in the basement but her foot still stuck out. When the royal footmen came, the stepsisters tried on the shoe, but their feet were too big. When they were about to leave one of the stepsisters tripped the footman. The shoe went flying up in the air and landed right on Minnie's foot. The prince had found his bride. And they lived happily ever after.

Abby Andrews
Age: 8

THE DAY OF EVIL

The day is January 1, 2010; we have just got home from a New Year's Day party. My family and I live in a town called Maxport, California. My town isn't the biggest town in California, but it is a pretty nice town. There are a lot of stores and big office buildings in the middle of the city. Around the main town are many neighborhoods with homes. For the most part the city and neighborhoods around it are very clean. People seem to like to live here and everyone knows everybody.

Our house is a two-story on Beetlesworth Avenue. My parents really take care of our house and so does everyone else in the neighborhood. I have always lived here and two of my friends, Lisa and Eoin live next-door, they are brother and sister. We have been friends for as long as I can remember. We grew up in this neighborhood and went to school together. We were always known as the Three Musketeers. That was until we met Tony. He lives on the other side of town.

Our town has two different areas to it. One is the east side, which I live in; it is the nice side of town. The other side is the west side, which is were Tony lives because his parents died in a car crash. He is eighteen now, so he stayed in his parents' house and he lives alone. Lisa, Eoin, and I go to Tony's all the time, but usually Tony comes to our houses because it is just a nicer place to hang out.

Today my friends and I are going on a hike in the Soranor Forest.

Ding-dong.

"I'll get it," I said. I opened the door and there was Tony.

"Hey Tony," I said.

"Hi," Tony said.

"Do you have everything for the hike trial today, Tony?" I asked.

"Yeah," Tony answered.

Ding-dong.

"I'll get that, it is probably Eoin and Lisa," I said.

I opened the door and Eoin and Lisa said, "Hi."

"Are you ready to go on the hike?" I asked.

"Yeah, we're ready to go," Lisa said.

"Then let's go," I said.

"Okay," we all replied.

So we started to walk to Soranor Forest, which was about one and one-fourth miles away from my house.

When we got to the forest it looked very dark and gloomy. I was the first to enter the forest. I was pretty scared because there are legends about the Soranor Forest. There was a disappearance a year ago in this forest. Second to enter was Tony. Then finally Lisa and Eoin both walked in. I could see in everyone's eyes that they were scared.

"This place is pretty scary, huh?" I asked.

"No, duh!!!" said Eoin.

"Let's go," Tony said.

"Okay," we said.

So we started out of the Soranor Forest. When we hiked about a half of a mile, we saw a path, which was weird because no one has been in this forest in a year.

"Should we go on the path?" asked Lisa.

We thought about it for a little bit and then I said, "Let's walk the path."

"I agree," said Tony.

"I guess I will go," said Eoin.

"Are you coming Lisa?" said Eoin.

"Uh, okay, I will go too," said Lisa.

So we headed down the path. About a half-hour after we started on the path, I heard a noise. It sounded like a horse.

"Do you hear that?" I asked.

"Yeah, I did," said Eoin.

"Me too," said Tony.

"Me three," said Lisa.

"It's getting louder; I think the horse is coming this way. Let's hide in these bushes," I said.

So we hid in the bushes and when the horse passed by we saw a man or a woman. We couldn't tell because whoever was riding the horse was wearing a black-hooded cape. The person on the horse dropped a box. The person looked like they meant to drop the box because they pushed the box off the horse. When the rider was out of sight, we got out of the bushes.

Tony looked at the box and said, "Look, there's a letter on it."

"Open it, Tony," said Eoin.

Tony opened the letter and read it.

> Dear Tony,
>   When you open the box you will find a green potion. Drink it or you will be cursed forever. Drink all of it!
>   Sincerely,
>   ???

Tony showed us the entire letter and said, "I'm going to drink the potion."

"Why risk your life, Tony?" Lisa asked.

"I have nothing to lose, if I die I will be with my mom and dad," said Tony. He opened the box and took out the green potion. He pulled the cap off and drank the potion in one gulp.

"Tony, do you feel all right?" I asked.

"No," said Tony.

"Tony!! He's out cold!" I yelled.

"Lisa, go back to the city and get help now," I said.

"Okay," said Lisa. Lisa ran off.

"Tony, can you hear me?" I said.

There was no response.

I said to Eoin, "Get my blanket that is in my backpack, he's freezing now."

"Okay, here you go," said Eoin.

I wrapped Tony up in the blanket to try to keep warm. I thought for a moment, "Eoin, did you bring a hatchet?"

"Yeah, why?" asked Eoin.

"So we can cut the branches off and put them under him parallel," I said.

"Oh," Eoin said.

"Give me that hatchet," I said.

He gave me that hatchet and I cut two long, thick branches. We slid the two branches under him and I told Eoin to lift the two branches and walk back home. When we were carrying Tony, for about a half an hour, we came upon Lisa's body, she was dead!

"What happened to Lisa?" I asked.

"Look, there's a deep stab wound on her neck," screamed Eoin.

"I bet the person on the horse did this!" said Eoin.

"Yeah, we have to leave her here because it is too much weight then," I said.

"Okay," said Eoin.

So we started off once more. When we got to the end of the path, we knew that we had to trail back trough the hardest part of the forest. It was hard because of all the rocks. Before we went the rest of the way we took a break. When we sat down I checked on Tony. He had developed brown scars.

"Hey Eoin, look at Tony," I said.

"Oh my, I read about this. He will turn into a hooded Sebrin. That is a person that is evil and tried to take over our city by killing everyone, including us. The only way to kill him is to stab him with arrows and swords. I have two swords and two bow and arrows in safekeeping," said Eoin.

We ran out of the forest and straight to Eoin's house. We went to his room and got the bows, the arrows, and swords. The arrows had a sharp edge and they were in a pouch that was able to fit around my neck and back. I would have to carry the bow. The sword was silver. The handle was black and it hooked onto my belt.

After we were all prepared we headed straight for the forest. When we were about ten feet away from Tony, we hid behind some tall dark bushes. We saw him standing there. He had a sword; it was the same size as mine. He was wearing a cape with a hood. He looked like he was looking at his sword. Suddenly I saw Eoin draw out one arrow, he put it in position on his bow. He pulled it back as far as he could and fired. It was a direct hit! I decided to help Eoin fight

Tony with arrows. I drew the string of the bow and aimed for him. I missed! Tony turned around, he pulled the arrow and threw it at us and hit Eoin.

Eoin said his last words, "Tell my parents I love them."

"Good-bye Eoin," I said.

I laid him back down on the floor and stood up. I drew my sword, out of the pouch, Tony looked at me. I tried to fight him off by hitting his sword with mine. For a moment he moved backwards and looked away, this was my chance to attack him. I quickly moved toward him and sliced off his leg. He fell to the ground and stared at me. While Tony was on the ground, he tried to reach for his sword. At that moment I saw what he was doing and I stabbed him in the arm. He screamed! Before my eyes he disintegrated and then he was gone. I never spoke about this day, to anyone, every again.

Alex C. Fosnot

WATERY GRAVE

Yellow River, Pennsylvania 1704

"Let's go play by the pond," said thirteen-year-old Amy.

"All right," said her best friends, Lily and Elizabeth. It was a very hot summer day. Amy, Lily, and Elizabeth were dying from the heat and needed to cool off. As fast as they could, Amy, Elizabeth, and Lily ran to the pond's small beach to play tag.

"Let's not get too close because I can't swim," said Amy with fear. Amy's father owned all the land, so they could play wherever they wanted to.

"Do you want to push Amy into the pond?" Mike asked his friend, Mark. Behind a bush far away, Mike and Mark were plotting to push Amy into the pond because it might be funny to watch. As the girls started to play tag, both boys decided that it was time to start the plan to push Amy into the pond.

"Hello," said Mark and Mike.

"What are you doing here?" said Lily.

"Earlier today I dropped my hat in this pond. I came back here to look for it. Since you are already here, would you three help us look for my hat?" said Mark.

The girls started to look at each other like the boys were up to something. After a few minutes they decided to help them look for Mark's hat.

Amy, Elizabeth, Lily, Mike, and Mark decided to split up into teams. Lily and Elizabeth looked on the left side of the pond, Mike and Mark looked on the right side of the pond and Amy looked at the deepest end of the pond. Once Mike and Mark were done looking on the right side of the pond, they decided to go help Amy.

"You have to get really close to the water so you can see all the way to the bottom," said Mike. Amy looked at them, but squatted down anyway.

"On my signal, we push her in. One, two, three!" said Mark and Mike.

As soon as they pushed Amy into the pond, Mark and Mike laughed their heads off. But Lily and Elizabeth rushed over to see if Amy was all right because they knew that Amy couldn't swim. You could hear Amy struggle underwater and see bubbles come up to the top. When Lily was just about to jump in and save her, Amy's lifeless body floated up to the surface.

"Amy? Ammmy? AMY!" yelled Elizabeth, but there was no reply.

"YOU TWO KILLED HER!" screamed Lily. In shock both Elizabeth and Lily started to cry. Mike and Mark were so shocked and horrified by what just happened, both ran away from the pond. Elizabeth and Lily cried all the way to Amy's house to tell her parents that their daughter was dead.

Yellow River, Pennsylvania 2004

"Oh, it's so beautiful," said thirteen-year-old Amy.

"Wow! This place is so great! What do you think of it Elizabeth?" asked Amy's ten-year-old brother, Mike.

"It's all right, I like New York City better," said sixteen-year-old Elizabeth.

"Could someone please help me with these bags!" said Mark, Amy's father.

"Sure honey, I'll help you. Amy will you help too?" said Lily, Amy's mother.

Quickly, Amy helped with the bags so she could explore their new house in the country. She unloaded the rest of the bags and put them on the ground and quickly took two of her bags and headed to the house. Inside the house, the rooms were all dusty and the furniture was covered by cloth to protect it from dust. The kitchen looked very old. Next, Amy walked through the dining room. The dining room was pretty basic. The last room Amy walked through was the living room.

She headed up the stairs right next to her room. When Amy walked into her room, she absolutely loved it. The walls had built-in bookshelves for all her books, and there were two windows in her room. One window had a view of the street that leads to their house and the other was a view of the pond. Amy, from looking and exploring the house, had forgotten that she was very hungry and rushed downstairs to eat dinner.

"Would anyone like to take a walk to the pond before it gets to dark outside?" asked Amy.

"Sure, that sounds nice. Let's go," said Amy's dad.

Everyone left the table and went for a walk. The pond was almost directly in their backyard. When they got to the pond, there was some kind of force that led Amy to one side of the pond. Amy looked in the water and even stuck her feet in to relax for a minute. When Amy got up from sticking her feet in the pond, she noticed a tree that had something written on it. The tree said: "May Amy not rest until the two who killed her, Mike and Mark die in this lake. Written by: Lily and Elizabeth, June 4, 1704"

"Mom! Dad! Mike! Elizabeth! You have to come see this!" yelled Amy. This is just too weird, Amy thought. Amy's dad's name is Mark, her brother's name is Mike, her mother and sister's names are Lily and Elizabeth, and her name is Amy.

"What, what is it?" gasped Amy's dad.

"Look at this." As Amy's family started to read the message on the tree, her family's faces started to show fear.

"Oh, don't pay attention to this message. We better go inside, it's starting to get dark," said Amy's dad. Even though he did not show it, you could hear fear in his voice. When Amy stepped away, she stepped on something hard. She brushed the leaves and dirt off of it and saw that it was a grave. It said: "May Amy rest in peace in her watery grave June 2, 1704"

"Daaaaaaaad, come look at this."

"Well, (gulp) I guess the message on the tree is true. That girl probably died in that pond right over there (gulp). We really should be getting back inside," said Amy's dad with fear that took over his voice. When the whole family came over to see the grave, you could see the hairs on their arms rise. On the way back to the house, everyone was very alert and scared.

That night right before Amy went to bed, she looked out the window that faced the pond and saw a girl in white standing next to the pond. Then, just as quickly as Amy saw her she was gone. Remembering the message on the tree, Amy went to her parents' bedroom to see if her dad was there. Her dad was lying in bed reading a book. Next, Amy went to Mike's room to see if he was there. When she looked in his bedroom, Amy saw that Mike was not there. Amy quickly ran back to her bedroom to look out the window to see if he was by the pond. Amy saw the white girl she saw earlier leading Mike to the pond. Amy ran and got her parents and her sister and told them what was happening. Everyone ran downstairs and out the door to the pond to try to save Mike. Mike was standing at the deepest end of the pond. His eyes were glowing white and the girl was standing right next to him.

"Let go of my brother!" Amy screamed at the ghost.

"I've waited three hundred years for this and I'm not going to let this opportunity pass me by," said the ghost with an evil voice. The ghost pushed Mike into the pond and just as quickly as he was pushed in, his body floated up to the surface.

"You're next Mark," said the ghost and then vanished. The whole family ran over to see if there was any chance that Mike was still alive. His body was cold and showed no signs of life. The family headed back to the house and started to cry.

The rest of the day was very silent. Nobody went outside the house. The whole day Amy had a feeling that something was going to happen that night.

Once it was time for bed, the whole family slept in the same room. Amy and Elizabeth slept on the floor while her parents slept in the bed.

A strange song woke Amy up. She checked her parents' bed to see if her dad was there, but he wasn't. Amy looked into the hallway and saw her dad following the ghost in the same trance that Mike had been in. Amy decided to go alone. Amy followed them all the way downstairs and to the pond. She was going to distract the ghost long enough for her dad to get away. Amy slowly and quietly hid behind a bush and waited for the right moment to jump out.

"Stop right there! Do not kill my father!"

"Like I said before, I must kill your father so I may rest in peace. I have waited three hundred years for this and I'm not going to wait any longer."

Amy started to run toward the ghost but right before she got to him, the ghost pushed him into the water and his dead body floated up to the surface.

"Now I can finally rest in peace," said the ghost and then vanished.

Amy ran over to see if her dad was still alive, but he was just the same as Mike, cold and lifeless. Amy started to cry over her dad's body because she saw the whole thing and yet she did not stop her dad from being killed. The sun started to rise as she was crying all the way to her house to tell her family that their father was dead.

Rebecca Warner

24

THE TALENT SHOW

"No! No! No!" said Sarah Maybelline to her best friend Samantha Wonder. "You are supposed to kick after you spin!"

They were practicing for the Parkwood Elementary Talent Show. Every year the girls had been in the talent show together. Even after all those years (they were in the fourth grade) they had always come in second place, Becca Richards had always won. She was a good dancer and Sarah and Samantha always sang. They had good voices but not good enough to beat Becca. She had never lost but this year that was going to change. This year Samantha and Sarah had an awesome dance routine to the song "Sweet Sixteen" by Hilary Duff. They had outfits that were awesome. Their outfits were black pants, boots and a shirt that said Sweet Sixteen in glitter! Now all that they had to do was get the dance right. Samantha kept messing up in the same spot but was slowly getting it.

"This year Becca is going down." said Samantha.

That night Samantha slept over at Sarah's house so that they could practice more than usual.

The next morning Samantha and Sarah woke up early. The same thought hit both of their minds... today is the talent show!

When they got to school Becca said, "I hope you are ready to lose because I'm going to win once more, what will you be singing, 'Ring-Around-The-Rosey'?"

Finally two o'clock came. Sarah and Samantha raced home to practice and get on their outfits and makeup for their big night.

When Sarah arrived Samantha was already at school. The gym was so crowded that the seats were all taken and people were up against the walls. This gave Sarah the chills. Becca was first up this year because she had awesome dance moves but instead she saw horrible ones. It was if Becca never even practiced. She usually did the splits and this year she could barely do a cartwheel. Next up was Sarah and Samantha. They did great and got all their moves perfect. Samantha didn't even mess up on the part she usually did.

Finally it was time to see who won.

"And our second place runner-up is Roger Elmers."

Becca's face went down and Samantha and Sarah's faces went up!

Finally the judge said, "And our winner is Sarah and Samantha."

The crowd went wild as they walked up on stage. Then everyone quieted down when they were ready to say their speech.

"All we want to say is thank you for the award."

Again the crowd roared and Sarah and Samantha had grins that went from ear to ear!

Emily Sparks
Age: 9

ATTACK!

Captain John Parker stared out at the wide blue sea as he steered his ship, the Elizabethan. Captain Parker was a tall sturdy man. He had long reddish-brown hair he kept pulled back in a pigtail at all times. He wore a normal outfit for merchants: black pants and a white shirt. The Elizabethan had recently been given to the British navy by the merchant Richard Milroy, after a woman had been killed on it. However, the navy had no need for a merchant ship.

They gave the ship to Captain Parker, because his old ship had recently been destroyed by vandals.

"Captain. Sir. Captain. CAPTAIN PARKER!"

"What?"

Parker spun around. There stood Ethan Smith. Ethan was an average height and slender boy. He had golden hair, of which he truly detested the color, that had grown to be just above his shoulders. He had managed to get on board after he had been discovered half-dead on the shore of an island.

"Sir, there's another ship approaching us," Ethan informed him.

"Okay. Go tell Lawson to try to see who's on board," Parker ordered.

"Yes, sir."

Ethan hurried off. He ran around two men who were mopping the floor and jumped over a pile of ropes lying on the ground. Once at the base of the main mast, he called up to Lawson.

"Lawson, I-I-I mean, Mister Lawson!" Ethan called, gasping for breath.

"Climb up here, boy. It's hard to hear in this wind."

Ethan scrambled up.

"Can you see the ship at all?" Ethan asked him.

Lawson squinted his jade green eyes and shaded them with his chubby fingers.

"It looks British. Yes, it's British all right," he replied looking at Ethan, who was the same height as he.

"Thank you, sir," Ethan said as he scurried down to report to Parker.

"It does look rather grimy for a navy ship though. Perhaps it's just a merchant ship," Lawson murmured after Ethan had left.

Captain Barlanta grinned, showing off his gold teeth, as his ship glided toward the Elizabethan. He was very dirty and was of average height. He had dark, almost black, hair with several gray hairs speckled here and there. As always, he wore a large hat he had stolen during his first attack. He was proud of his skills as a captain and had looted many towns. He steered the ship slowly toward the other ship and stroked the handle of the sword he kept at his side at all times.

"This should be very easy. It's just a merchant ship. Most likely, they aren't prepared for an attack," Barlanta murmured to himself. "Everyone, prepare to attack!" he yelled, looking around at his crew who, at the moment, was silently watching the ship's progress toward the Elizabethan. "You may keep a quarter of the plunder."

A cheer arose as the pirates hurried to obey the order. Some rushed to load their muskets in preparation. Others hurried to prepare ropes to swing across to the Elizabethan when they caught up. Still others ran below to man the cannons. For a while, the ship was filled with the sounds of pirates beginning to prepare for battle and swords being sharpened.

The two ships pulled up next to each other. Captain Barlanta unsheathed his sword. Quickly a member of the pirate crew raised the flag with the Jolly Roger on it.

Suddenly, a round of cannon fire fired from the Black Rose sending cannonballs flying towards the Elizabethan. Hundreds of rounds of muskets were fired toward the Elizabethan. Men fell off the ship as they were hit with the musket fire. As the crew of the Elizabethan hurried to find swords and muskets with which to defend themselves, pirates swung across to the Elizabethan on ropes. Ethan hid behind the main mast of the Elizabethan, where he thought he could be safe. All around him, men fell having been shot or stabbed by another person. The crew of the Elizabethan would now know just how accomplished they were at fighting. Captain Parker showed his talent when he got into a wild sword fight with a pirate in which they were both nearly decapitated several times. This ended only when Parker acted as if he was wounded and then stabbed the pirate in the gut. A pirate grabbed Ethan around the middle and holding onto him, swung across to the Black Rose. Several other of the Elizabethan's crew were swung across also. The rest of the crew, that had survived, were pushed and shoved across the planks of wood set up by the pirates. Unfortunately, several of the pirates had found all of the spare ammunition and had set it on fire. Eventually, the Elizabethan began to sink, her mast having fallen. Flames licked her sides as the two crews watched from a safe distance on the pirate ship. When they had been rushed on the ship, Captain Parker got only a glimpse of the name of the ship before a tall man with unruly black hair shoved him forward. In peeling letters were the words: The Black Rose

It was at that moment that Captain Parker saw Ethan being pushed by a grinning pirate right past him.

"It's okay. Just be brave," Parker told him under his breath. Ethan stared at him and knew that if he survived, he would want to be as brave as Captain Parker. Captain Parker was still able to give hope to his crew even as they were pushed around by the fiercest pirate crew in the Caribbean.

Everyone was locked in the brig, below deck, all in one cell except for Captain Parker, who, out of respect of his position, got his own tiny cell. Below deck, it stank of rotting wood. The floor was so dirty it was impossible to see the floor. Wetness on some of the floor showed that there had been attempts to clean the floor, which had been unsuccessful. Bones littered one of the cells in which a large number of flies had made their home. On the opposite end of the brig, there was a large pile of crates of different sizes filled with items such as bread, ham, and other foods and drinks, mostly wine and rum. The ship tossed and turned causing barrels of black powder to roll across the floor.

"'ello," growled a pirate coming down the steps. "Capt'n Barlanta wants yer to come up on deck. He wants to talk to you."

Peter took a deep breath and followed the pirate up. Once on deck, Barlanta rushed over to Parker.

"Look! There's a ship following us," Barlanta cried accusingly.

"It seems so," replied Parker.

"Do you know why?" Barlanta questioned.

"No. I don't know why. This is the Caribbean. You often see other ships of course. No need to worry," Parker replied matter-of-factly.

WHACK! Barlanta smacked Parker across the face.

"Don't you get sarcastic with me," Barlanta cried angrily.

"I wouldn't dream of it," Parker replied.

"Go back below!" yelled Barlanta, shoving him towards the pirate who had dragged him up.

The other ship, the Regulator, rolled towards the Black Rose. Sailors scurried about on it preparing for a fierce battle. The Black Rose was one of the fiercest ships in the Caribbean. In half an hour, they had nearly caught up. They could see infamous Captain Barlanta staring in horror at the ship.

The Black Rose fired first. A cannonball flew into the water by the Regulator. The air was soon filled with the sounds of the explosions of cannons and the shots of muskets. Pirates swarmed onto the Regulator and sailors swarmed onto the Black Rose and immersed themselves in hand to hand combat. The air was filled with the sounds of swords clanking against each other. A small bank of sailors hurried below deck to release the prisoners. As soon as they got back on deck, the prisoners joined the fight. The sailors hurried to light the black powder below deck. The crew of the Elizabethan was hurried on board the Regulator. The pirates were locked up below the deck of the Regulator. The Black Rose was in ruins, flames over one hundred feet high.

The pirates had been captured and Captain Parker's crew had been rescued. The Regulator headed towards Kingston where the pirates' fate awaited them. When they arrived back at Kingston, the men hurried into the arms of awaiting ladies and were rushed to be treated for their injuries. The story was told many times in bars and pubs. Those men who did not survive were honored for their bravery. Soon after they got to Kingston, all but one pirate was hung. Captain Barlanta had managed to escape from the prison. He fled to an island far away and perished when pirates raided the island. It is said that he, even now, roams the Caribbean, looking for revenge for his one loss, the loss that brought about the end of his piracy and the rest of his life.

Sarah Marks

THE SMILING FROG

Once there were two children and every summer, they would go visit their grandma and grandpa in Kentucky. Every summer, it was the same; they would eat Grandma Jo's awesome cooking and go fishing with Grandpa Guy, only this summer was a summer they would never forget. Paul and Dale, the two children, got to Grandma and Grandpa's house late one evening. They said good night and went to bed. Early the next morning, Grandpa Guy was sitting by the window and he was putting some pepper on his biscuits and gravy, when a gust of wind came through the window and made Grandpa sneeze. Grandpa let out a big "ahchoo" and his dentures flew out the window. A small frog jumped up to catch a fly when Grandpa's teeth landed in the frog's mouth. Grandpa told Paul and Dale to go outside and look for his teeth so he could eat his breakfast.

Paul and Dale got dressed and went outside and looked on the ground, under the window for his teeth, but they had no luck. They all looked everywhere. Inside, outside, in the pond, on the ground, but they gave up soon. Later that afternoon when it was almost dinnertime, Mr. Francis Newman, the farmer who lived down the road, was bringing home some hay to feed to his cows when he saw a strange frog who seemed to be smiling at him. He quickly drove up to Grandma and Grandpa's house and walked up to their door. Grandpa Guy opened the door and saw that Francis had a strange look on his face. Mr. Newman told Grandpa that he just saw a frog sitting on a lily pad smiling at him as he drove past. Grandpa grabbed his old coat and hat and ran out the door to the pond. Paul and Dale followed not too far behind. They soon saw the frog and tried to catch it.

There were many trees by the pond so Paul went back to the house and got the pepper, came back, climbed out onto a limb of the tree that the frog was sitting under. He shook the pepper shaker and told Dale to catch the teeth. Paul quickly shook the shaker and the frog sneezed and out popped the teeth. Dale caught the teeth and the frog jumped back into the water. Grandpa wiped off his teeth and put them back into his mouth. They all went back up to the house, invited Mr. Newman to eat with them, and ate supper with the window closed. Nobody ever saw the frog again and Grandpa never lost his teeth again. Well not for a little while.

Kelley Virginia Wilbur
Age: 12

29

"What do you think, Philip?"

"Well Sam, it's very easy. Mr. Brooke said he would see the lady later. He did, but not as formal as the first time. You see, Mr. Brooke had the knife in her arm to not get rid of the evidence, but so he could use it on the other lady, too. I noticed that your picture of her over your mantle must have been about ten years old. That's when I knew you were the murderer. Therefore, this man is the killer of these two young, innocent women."

Philip rested and rested that night until he awoke with a fright. He was scared that he showed the wrong proof at his case; but remembered what it was and got up, made himself some coffee, and started to cook himself some breakfast. He caught up with Sam as he walked out of his apartment down the street.

"Hello, Sam!"

Sam was a shorter lady who was fairly skinny. She had light brown-reddish hair, dark blue-green eyes, and a smile that always brightened Philip's day. Her accent matched her personality -- cheerful, yet comical at times. Yet, she had the oddest kind of hackle. You might say that made you laugh just by her laugh.

"Hello, Philip. The captain's giving us a new case."

"Rats," whispered Philip under his breath. "I was hoping we would get a break."

"Someone as good as you should never get a break," Sam giggled.

"Here's your new case," said the captain. "It's said to be the most unusual homicide this country has ever seen!"

"A clown murder?" explained Philip with an expression of feeling stupid on his face. "What do you think we do? I mean, this is so stupid, I feel stupid!"

"Try that again," spoke the captain with confidence. "This murder was done and we have not but one clue as to who did it, how, and why. The clue is this." He takes a painting and hands it to Philip. "This was sold to someone on the force. He gave it to us because he said he found a connection between this painting and the murder, can you see any clues that might have to do with the murder?" He waits for a reply from Philip.

"Well," sighed Philip, "what year did you say this was painted?"

"1848. Why?" asked the captain.

"Well, it says right there on that box of balloons: October 5, 2003. This was the date of the murder."

"Nice work, sir!" exclaimed Sam.

"I'm not done, Sam. The knife that this clown is using is the murder weapon. I see the man outside, looking through the window. This might be the murderer. Captain, just out of curiosity, do you know where this was found?"

"The man that gave it to us was Bill, from the force. He said he bought it at an auction for public officials and their families."

"I think we should attend the next one, how about you, Sam?"

"Yes, that would help us before the next murder occurs."

"This painting is a nineteenth-century oil done by an unknown artist. As you can see, it contains a cowboy shaving with a straight razor, like they used in the old West. The bidding will start at $1550. Do I have 1550?"

Philip raised his hand.

"1550. Do I have 1600? 1600? 1600? "The man paused for a few seconds. "Going once..."

Philip, the captain, and Sam were now excited.

"Sold to..."

"Inspector Phillip."

"Sold to Inspector Philip everyone, for $1550."

"Now to do my job," Philip proclaimed as he got up.

The next day, he told their captain everything.

"You see, the man isn't a cowboy, but dressed as one. There is a journal on the desk that contains the true date, which is November 2, 2003. That must be when the murder takes place. In the reflection, there is a man pushing a cart and appears to be reaching for a gun on the cart. The murder weapon has to be the gun."

If Philip could find out where to go for the murder, they might be able to stop the man from killing someone else.

He tried to find more clues that might help him to find the place of murder, but nothing came to him.

As he was getting dressed for work the next day, he heard the television, "There was another bizarre murder that, according to Captain Carl Frankman, 'is a classified case that is probably the most unusual collection of murders of this country's history.' A man dressed as a cowboy died in his dressing room by a straight razor while he was shaving. The man was just about to go on stage."

"Well, Captain, we might as well try the next auction."

"We're late!" Yelled the captain under his breath. "We have to catch the person who bought the painting before it's too late!"

When they found the woman's house, they stepped to the door. They came in and snuck around very quietly. Finally, they came to a doorway and Philip peeked his head into a room to find a woman that has a corset on her by another lady. He knocked.

"Hello, Philip. I was wondering if you would like some tea. Would you?"

"Yes, I would, but I have come here to really see the painting you bought today."

"Well, stay here and I will go make you tea."

"Hurry back now."

He finds the painting. Philip picks it up and is puzzled by the scene. It is a picture of the lady putting on the corset on the other woman. In a mirror that is peeping his head through the doorway. It looked like Philip.

He heard a faint scream. Then a crash. There was a busting of a window. Philip, Sam, and the captain all entered the kitchen. They found the lady on the floor with no stabs or marks except on the strings of the corset. They were untied. The strings were worn. They looked like they were pulled tightly.

He was puzzled.

There was one "last" painting. It was taken by Philip to look at very carefully. This painting was probably the most interesting of all. It contained a priest being hung on stage. The painting was called The Performance Of The Priest From The Church Of The Jesuits. Philip discovers that there is a piece of writing in the picture that says, "Go to this church." So, they all decide to go to the church of the Jesuits."

"You have come!" exclaimed the priest with joy. "I am a Jesuit and highly educated. I love to paint. A man has been coming to me and confessing the thought of these murders and all of his plans for them. I am not allowed to tell people his confessions, so I tried to communicate them through paintings. The next murder is me. He has discovered that I was doing this. Could you please help me?"

"We will help," spoke the captain.

"We will trap him," said Philip and Sam.

They waited. Then, there was a rush of an opening door. A man walked up with a gun.

"Come on old man, I know you are in here! You told people what was supposed to be a secret!" His gun was now loaded.

Philip came out with a priest outfit on him. He turned real fast and shot the man in the leg.

"We got him!"

"We have a witness!" exclaimed Philip. "This witness is a Jesuit priest by the name of Thomas Harris. He has told us by painting that this man has or is going to commit these murders. Each painting contains clues that would help to discover the murder weapon -- the first is a pair of scissors, the murderer -- a mysterious man like in the second picture, and the victim -- the third was a lady getting ready for a play. The lady getting ready for the play reminds me about the victims' connections. They were all dressing for some type of performance."

"They might need to know the motive for the murders, Philip," spoke Sam definitely.

"Aw, yes, well, they all knew him. It's very simple to find, Sam. It's right in these records." He handed her an off-white folder. "I think you'll find that they all were good friends to him, and they had all taken his dream of an occupation after he told them about it. He's also very religious, too religious for that matter."

"Why do you say that?"

"He thought they were too sinful to live. He's a crazy man."

Philip went home the next night and sat down on his couch, sighed, then got up again. He put up an award for service on his wall. He fixed its position until straight. He went to bed. Another case solved.

Cameron Ingram

THE LUCKY ONE

About three years ago some old roughneck's dog had had a litter of pups, three in fact! They kept one, one male and dumped the other two, two females. But before the two were dropped off the old man that was the owner of the dogs he was the town drunk, he decided that before he drops the pups off he would give them a chance. But being pups they got into a whole lot of mischief the old man would then beat the dogs, and because he said they were bein' bad! So the old man got tired of foolin' with the pups and dumped them off on an old country road where no one could find them and they would eventually die.

About one week after that a lady by the name of Mrs. O'Deal was going down her driveway to get her mail when suddenly she heard whining and barking coming out of an old tattered beer box. She looked in and saw two puppies. One looked like a yellow Lab and the other like a basset hound. She kept them for a while but she knew she couldn't keep them forever because she had already owned a Saint Bernard named Sadie. So Mrs. O'Deal put an ad in the local paper about the puppies.

Then someone replied! Their names were Tim, Nora, and Holly Brown. Holly had wanted a puppy for about a year! Tim had promised Holly that if she had kept her school grades up he would get her a puppy. So, the next day he and Holly went to Mrs. O'Deal's house to look at the puppies. Holly got to her house and when she saw the puppies she fell in love with the Lab-like one, she was small, and very shy. Holly told her dad that she wanted that puppy for her very own. Then, they took her home, fed her and gave her a bath. Next, Holly told Tim that the puppy needed a name, she looked in a book of names and she liked the name Robin. So, Robin was her name.

One or two months after that, on Labor Day, Holly had a day off of school and nobody was at work, Tim was mowing hay and Robin was chasing a butterfly then suddenly she jumped over the mower and it cut three of her legs very badly. Tim had tried to call every veterinarian but everyone was off work. Just when Tim and Holly had given up almost all hope, they heard the phone ring. It was Dr. Teresa Hendersen she had gotten the message from her assistant. They took Robin into her office to be checked on. Dr. Hendersen had to amputate her front leg. When Nora and Holly took Robin home from the vet's office Holly made Robin a bed in Tim's barn out of straw. And every day Holly's cat Oscar would come and visit her on her bed.

Robin is now running faster than Tim's other dogs and is very happy at her home. Many, many years from now Robin will die on Tim's farm dreaming of chasing butterflies and running in the fields.

For my sweet dog Robin

Molly Lynn Brown
Age: 13

"Cate, time to eat!" yelled Cate's mom from the kitchen.

Cate got off her horse and came to eat. I peeked around the corner of the stable. Her horse was just standing there. I snuck over.

"Hello," said a voice.

I looked around, no people.

"Over here, little boy," it said again.

"Who are you?" I yelled. Then I turned my head and saw the horse talking to me.

"What?" the horse asked.

"You... you are talking to me?" I said.

"So," said the horse.

"So, you're talking to me and horses don't talk," I said.

"You are one weird boy," the horse said.

"I am not the weird one, you are the weird one!" I said.

"What do you expect me to say? Neigh!" said the horse.

"Yeah, normal horses say neigh," I said.

"Well, meet my friends," the horse said.

"Hi."

"Hello," they said.

"Wait, they are all talking to me. What's going on?" I said.

"Well, there's a planet of all horses. And we live there. The end," said the horse.

"Fine," I said, "I'm Brian."

"And I'm Coca," he said. "Do you want to stay for some hay?" Coca asked.

"No way!" I yelled. "You eat hay, I eat apples, carrots, mashed potatoes," I said.

"Mmm, apples and carrots!" Coca yelled. "What do you like best, bitten off or slobbered on?" Coca asked.

"Ew gross!" I yelled.

"Brian, they are very good!"

"Maybe you like them that way, but that is so gross! Anyways I have to go. Bye!"

The next day I snuck out to the barn again. This time Cate caught me. "Brian, what are you doing, stealing my horse!"

"I wanted to take him out to the field," I said.

"Fine, just don't lose him. I'll just ride another horse," she said.

"So, there's another planet out there with only horses?" I asked Coca.

"Yep," he said. "I've never been there, but I've heard it's a horse paradise. I wish to go there one day," Coca said. "My family's up there, all of them."

"Cool," I said. "When you go, can I go?" I asked.

"No. I don't know if I will stay up there or if I'll come back," said Coca.

"I know I can help you get up there to horse planet!" I said.

"How?" he asked.

"Good question," I answered. I led him back and went home.

I took him out again the next day. "Today you go to horse planet!" I yelled. I tried to explain to Cate, but she just said that I was such a knucklehead.

Then Coca and I went to the top of a hill. He got in a spaceship.

"Bye!" he said. "Tell Cate I said bye!" He blasted off.

When I got back, Cate yelled, "What did you do with Coca?"

"I told you he went to horse planet. Look, it is just to the right of that star."

We saw his spaceship zoom by.

"He told me to tell you bye."

Emily Nurrenbrock
Age: 10

THE DRAGON THIEF

More than one hundred years ago lived a young girl named Miranda who worked in King Arthur's castle. One afternoon, she was exploring the castle library, but when she pulled out a book, about three feet of the wall above Miranda's head disappeared.

Miranda stepped inside the darkness and screamed for she was falling down deep into the passage. Finally, her head struck solid ground.

When Miranda awoke, she found herself on a huge mountainside with small huts scattered all around. They were connected by stone bridges with strange creatures running back and forth on them. After a while, she realized they were tiny wizards.

She stood up and looked around. There were not many trees, just a few by the muddy ponds, their gnarled branches twisted in a position to capture any young girl who came too close. Soon, she saw a little cottage next to a trickling stream. A beautiful young woman stepped out. She had long, curly brown hair and brown eyes that twinkled in the sunlight. A canvas shoulder bag hung around her shoulders full of books with wrinkled-up pages.

"Read all about it!" she shouted.

Miranda ran over to her.

"Would you like one?" the woman asked.

"Yes, please," replied Miranda. "Do you know what the name of this place is?"

The woman looked down, her eyes sparkling with delight. "Sure do!!" she answered. "It's called Oakman Village, the village with only oak trees, no other kind of trees. Anyway, here's your book!" She handed her the book.

It had a page about the king and queen. Miranda scanned the pages. She raised her eyebrows, and then she looked up at the window.

"Ma'am? Did that really happen?" Miranda asked.

"Princess Rose is the name," she said. "And did what really happen?"

"A dragon from Nogard stole a bag of the king and queen's gold."

The two of them sat down on the steps that led to the cottage door.

"Yes," she answered. "A young dragon named Meeka stole some of the king and queen's gold. You see, Meeka loved to draw, but she could not afford cloth to draw on or a feather pen. So she stole some gold from the king and queen."

Miranda stood up. "I must get it back," she said.

Princess Rose stood up also. "Then you will need a few things for your journey. Here is a torch flashlight," she said, reaching into her shoulder bag. "As soon as you turn it on, you turn invisible. You will need this magic diamond that lights up in dark places. This amulet helps you against evil. Oh, and one more thing, you can ride my unicorn to Father William's cottage to hear some information about Meeka."

Miranda put her supplies in a black canvas bag and got her unicorn. Miranda rode until late afternoon, when she found a small cottage by an oak tree forest.

An old man leaned over a flower bed watering daisies. He had pebble-sized hazel eyes and wore a weatherworn straw hat and stood on two of the scrawniest legs Miranda had ever seen. He was also humming a soft song that sounded like the robins chirping in the treetops.

He suddenly looked up at Miranda. She looked back at him.

"Are you Father William?" Miranda asked.

He nodded, "The same."

Miranda slid down the side of the unicorn and went over to him.

"Where are you headed?" he asked.

"I'm going to Nogard to retrieve the gold that Meeka, the young dragon, stole from the king and queen."

The man nodded and took Miranda's hand. He led her into the cottage.

"Who is this?" asked an old woman.

"Hilda," said Father William, "this young lady is on her way to Nogard to get back the gold."

Mother Hilda, as she said to call her, and Miranda sat on a split log.

"You see, child, long ago, we were friends with the dragons. But one day, the dragons wanted more land. The king refused. Soon after that, a war began. Since the dragons lost, they agreed they didn't want to live on the surface of the earth. They dug a village they now call Nogard," she explained.

"Thank you, ma'am," Miranda said on her way out.

Father William gave her a map. "Be warned of the toads of death, and do not eat any plants!" he said.

Miranda set off. By nightfall, the toads of death came out. Miranda clicked on the torch flashlight and instantly disappeared. She made sure neither her nor the unicorn ate the plants. Miranda looked at the map and told the unicorn which way to go.

Soon she arrived at a huge castle. Its bricks were as gray as smoke in the sky. All by itself, the portcullis raised. Miranda cautiously entered the castle, though it was very dark. She used the magic diamond to light her way and wore the amulet to make sure evil could not harm her.

After a walk through the great hall, came a door that had in red letters, Meeka. Miranda cautiously opened the door. The dragon was snoring soundly. On a stone desk sat a bag of gold. Miranda snatched it off the desk and ran to the unicorn.

She set off with a snort. When she arrived at the passage, the unicorn gave her a boost. Miranda climbed into the castle library and gave the gold to the king.

Then she snuggled in the chair and read her favorite book. And that is how Miranda retrieved the gold for the king.

Emma Barthold
Age: 9

WHAT ARE FRIENDS FOR?

I was walking home from school with my best friend Brooke. We were looking through the windows of the stores and I noticed a boy shopping for shoes.

He turned around and saw Brooke and I looking at him. I ducked real fast and pulled Brooke down with me. "He saw us!" I said. He was the most popular boy in school and was very nice. Well, those were the rumors!?

We ran away as fast as we could and then into the video arcade. All of the boys were there and were playing a new game called the Muncher 2000.

We saw Josh (the boy we saw shopping for shoes) walk into the video arcade. We ran and hid behind the Pac-Man game. I asked Brooke why she won't talk to him and she told me that she had an embarrassing moment right in front of him and he laughed at her so much that a crowd began to form.

"Are you serious," I asked.

"Well yeah! I just think he'll laugh at me again!"

"C'mon we are going to talk to him," I said.

"No! No! No! No I am not going to talk to Josh for a million bucks," said Brooke.

"Oh yes you are going to talk to him, just not for a million bucks. What did you do anyway when you got embarrassed in front of Josh."

"Well... I kind of went into the boys' bathroom and came out screaming," said Brooke.

"That's not... too... embarrassing!" I said.

"Can you at least go up and say hi."

"Yeah I guess that's not too bad."

So she went up to him and slipped on spilt mustard all over the tile floor.

"Hi," said Brooke to Josh.

"Oh no," I said.

"You.. wa... wa... want t... t... to g... et a milkshake at the G... Greator's next d... d... door?" said Brooke.

"Sorry," said Josh. "That was lame."

"Arrgg!" growled Brooke. "Why does it have to happen to me?"

"Well, you are kind of a klutz."

"OK! So maybe I have had my moments," said Brooke.

"Yeah, like all the time. Let's go clean you up," I said.

"OK," said Brooke.

"Why did you come help me up off of all that mustard and risk the chance of being embarrassed with me?" said Brooke.

"Well... that's what friends do. They risk every single chance they can get whether it's scary, funny or sad," I said.

"Thanks," said Brooke.

"Yeah, well what are friends for?!" I said.

"Well, they are for..."

"OK, I didn't really mean you naming what friends are for," I said.

"Ha ha," Brooke said.

"So, what do you want to do?" I asked.

"Well, we can look through store windows," said Brooke with sarcasm.

So instead we went into the Greator's next door and there lying on the floor was Josh, covered with ice cream. And a huge crowd was beginning to form.

"I guess that's what he deserves after what he did to me!" Brooke giggled.

Taylor Ann Sheaffer
Age: 10

THE PSYCHIC BEST FRIEND

"Really? Oh my, Shay! That is so cool! I can't believe it! Yeah, sure Shay. See ya." I was talking to one of my best friends, Sharaya Wave White Ramage, (Shay for short). I just couldn't believe I had such a good friend... that was psychic! I ran to tell my mom, then stopped. I realized I shouldn't tell anyone without her permission. That would be unfair, cruel, and mean.

She might have told me her secret because I'm a professional secret keeper. Plus, as vice-president of our club that we have with Chelesey Eads, she could discuss the matter with Chels (our president), and kick me out if I told anyone!

I ran over to the phone and dialed Shay's phone number. Busy, I thought of course. Then, about five minutes later, I heard the phone ring. "Hello?" I asked.

"Jen? This is Shay. Did you call about five minutes ago?"

"Yes," I answered. "Yeah, I called. I've got a question. Did you want me to keep your being psychic secret? 'Cause I almost told my mom," I said.

Shay immediately replied, "No, no! Do NOT tell anyone! I'm not even sure I'll tell my parents!"

I calmly told her to take some deep breaths and she turned out to be fine.

Shay said, "I just heard 'told my mom' and I was frantic. Sorry, Jen."

"It's okay, Shay. No worries. All right?"

"All right."

"See ya, Jen."

"See ya, Shay."

I went to my room and thought. My main thought was: It's pretty weird, having a psychic best friend.

Jennifer Rae Robinson

AN INDIAN GETAWAY!

The plane was just about to leave for India! I was so excited! I finally get to meet my family again! I'm staying for six weeks! I would miss my friends, but, when I thought about them I could see them right in front of me.

Now the plane is taking off, wee ha! I love to feel myself soaring in the air like a bird. We had to go to Chicago, London, and India. Phew, that's a long way from little Dayton, Ohio.

In no time we were in Chicago. We didn't have to wait long before our next flight. We got onto the plane just in time. (Thankfully!) The flight attendant told us that it would take seven hours to get to London.

> Question: What time would it be in America when we got to London if the time
> we left was two hours after 12:15?

The coolest thing about the plane was that it had TV's! Most of the time I read, slept, or watched TV on the plane.

The plane ride from London to Delhi was about the same, quite boring actually! The next morning... Namaste! Which means hello in India. We landed in Delhi, the capital of India!

Everything was so different here! There were no carpets and there weren't as many stores in the airport. We were even allowed to drink coffee! Finally we got on the plane to Calcutta. That's where my dad's side of the family lives.

My cousin Sonty Dada was waiting for us with a taxi.

I said, "I thought I remembered you, but I don't think I do. You look different."

He said (looking disgusted), "We made a promise, you were supposed to remember me and I was supposed to remember you."

When we got to the house everybody was waiting for us. Rohit is seven years old. So we usually played with him. Later Sonty gave me a tour of Calcutta. It's very polluted and there is a lot of traffic, but in some places it is very beautiful. For example, Victoria is a wonderful place. It is two-hundred-feet tall. They show light and sound shows there. We went to Belur Math by the banks of river Hooghly. Swami Vivekananda consecrated the Math on the ninth of December, 1898 and it is home to the monks now. It is a very peaceful place. On our way to the Belur Math we saw an elephant sharing the roads with us! I thought that was so cool. Did I forget to mention that there are stray dogs and stray cats everywhere?

Anyway, most of the time Rohit, Neil and I played five hundred, cricket, catch, or in the sand by Grandma's house. Sometimes my mom went shopping with me, (boring!).

> Question: If my mom is going shopping at 1:23 and said she'd be gone for two
> hours and thirty-three minutes, what time would she be back?

Then it was time to leave for Bangalore. I would miss Calcutta very much. When we got on the plane to Bangalore it was dinnertime. We got some gourmet dinner! I was so tired when we got to Bangalore because it was around midnight. If I were in America, I would be in school!

Bangalore only looked like America. But, it has a lot of Indian culture. There were two boys waiting for us at the house. Deepak was older than us and was always in and out of the house. Obviously, we didn't play with him. Jayant was ten and he liked to scare Neil, so we played with him.

We went to a bird sanctuary, Ranganathittu. It is filled with hundreds of species of birds, from all over the world. It is gorgeous. We even saw a crocodile lazing in the afternoon sun in the lake, as our rowboat passed by!

After that we went on a safari in an open Jeep in Nagarhole National Forest. There were elephants, bison, deer, wild pigs, sloth bear, all sorts of birds, plants, etc. We saw the tigers only on TV!

> Question: If we saw five elephants, twelve bison, twenty-six flowers, and thirty-eight birds, how many animals did we see?

Guess what? We got to stay in a hotel in the jungle! It was so cool! Even though we stayed there for only one night, I had the time of my life! It was so beautiful. There was no pollution so you could see all the stars and constellations there were in the sky. We sat around a bonfire and the food was delicious.

We also went to the Mysore Palace. It has exquisite carvings and art from all over the world. It is one-hundred-twenty-four-feet in diameter and it is simply beautiful. It is truly a palace worth seeing. Imagine if you lived in it!

The next morning... we ate breakfast and left because, we didn't want to miss our flight early the next morning. It was a very short flight from Bangalore to Cochin.

> Question: Find Bangalore and Cochin on the map. How long do you think it would take to get to Cochin from Bangalore? Why?

I would miss Bangalore very much, but I couldn't wait to get to Cochin, where my mom's family lives. Now let me tell you why I wanted to go to Cochin so bad. It's because the only people my brother could play with are girls! They are Richa, Sneha, and I. Neil got really upset and wanted to go home. We all laughed!

We got to do some things with my mom and dad. We got to celebrate Christmas there, we went to Veega Land, we went to Munnar, and we went to the backwaters.

Well, everybody knows what Christmas is, right? So I don't have to explain that to you.

Veega Land is an amusement park. It comes with nice water features, a fairy castle, and a caterpillar village.

Munnar is a tea estate. It is sixteen hundred miles above sea level and it turns blue every twelve years and it is a wonderful sight to see. We saw regional folk dancers dancing with fire and snakes.

The backwaters are the waters that connect to the Arabian Sea. It is delightful to be on a boat ride with your family and have the boatman drop you off wherever you please!

But now it was time to go to Delhi. We woke up at 3:00 in the morning because there was a strike in the area. If we got up too late the roads would be blocked. The airport was closed when we got there.

> Question: We got there at 3:25 a.m. The airport opens at 6:00 a.m. How much time did we wait?

Finally the airport opened. We had to wait for our plane to arrive. Finally, we were off to Delhi.

> Question: What is Cochin's temperature compared to Dayton's temperature in January?

We stayed in a hotel called The Intercontinental Grand. The next morning was very special! We got to see the Taj Mahal and Fatehpur Sikri!

Taj Mahal was built by Shah Jehan in memory of his wife Mumtaz. It is made of white marble and had precious stones of all kinds, it changes colors from night to day and is fantastic!

Fatehpur Sikri is a world heritage site. It has the world's largest gate called the Bulund Darwaaza (big door).

The following day we saw the India gate which is a monument of the unknown soldiers who died in World War II.

The Rashtrapati Bhavan is the president's house. It has beautiful gardens and fountains. Fifty people are employed just to chase off the birds!

The Jantar Mantar in Connaught Place is an observatory built in 1724 by the Maharaja of Jaipur. It helped people calculate the time of day.

The Qutab Minar stands two hundred thirty-nine feet tall and is beautiful any time of day. It was built in 1310 and even to this day you can see the intricate carvings on the pillars. In the courtyard stands an iron pillar built in the fourth century and the inscription records "Chandra" after the famous King Chandragupta II and... it has never rusted for that many years!

Later, we went to Humayun's tomb designed by his widow. This was the inspiration for the Taj Mahal.

The Red Fort built in 1638 was next in line. It has red sandstone walls and the beautiful Diwan-I-Khas, was once home to the peacock throne.

The next stop was the Bahai Temple that looks like a lotus in a pond. It was built in 1986 and is an architectural marvel of recent times.

It was time to come back home. Our trip back was the same as before, except we got to stay overnight in London. At school the next day I talked to my friends, felt very lucky and when I got back home I said, "Hey, why not write a story about my trip to India...?"

Dedicated to: My friends and family!

Shirin Ann Dey
Age: 9

THE PAINTINGS

"I can't believe your mom actually let me come over," said my absolute best friend Melissa.

Melissa was tall with bright blue eyes that lit up every time she heard my name. She had a petite figure and shoulder-length dirty blonde hair. A model type. Me being envious of her with my normal looks; a lanky but short body, dull green eyes with short, and frizzy chestnut brown hair.

"Yeah I had to promise her I would actually do my chores."

"Ouch, that hurts," she replied.

"Well what should we do?" I asked tiredly.

"TRUTH OR DARE," Melissa replied excitedly.

"Okay, sounds like fun," I said.

Well I picked dare and guess what? Melissa dared me to go into the old, deserted, ghastly house in the woods behind my house.

"NO WAY!" I yelled quickly.

"C-H-I-C-K-E-N," Melissa said slowly as she stood up and waved her arms around in a birdlike fashion.

"Chicken, bawk, bawk, bawk."

She kept repeating this until I said, "Fine, all right, but my mom will kill me if she finds out I'm gone."

"I promise we'll be really quiet then," Melissa said.

It was the dead of fall so Melissa and I got into hats, gloves, scarves, turtlenecks, warm pants, coats, and boots. We started out past my mother who was watching "She's Too Young" on Lifetime. We clattered down the stairs and out the door. We slowed down our stride when we were on the path in the woods. Melissa's voice broke the silence. Her voice was in tune with the rustle of the leaves.

"What do you think is inside the house?" she asked.

"I don't --" my whispering voice broke off at the sound of a scream.

My head jerked toward Melissa. No; not Melissa. I heard it again and I took off running. I ran past Melissa leaving her behind, enclosed in the darkness. I stumbled on a rock and slipped down the hill. I landed in front of the ghastly house. I heard footsteps behind me as Melissa appeared.

"Why did you leave me behind?" Melissa asked out of breath.

"I don't know I just started running, but what do you think that noise was?"

When Melissa didn't answer I followed her gaze toward the doorway of the house. Someone was going inside. I knew it was coming and it did.

Melissa said, "Well, let's go see what's in there."

I never understood why she got excited over dangerous things. She grabbed my arm and dragged me toward the front door. I slowly turned the knob and the door flew open. We tiptoed inside and silently closed the door. I looked around and saw dusty cobwebbed stair banisters and yellowed, stained sheets thrown over Victorian flower couches and chairs. Melissa and I both strutted across the squeaking floor and climbed the stairs. Melissa was in front of me as she stepped on an unsturdy step. It broke, but luckily the railing was strong enough to support her weight as she regained her footing. I jumped over the broken step while leaning on the railing for support. I was now leading the way and was more careful of my footing. We finally made it upstairs. The hallway was narrow and seemed to go on forever. There was one door up ahead. Melissa and I both tried to squeeze through the hallway but found out that we had to go single file. We got inside the room and I stood there waiting for my eyes to adjust to the darkness surrounding me. I looked around and I saw pictures, pictures that made me scream. These pictures were not ordinary. They were paintings of people. People with rotting flesh, no eyes and, decaying teeth. I heard a faint sound escape Melissa's lips. As I turned around I saw Melissa slumped over with a man standing behind her. The man I recognized. I also recognized the woman standing behind him. They were from the paintings on the walls. Yes, the paintings on the walls were old but I could tell it was them because of some very distinct features. For instance the man had a chin jutting out of his face and the woman had a very tiny nose. Both of them started to approach me and I reacted with a scream. They both covered and uncovered their ears quickly. They then began to shuffle toward me awkwardly but rapidly. I backed up as I heard a groan escape Melissa's mouth. I looked over at her and saw thick red blood escaping her left nostril. She began wiping it repeatedly as it was coming down very quickly. She struggled to get to her feet but failed. The two people then cornered me between an old oak desk and a phonograph. I looked to Melissa for help but she was still slumped over moaning. I was turning away as something caught my eye. My painting on the wall! It was not as old as the others but was still considerably ugly. I got sick on the female. She looked shocked. I couldn't help it, this was gross. Then everything happened so fast. The two people were lying on the ground. Melissa was up again and had saved me from them. I jumped over to her as she hit me on the head with a desk chair. She did this with great force. I woke up a little woozy and dazed. Trying to get my vision back she started talking. My family used to be good friends with her family until we stole her family's secret of immortality. Everyone in their family was painted with special paints when they were babies. The paintings grew older instead of them. They stopped getting older at twenty years old. My family found their secret, stole it and disabled them so that they could never use their secret formula again. Melissa's job was to uncover the secret and destroy my family.

"Of course I could never do that you're my best friend," she said.

"But I can destroy you Melissa," a voiced hissed.

It belonged to my mother. She walked in with Melissa's painting. She heaved it at the ground and right before my eyes Melissa disintegrated. I started crying, tears streaming down my face. My mother told me I was painted right after I was born and I didn't know it but I was actually five hundred and sixty-three years old. I looked around at the paintings and spotted my mother's picture. I walked over to it as my mother opened her arms up wide. She must have thought I was going to give her a hug. An astonished look came upon her face as I grabbed her painting and said, "This is for Melissa," and threw down the picture. My mother uttered a soft cry before turning to ashes. I looked at Melissa's painting on the wooden floor. It was beautiful again. Youth restored. I sat down on the hard, cold floor but suddenly got back up and dragged myself across the floor toward my painting. I grabbed it with sweaty hands and said, "This is for me and to end all this." As I threw it down I disintegrated too.

Victoria VanGhle
Age: 12

WHEN I WAS THREE

When I was three years old, I was playing with my sister Tiffany. We played in our room, our room was covered with toys. Tiffany got in the box. Then we saw a snake. The snake was trying to get Tiffany when she was in the box.
So I ran to the living room and said, Mommy Mommy snake going to eat Tiff.
Mommy said, there is no snake in the room.
So I went back to the room. The snake was still trying to get Tiff.
So I went to the living room and said, Mommy Mommy snake going to eat Tiff.
So Mommy came in the room and saw the snake and got Tiffany out of the box. We got out of the house to get our papaw to kill the snakes that were in the house. Papaw killed three snakes from our bedroom.

Krystal Michelle Justice
Age: 12

MATILDA'S SECRET

Once upon a time there was a strange girl named Matilda. She lived on the planet Squakledwarf. One day Matilda moved to Earth. She always wanted to live in Florida. Nobody knew she could do magic. She had friends named Anne and Ella. They liked Matilda so much.

One day Anne and Ella went to go find Matilda. She was at Florida Beach doing magic! Her friends saw her and then they ran to the police station. They told Officer Limetrain to follow them to Florida Beach. Officer Limetrain saw Matilda making her cat, Pumpkin, fly!

Officer Limetrain said, "What is the meaning of this?"

Matilda turned around leaving Pumpkin falling into the ocean! Matilda got Pumpkin out of the ocean using her magic.

Ella said, "How did you do that?"

Officer Limetrain made Ella and Anne go home. Then, he called the rest of the police force to come to Florida Beach. Matilda didn't know what to do. She tried zapping the police, but they always dodged her blows.

Then everyone heard a small boy crying in a drowning voice! Matilda formed the water into a ball so it would stay out of her way. She told the boy to run to the beach as fast as he could. The boy tripped. Matilda couldn't hold the water any longer. The water splashed all over the boy. Matilda got the water above her again in a ball.

Matilda said, "Hurry before I drop it again!"

So the boy ran very fast, and he made it.

His mom came running with happiness because her son was all right. The police still wouldn't let her go. The war between magic and mortals lasted for a week.

Matilda said, "Why are we fighting? It shouldn't be like this."

Officer Limetrain said, "Well, you are very strange."

Matilda said, "So what if I'm strange."

Everyone looked at each other in shock. Matilda talked back to a sheriff!

Officer Limetrain said, "Well then, you are free to go."

Ella said, "How come you never told us you had magic powers?"

Matilda said nothing.

Anne said, "C'mon we won't make fun of you."

Matilda said, "I was afraid you guys would make fun of me."

Ella said, "Why did you think that?"

Matilda shrugged.

Anne said, "Who wants to go get some ice cream?"

Matilda and Ella said, "Me!"

And they lived happily ever after.

Alyssa Mason
Age: 10

47

SECRET OF THE FOREST

"The field trip is here, yes!" bursted Jake. He waited all month for this day to come.

"Wouldn't you rather study?" smiled Mrs. Souvers.

"Okay class let me tell you what animals you should look for in the forest."

The teacher picked up her list and started to read. Jake yawned and turned away.

When they got outside, the early morning fog was so heavy it was hard to see anything. The two buses were waiting.

"We are going on the second bus," said Mrs. Souvers.

Pushing and shoving the kids crammed through the door. Jake sat next to his best friend Kevin; they had known each other since first grade.

"Hey, Kevin look at this!" said Jake, pulling a bug jar out of his pocket.

"What is that for?"

"I'm going to pick up some spiders to scare my older sister. I want to dump them in her room." smirked Jake.

After traveling for a while, the two buses turned into a long narrow road leading to the park entrance, when suddenly they bumped to a stop. Jake looked ahead, but all he could see were the blinking lights of the first bus. He heard the breaking-up voice on the radio, and watched the bus driver leave. Meanwhile, the kids were getting restless. Jake noticed that the fog in front of them turned black.

"Is it a fire?" asked Jake.

He heard the noise on the radio.

"Shh...shh..shh..H..p, we..., lp...shh...," then silence. The connection was lost.

"I want everyone to get back to their seats!" said Mrs. Souvers sternly.

"Roger and Maggie will stay in charge while I'm going to check on the problem," she added.

Jake stuck his head out the open door. "It doesn't smell like smoke, but I can't see anything."

"Why don't you go and check it yourself?" asked Roger, pushing Jake out of the bus.

"Everyone else get back!" yelled Roger to the kids.

"Nobody should leave!" frowned Maggie at Roger.

Jake glanced around and noticed that he was standing next to an overgrown driveway. The fog seemed to be less dense there. He took a few steps and tripped over an old rusted chain. Jake spotted a banged-up truck ahead of him with a lot of tools scattered on the ground. Jake had a strange feeling that someone had left everything in the middle of work years ago and never came back. The smell of mildew filled up the air. Weeds and tree roots were cracking through the driveway, taking it over. All of a sudden Jake heard something move in the bushes next to him. He peered closer and saw a clear blue Jell-O-looking blob, the size of a tennis ball. It rolled under a leaf. Jake picked up a stick and poked the thing. It squeaked and slowly started to roll away. Jake grabbed it. It felt cold. The ball drooped in his hand and began to slide off. Jake looked around and noticed a few more blue spots moving in the bushes. He got an idea. Jake formed the thing into a ball and ran back to the bus.

"Who cares for a Jell-O fight?" shouted Jake, directing the ball right into Roger's head. Roger ducked and the blob hit Maggie.

"Aaaaah!" She screamed. "What are you doing?"

"Sorry," muttered Jake.

Down on the floor the blue ball was slowly rolling around. Kids were pushing each other to see it.

"There are a lot more of them in the forest!" said Jake, excitedly.

"Can we see?"

"I want to see it!"

"We have to stay on the bus!" ordered Maggie, brushing off her jacket.

"Nobody is supposed to leave!" added Roger, kicking the creature. Then he hung out of the door.

"Mrs. Soouuveeers!" he called.

"Tattletale!" snapped Jake.

"Come on, Kevin! Don't you want to see it?" he shouted, waving to his friend. Some kids forced their way out of the bus, swarming around Jake.

"Let me give you a tour," said Jake proudly. The kids followed Jake to the forest.

"Where are they?" asked Annie, as she pushed up her glasses.

"Look!" gasped Kevin. "Over there!"

"I see another one!"

"There are more!"

Shouting and laughing the kids were chasing the blue creatures, tossing small balls back and forth. Before long the Jell-O fight began. The kids did not notice that they were getting surrounded. Meanwhile Jake was chasing a very large gelatin-looking blob away from the group. All of a sudden he heard cries. Jake turned around and rushed toward the distant voices. What he saw stunned him. A blue shimmering wall encircled the terrified kids. As soon as someone would try to break through, the wall rose and pushed them back inside.

"Jake, help!" cried Kevin.

"Help us to get out!"

"C-can you break it?" asked Jake, coming closer and kicking the wall from his side. It felt like thick rubber. He could not make one dent. All the kids were in tears. Jake's heart dropped, the black hole swirled in his stomach.

He looked around. More and more little blue balls were rolling from the forest and were merging with the wall. He had to hurry.

"I'll get the teachers! Hold on!" shouted Jake, forcing himself to sound confident.

He ran to the buses. As he was passing the old truck, Jake tripped again over the rusted chain. Another idea popped in his head. "I wonder if this would work?" Jake's heart was pounding as he pulled the end of the heavy chain. His hands were shaking, his mind spun. As fast as he could Jake dragged the chain back into the forest. The wall around the kids seemed to get even bigger.

"Did you get the teachers?" yelled Kevin anxiously.

"Kevin, hold on to this!" called Jake, throwing the chain to his friend. With a hissing sound, the wall began to break up where the chain hit.

"Kevin, look, the blobs don't like it!" said Jake, as he was hitting the wall. They broke enough of it so that Kevin could get out. Then the wall started to close back. The kids scrambled toward the opening.

"Somebody grab the chain!" yelled Jake. "Do the same thing that Kevin did!"

Annie took the chain. As soon as the opening was big enough, she climbed out.

"My glasses!" cried Annie.

"Forget about it!" yelled Zack, reaching for his end of the chain.

Inside the wall kids were still fighting each other to get out. Finally, one by one they struggled their way out and ran to the bus. The fog was getting less dense. When Jake was close to the bus he saw his teacher and driver walking back. He quickly stepped in, found Kevin, and sat next to him. Soon, the driver and Mrs. Souvers got in too.

"Mrs. Souvers..." blurted Roger.

"Not right now Roger. Please take your seat," said the teacher.

"Everybody please be quiet, and take your seats. We have some mechanical difficulties. The first bus is broken down and we have to make room for the other two classes. Unfortunately, our trip today will have to be postponed until next week."

The kids on the bus were very quiet. Then Jake heard somebody whimpering.

"What's wrong Annie?" asked the teacher. The girl kept on crying.

"She went into the forest," exclaimed Roger.

"Annie?" the teacher said angrily.

"Her glasses were left in the forest," added Katherine.

"We don't have much time. Let's go Annie!" urged Mrs. Souvers. But the girl, with a terrified look, just shook her head no.

"Jake knows where it is." said Roger, pointing at Jake.

"Jake?" questioned the teacher.

With a sigh Jake got up, feeling sick to his stomach. He and Mrs. Souvers started into the forest. The sun was streaming through the trees. The fog was nearly gone. When they arrived, Jake was stunned to see there wasn't a trace of the creatures left. On the brightly sunlit area, he saw the rusted chain and Annie's glasses. Jake picked up the glasses and gave them to Mrs. Souvers.

"We're going to have a long discussion about this when we get back to school." she scolded.

When they got back to the bus, Jake sat next to Kevin. They looked at each other without saying a word. Then Jake's foot hit something soft. He looked down and noticed a little blue blob rolling under his seat. Jake reached for it, opened his bug jar and stuffed the creature inside. Kevin stared at him, his eyes filled with fear. The kids from the first bus started to pour in, pushing and shoving, trying to get the best seats. Jake quickly hid the jar in his pocket. All the way back Jake's hand was in his pocket feeling the creature rolling in the jar.

Eric Black
Age: 9

THE HAUNTED HOUSE

One day I went to a haunted house. It was scary but then again it was funny and fun. My mom didn't go because she was sick and my dad had to work. He works really really late. So I decided to go by myself.

It seemed a little funny because it wasn't Halloween and haunted houses were open, but I said, "Who cares," and went in.

This is where it all began. It seemed all right at first, but the doors boarded up and shut by themselves. I was really scared. Then I saw a skeleton and a mummy. I was so scared I couldn't move. Then the lights went out so I could not see. Suddenly, something touched me and I jumped back and landed flat on my face.

It hurt. Then they got me and took me to a secret place in the house. It was the scariest place I've ever seen. There were mummies and vampires and wolves. They put me in a non-air tube. I escaped. I thought I was going to die, but I didn't die after all. Then I left the house and never came back.

Wesley Jones and Peter Bechtel
Ages: 10

51

PLANET-X

Today is the day, June 14, 2064. Christa and her family have to leave their homes as well as billions of other people on this Earth. Everyone who sees Christa can tell she's nervous and scared about leaving this planet and the tears in her eyes say that she will miss it deeply. She still has a ton to pack and so many things to take pictures of for memories. Christa is adark-haired girl, tall and thin, and the most athletic of her family of six.

Christa, and the others, know they have to leave Earth. The Earth is getting closer and closer to the sun every day and in the next twelve hours our precious and beautiful Mother Earth will fall into the sun's gravity, burn up, and be swallowed up by the sun.

Researchers thought it was best to try to save what species they could, and move everything on Earth to Planet X, instead of waiting for us and everything else to die, and every living species to be destroyed. NASA has built us 550,000 spaceship carriers to transport everything into our new home planet, Planet X. Those carriers hold about 500,000 people each.

Planet X is very far away from our sun, and it will be deathly cold. We have only one hope. Top astronomers have a theory that Planet X, which is past the ninth planet Pluto, may actually be the last planet in another solar system. They are holding out hope that Planet X is revolving around its own star, or sun, and that we will have a chance at survival. To help us, scientists have paired up with the latest fashion designers to make us special clothes and masks that will protect us from the most dangerous and fierce weather that we may encounter.

The time has come for Christa and her family. She is helping her mom and dad pack the car with their most valuable possessions. And after that, into the car and away they go! She is so nervous! They wonder what Planet X will be like? What will the ground be like? What will the air be like? She wonders how dramatically her life will change? Everyone hopes that it will all go well.

After it was discovered that the Earth's orbit was disintegrating, and moving closer to the sun, experts desperately tried to think of ways to save all the living things on Earth. There were many reasons why they couldn't choose another planet in our own solar system. Mercury had already fallen into the sun and been destroyed. Venus was very close being destroyed. They would not have survived the heat anyway, even with special equipment. Mars may not be far behind the Earth in falling into the sun, so it would be pretty pointless to spend all that heartbreak, time, and money trying to settle on Mars. Jupiter and Saturn are great gas giants, so they don't actually have land that they could build houses, work, and play on. Neptune, Uranus, and Pluto are all so cold, so very cold. They would not survive long, and it would be more than a lifetime before their orbits came around again to the sun.

So, it was decided. They would shoot for the mysterious Planet X, and hope that the scientists' theories were right. It is their only chance.

Christa has only one hour left on this Earth. She has so many butterflies in her stomach and ants in her pants, that she is acting like she forgot to take her medication. Christa, her family and her cat, Kelly, are at the docking station, and are ready to board the ship. Thousands and thousands of police officers are loading the goods, people, animals, and every other living thing and packing them into the spaceships like sardines. It is Christa's turn. They will all pray for good luck and a quick trip.

I have to back up so everyone will understand who was chosen for this dangerous trip, and how. But first I pray for the others left behind, who will meet a terrible and fiery death.

The leader of the United Nations took every registered person and put his or her name into this special computer. First, they deleted anyone who committed a serious crime so that we would have a better and less crime-filled "new" world. Then they deleted anyone who wrote a letter saying that no matter what, they were not going to leave. After their letters were double-checked, if they still wanted to stay, they were taken off the list.

Then they made a list of who definitely would go on the dangerous trip. They first put in all of the important religious leaders from around the world. This group included people like deacons, monks, priests, bishops, cardinals, nuns, brothers, rabbis, clerics, and most importantly the Pope. Many gave up their seats to help the people that were staying on Earth. Next, all the people that had to do with in any way, the government, armed forces, or important leaders.

The leader of the United Nations sat in this dark, musty, and very lonely room and pondered about what category of people to pass through next. After an hour had passed, an idea came to him. Since they were going to practically create a "new world to live in," which they knew nothing about, he was expecting that many people would get sick, badly injured, or seriously hurt, so he thought that it was best to pass all of the doctors that were of any category or skill. Then in case of a dispute he had to pass all of the judges and lawyers. He also found it quite necessary to pass the people with professions like policemen, firemen, and especially paramedics.

He quit because when he looked at it, he was going to eventually pass everyone so he looked at his elimination list closer. He thought and thought but nothing would come to him. He really hated to do what he was about to do, but it was necessary to cut many more people from the list.

An obvious cut that popped into his head was to cut the people with the diseases that would kill them in less than five years or required special medical facilities to survive. This also included those that required special or permanent medicines, because it would be years before they could make those medicines again. But then he thought. Since the trip would take many years, and the conditions and survival was going to be brutal and very tough, he decided with a long and deep moan, that he would cut those who were ninety years old or older since they were going to be traveling towards the light at the end of the dark tunnel shortly anyway. Also because most people who were ninety years old and older cannot put up with a brutal survival, they would probably not make it. The older people get, the harder it is for them to stay tough and stable. With the many harsh cuts that the leader of the United Nations had to make, there was no need for any more. All the seats were full and all the cuts that were necessary were made.

As I return to the present, where the many police officers were packing the spaceships one by one and two by two, I bless those who cannot go on the trip and that they may find peace, and I pray for those who get to go, that they have a safe trip and a safe "new" life.

In the spaceships, the safety belts locked in place and the takeoff light turned on as many people wave good-bye with tears streaming down their faces and prayers going through their head at a rapid speed. As they were about to count down for takeoff, they got a radio message saying that Venus had just been sucked into the sun, and Earth was soon to follow.

The countdown began. FIVE, FOUR, THREE, TWO -- WAIT! Another radio message was sent to each spaceship. They reported since Venus was sucked in, it disturbed the gravitational pull of the sun so much that the Earth was slowly going back into its original orbit. They were saved! The Earth was not going to be sucked into the sun! But it was too late. Some of the ships had already taken off and were in space heading for Planet-X, but the navigators were quickly brainstorming on how to turn themselves around and go back to Earth. The people on Earth were jumping for joy! With the new orbit, the summers were going to be hotter and the winters colder, but that is OK. They were not going to die and they were going to get to see and live once again with their loved ones just like it used to be before the solar system started collapsing.

Samantha Zimmerman

EXERCISE MACHINE

While I was sweating from a grueling workout at the gym I saw the weather dude on the TV. He showed the five day forecast and he explained that the nimbostratus clouds were going to be over the area and there was a ninety-nine percent chance of rain. Since the weather was not cooperating with my plans, I decided to go back to the gym.

While I was sitting in the gym doing unbearable sit-ups I heard a big blast of thunder. When I saw the enormous flash of lightning the Lean Mean Thigh Eating Machine turned into a person. I was so frightened I jumped up as high as a man on stilts. I had no idea what to do. I slowly walked over to the person and asked if he was okay.

He said, "Yes I am okay and my name is Bob."

He has short black hair, glistening blue eyes, and wearing a green suit.

We started talking and I figured out he was from Pig Palace, the supermarket next door. He was posing as an alien for the new improved alien cereal. We figured the lightning must have carried him from the supermarket to the gym. But where was the Lean Mean Thigh Eating Machine I asked. He had no idea where it went. So, we went on a walk curvy dark block. As we walked past Cow Castle, the shoe store, I saw it out of the corner of my eye, the Lean Mean Thigh Eating Machine was sitting out of Cow Castle's doors. It was still intact so, we decided to transport it back to the gym.

On our way back to the gym, we stopped and talked to a boy named Fred. He said he saw the whole thing while he was standing inside Pig Palace waiting on the thunder and lightning to stop. After a long time he finally told us that the lightning picked up Bob and carried him to the gym and took the Lean Mean Thigh Eating Machine to Cow Castle.

Fred ended up going home and Bob and I took the Lean Mean Thigh Eating Machine back to the gym. We were relieved that we knew what happened and everybody was safe.

After we got the Lean Mean Thigh Eating Machine back to the gym, Bob and I talked for a couple hours. I realized he was a member of the gym too. We decided to work out together a few times a week. It should be a lot of fun working out with the company of Bob.

Natalie L. Pendleton

THE NEW PUPPY

The Johnson family had always wanted a puppy. All four children wanted their very own, especially Ashley. Ashley had many friends who had dogs. Some had huge dogs, some had little, and some were in-between. Ashley's best friend, Megan, had a little, white, miniature poodle. The poodle's name was Kisses. Megan named her that because she always gave kisses. Ashley loved going over to Megan's house and playing with Kisses. She went to her house almost every day after school. Ashley loved animals, especially dogs. When her class did projects on animals, Ashley chose to write about dogs. She loved doing research on dogs. She would go on Websites like www.puppies.com and www.dogs.com. She was always looking for signs that said: PUPPIES FOR SALE or FREE PUPPIES.

One day Ashley was walking home from school with Megan, and she saw it. A sign that read:

NEW LITTER
LITTLE WHITE MALTESE PUPPIES
Call 555-9999

Ashley was so excited. She had always wanted a little white puppy. One time when she was watching a dog show, she saw a Maltese. It had long, white, beautiful hair. When she first glanced at it, she almost thought it was a little white mop! It was a dream come true. She said good-bye to Megan and raced home to tell her parents.

When Ashley got home, she ran into her mom and dad's room looking for them. They were not there so she looked in the study. Her mom and dad were there. She leaped for joy, and she stuttered, "M-M-M-M-M-Mom and D-D-Dad, may I get a puppy?"

There was a moment of silence. Her parents looked at her, and she looked at her parents anxiously.

Finally her dad said, "Ashley, it takes a lot of responsibility to have a dog. It would take a lot of money to buy the dog and its food, and after you buy it, you would have to take it to obedience school."

Ashley thought, and then responded, "I would really like a puppy. I would do extra work around the house to earn money. I'll do anything for a puppy!"

After that sincere explanation, Ashley's dad said, "Your mother and I will think about it and let you know in a few days."

Ashley left the study feeling bubbly inside. She didn't receive the answer she wanted, but her parents had not said no yet. She went to her room and started to think about the little puppies.

***

A few days later, after Ashley got home from school, her parents called her into their bedroom. When she walked in, her parents were smiling; she knew that was a good sign. Then her mom spoke up, "Your dad and I have been thinking, and we think that you are very responsible and old enough to have a pet, so... YES, you..."

That was all that needed to be said! Ashley jumped up and hugged her parents. She was so happy! Then she ran to her room to call the breeder of the puppies.

When Ashley called the number, the breeder started asking her questions. Questions like: what is your name, what are your parent's names, how old are you, and do you have any pets? After the breeder was finished asking questions, he told her that she could come pick out a puppy the next day after school.

The next day after school, Ashley and Megan went to pick out a puppy. When they rang the doorbell, the breeder, Mr. Fizz and three tiny puppies greeted them. Ashley and Megan laughed at the little fur balls. There were two girls and one boy. The puppies were so cute. Each one was very unique and special.

Ashley and Megan talked to Mr. Fizz and played with the puppies. Ashley had taken off her shoes, and the biggest girl was gnawing on her toes. Ashley thought it was so cute. She told Mr. Fizz, "That is the puppy I want."

Mr. Fizz took the little puppy, picked her up, put on a collar, and handed her to Ashley. Ashley thanked Mr. Fizz, and then Megan and she walked out the door.

When Ashley and Megan were walking home, they thought of names for the puppy. They thought of many names: some like Snowy, Mazy, Candy, Jazzy, Princess, Scottie, Sassy, Blanco, Fetch, Butch, Rufus, Eli, Tory, Lassy, Bruno, Flora, Duke, Dudly, Daisy, Yankee, Sketcher, and Sheltie. But none of the names seemed right.

Then just before they walked in the door, Ashley said, "I've got it! I can name her Angel!"

The puppy did a tiny little squeak. The name was decided. Ashley's new puppy would be called Angel.

When Ashley and Megan walked in the door, the whole family gathered around Angel.

Questions surrounded Ashley: "What is its name? Is it a girl or a boy? How many puppies were there,? May I hold it?"

Angel was surrounded by love. Ashley answered the questions one at a time. Then they set Angel down to explore the house.

Everyone was so happy, especially Ashley. She finally got a puppy of her very own, to take care of and love.

Jaclyn Marie Demeter
Age: 11

57

Chapter One, The Hero Awakens

In the beginning of time, there was a sword that was forged in the heart of Mt. Vellange. The maker of the sword forged it out of pure crystal. It was a beautiful sword and very sharp too. The maker set the sword on an altar in the middle of the biggest cathedral, on a planet far away from Earth.

"Eeeeeep! That was a close one," huffed a boy of about the age of ten with a piece of meat clutched close to his chest. An enormous butcher knife had passed the boy's head by mere centimeters. The boy stumbled and fell on cold hard concrete in an alleyway.

"You'd better give me that piece of lizard man meat," growled a butcher with a very rough voice. He also wore a bloodstained apron and was walking towards the boy.

"No," squeaked the little boy. "I bought it from you fair and square so you can't have it."

"The only problems are that first: you paid me too little and second: you gave me fake money. Soooo, if you've got a brain you're going to hand me that lizard man meat," said the butcher realizing for the first time who he was talking to and trying to sound a little more gentle.

"No, No, No, No, No, No, Nooo. I'm hungry and I paid for it fair and square. So go back before someone really steals from you. You Lakama Fouke," shouted the young boy at the butcher.

That pushed the butcher way over the line of patience. He howled a curse, picked up his knife and started chasing the young boy. He threw his gigantic knife straight at the boy's head but the boy jumped to the side and ran on. He nearly escaped the butcher's fury.

When the young boy was safely away from the butcher, he started to inhale his stolen prize. The boy's name was Brimagon, the best street rat in all of Tipany. A city on the planet of Tidamal. The year Brimagon was born in was the year 5665 A.D. which makes it the year 5675 A.D. He was very short for his age but he didn't mind this just meant he could pick pockets much easier. Mankind can go fifteen times faster than the speed of light. Therefore, they have journeyed farther than we could ever possibly imagine.

Tidamal is a vast world... Almost if not just as big as our own sun. Unfortunately, only a small amount of it is actually inhabited by humans and the reason for that is because there are so many strange and mythical creatures such as dragons, unicorns, centaur, and even more than that. There is also an enormous amount of rain forest and even more of it is desert. And for some strange reason the trees would not allow themselves to be cut down. So humans went for less-wooded areas of the planet. Tipany is the capital of Tidamal because it has so much more money than any of the other cities and it has the best defensive perimeter than any other city. Tipany is divided into two parts: Modern Heaven which is where all the soldiers, rich, and anyone that can afford this part of Tidamal, and Medieval Hell: the not-so-good section of Tidamal. This section is exactly like the medieval ages with all the manure on the streets, garbage on all corners of the streets, and the water runs straight through the streets collecting all the junk along the way. This is where Brimagon was, in Medieval Hell.

When Brimagon was finished with his lizard man meat he set off in search of someone suitable to pickpocket. He didn't want to get caught using fake money for as long as he could. He left the foul-smelling alley in search of money. He wandered the streets for what seemed like hours when he finally found a vulnerable target. A man who seemed to be in his fifties was twitching as if there was no tomorrow, looking, as if expecting somebody was going to attack him right then and there. Brimagon did see the sword sheath at the man's side which didn't frighten Brimagon at all. Instead of worrying about it, he crept as silently as he could to get within stealing distance of the man. His hand was hovering over the pocket when suddenly he slipped and fell onto the man.

"Whoa... wa, wa, watch where y'ere go, go, going Sonny. Do, do, don't want to surprise someone wi, wi, wi, with a sw, sw, sw, sword ya'know," stuttered the man still twitching and looking around. His voice was very entrancing, almost like an elven voice, which is the most beautiful sound on Tidamal.

"Move over ya old gizard. Yer in my way. I gotta go to me friend's house all right," snapped Brimagon, praising himself for his perfect act.

"Al, al, al, all right you can go." said the old man as he pushed Brimagon along. "Kids these days... Always in a hurry to get where they think they need to be."

When Brimagon thought he was far enough away he withdrew the man's wallet that he had stolen.

"You don't have to give me that but I would highly suggest that you get caught next time."

Brimagon was furious at this comment. So furious, that he threw the wallet back at the man he had just stolen it from.

"Do you really think I need your pity to live in this cruel world? Well? No I don't so if you don't mind you can give your wallet to someone who does," shouted Brimagon to the man as loud as his voice would allow him too.

"Fine I'll leave," replied the man very coolly.

Just who did this man think he was? thought Brimagon. His reply made Brimagon so mad that he attacked the man with his hidden knife. As Brimagon drew his knife he saw the man disappear in front of his very eyes. Brimagon was relieved that he didn't want to fight him. He put his knife back and took one step when he suddenly flew back and yelped in pain. He had just walked right into a barrier that wasn't there when he walked into the alley. Brimagon stopped and listened intently for anything weird or unusual. He listened for three minutes before he finally found the sound that he was listening for. Faint footsteps could be heard as he concentrated with all his might as to where it was coming from.

"Where are you, you old man? Huh! There you are," shouted Brimagon with triumph in his voice. He threw the knife as hard as he could at a wall that was graffitied. The footsteps stopped. Right after that, there was a sound of metal on metal as the man suddenly appeared in front of Brimagon. Brimagon's knife landed right next in front of him and the man's sword was drawn out of its sheath.

"THAT'S IT YOU STUPID STREET RAT. I WAS GOING TO SPARE YOUR LIFE BUT

YOU JUST HAD TO MAKE THINGS MORE DIFFICULT DIDN'T YOU," bellowed the man with his face starting to turn red.

"I didn't mean to," whimpered Brimagon backing away from the enraged man. But the man wasn't listening for he was charging forward with extreme speed, his sword raised as if to kill, screaming at the top of his lungs.

"You can't escape me now you little twerp not at all."

Brimagon shrunk back against the wall. Just as the man was about to strike, Brimagon put his hands up as if to stop the sword from striking. Brimagon waited for darkness to take him but it never did. He looked up to see if the man was stopped only to find the sword caught between his palms. His wrist bloodied so badly that Brimagon thought that he was going to die of blood loss. He lived but instead broke the blade in half. Then looked astounded at the sudden change in events. The man fell to the ground shaking his head vigorously. Brimagon took that chance and ran away. As he was exiting the alley, he picked up a dirty washcloth and wrapped it around his injured hand, wincing at the pain that his action caused.

I'm sorry but I will not reveal any more of my future book for fear of spoiling it way too early. If you wish to finish this story, look for a book written by me in the near future. Thanks.

Benjamin Helstad
Age: 14

THE PARTY

I was invited to a Halloween party at Doug's house. Everyone from my class was invited to the party. We had so much fun at his party!

Doug's mother Sally made a lot of good food such as: kitty litter cake, bat's eye candy which is made with peanut butter and chocolate, and blood juice which was red. All of the food was delicious. I can't wait to eat some more of her food if they have another party.

We played all kinds of games like: bobbing for apples, and playing hide-and-seek. We also played on the trampoline and swings. It was so much fun playing all of those games.

When I went to the party I made a lot of friends. I am glad that I went because I would not have met these people. I met Heather, Josh and Doug's family. I had so much fun meeting and talking to them.

The children at the party were scared of some of the costumes such as: clowns, skeletons, and the big gorilla. You should have seen the children's faces. They all jumped out of their seats. We had tons and tons of fun. It was great!

The children wore all kinds of costumes like: a dead person, hippy, p.j. girl, clown, and a lot of other cool costumes.

I can hardly wait to go to another one of Doug's parties.

Hannah Romanowski
Age: 11

THE GIRL AND HER GUITAR

The cold wind hit her face and whipped her flowing brown hair into disarray. She longed to be somewhere warm and out of the biting cold wind of early winter. Her long black boots slushed through dirty snow and made her feet feel cold as ice. It was at least two or more blocks to the café where she would be performing. More than anything else in this world, she loved her guitar and the glorious folk music that came from it. She was proud of her guitar and her wide sashes festooned with third world embroidery on it. To her, all this was magical.

As she walked down the street, memories of her past flooded her mind, as a lonely tear trickled down her cheek. How could she forget that day she left home forever? So many memories; how could she ever forget.

It was a late autumn day in October of '62 when she left home for the first time, with only twenty dollars in her pocket. She went down the long street, with only a backpack of clothes on her back. She was leaving New Jersey and heading for New York City in search of a new life. When she finally reached the bus station, she purchased a ticket for New York City. She stepped into the bus and went to sit next to a girl about her age.

"Hi, my name is Corin," she said.

"Hi, I'm Margo."

"Are you bound for New York?" Margo asked.

"Yes I am. I thought maybe I would go to Greenwich Village. I heard that is where all the folk singers live. I've always wanted to be a folk singer. I have a guitar and some music I wrote and brought it with me."

"That's where I'm headed, too. I have ambitions of becoming an artist. I heard that many artists go there to become inspired by what they see and hear in the village," Margo replied.

They soon got acquainted with each other and shared their dreams of a new life. Since they were going to the same city, they decided they should share an apartment together.

"We're both new to this sort of life. It might be easier than finding places on our own don't you think?" Margo said.

"Yeah, that would be a good idea. Let's try to find an apartment with a skylight so you can make it into a studio and I can also enjoy looking at the stars at night," Corin replied.

"Yeah, I like that idea Corin. I really do," Margo replied enthusiastically.

As she rode along, the beautiful scenery engulfed her, farmland ready for harvest and trees the color of red, orange, yellow and the most lovely shade of green. She sat there pondering, was she doing the right thing? Then she went into a fitful sleep.

It was morning when they arrived at their new destination. It took them a little while to get settled, but they finally found a perfect little flat with a skylight. Margo started her painting and Corin started practicing on her guitar. They loved life in the village. The village was always filled with excitement and intrigue. As weeks went by, Corin enjoyed playing her guitar and singing folk songs as people gathered around to listen. Soon she was invited to play at a little café.

When Corin reached the little cafe, lively folk music filled the air as people sat around talking or listening. Corin found a small table and sat down.

"Corin!" A voice yelled from across the café; it was Margo. She walked over to Corin's table.

"Guess what?" Margo asked.

"What?" Corin answered.

"Bob Dylan is coming here tonight to listen to those who want to pursue a music career!" Margo said excitedly.

"Who's Bob Dylan?" Corin asked.

"You mean you don't know who he is?" Margo said in astonishment.

"No, tell me," Corin said in an agitated voice.

"Well, he's a folk singer and has just made a new record called "The Freewheelin' Bob Dylan." He lives here in the village and is very good looking," Margo replied swooning at the thought of him.

"Oh, Margo, you think every guy is good looking," Corin said rolling her eyes.

"Well, Bob Dylan's different! He knows how to connect people by being honest about life in his songs. What made you so late?" Margo then asked.

"I decided to walk; I wanted to think," Corin replied.

"I was getting worried, you wouldn't show up," Margo said.

"I'm fine, Margo, really," Corin said in a subdued voice.

Just then Bob Dylan walked into the café; all eyes were on him. He found a seat and sat down. As soon as he sat down, everyone started talking again.

"Do you want coffee?" asked Corin.

"Yeah, that would be great," Margo replied watching Bob Dylan's every movement.

Corin ordered two cups, one with cream and sugar; the other strong and black. The waitress placed the two mugs in front of them. Corin took a sip. It was very hot, strong and black, just the way she liked it. Just then a guy came over to where they were sitting.

"You better get ready, you're on in five minutes," he said hurriedly and then left.

"OK, I'm coming," Corin replied in a nervous voice.

Corin got up and took out her guitar from its case. The beautiful sashes hung from it, so colorful and so full of life. She was shaking and her hands were sweaty.

Why am I so nervous? she thought to herself.

"Are you okay Corin?" Margo asked.

"I'm fine; I'm just terribly nervous," Corin said in a shaky tone.

"You'll do fine. You're just nervous 'cause Bob Dylan's here and he'll be watching you perform," Margo replied encouragingly.

"I guess," Corin replied, not really believing her. "Wish me luck," Corin said and walked away.

"Good luck; knock 'em dead!" Margo yelled to her.

Corin fixed her shirt. All night long she had stressed over what to wear. She finally decided on a magenta-colored turtleneck, her navy blue surplus peacoat and a faded pair of jeans.

She walked up to the front; everyone grew quiet. She pushed her hair out of her face, sat down on the stool and began to play. The music and the words flowed freely from her voice and her fingers glided over the strings gracefully. A loud applause rang out after the song was over. Corin got down off the stool and sat down with Margo.

"You were fabulous, Corin. Everyone loved it. I always loved that song!" Margo replied enthusiastically.

"Thanks, Margo, you're sweet," Corin replied.

Just then Bob Dylan came over to their table.

"You did a great job; you really know how to play the guitar and have a great voice for singing," Bob Dylan said.

"Thank you," Corin replied.

Bob Dylan nodded and walked away. He was heading out the door and he turned around and waved to her and then he left. Corin was so in awe, she couldn't speak. She had never met a man like him before and never would again. Just then her thoughts were interrupted by Margo's voice.

"I can't believe he actually talked to you. He must have liked you to come over and tell you how good you were." Margo said.

"Yes, he must have," Corin replied.

As they left the café together, they began to talk about how coming to Greenwich Village had changed their lives and seeing their dreams come true. Corin would always remember the words of encouragement by the famous Bob Dylan that changed her life forever. While Corin continued with her folk singing, Margo would become the artist that she had always dreamed about becoming. They were able to experience the new life they went searching for.

Lisa Hamilton
Age: 14

THE LUCKY RACE

Mark is a boy in the sixth grade. He has a friend named John, a mom, a dad, a brother, and a sister. He goes to a big school and he loves to learn. Mark has been training for a race, with help from his family. He also has a good luck charm.

One sunny Tuesday morning, Mark was about to leave his house to go to school. He ate breakfast and talked about school with his parents. Then the bus came and he got on it after saying good-bye to his family. He sat by his best friend John.

"Hi John," said Mark.

"Hi," said John. "I'm getting ready for the race tomorrow, are you?"

"Yes," answered John.

They said nothing else to each other the rest of the day.

After school, Mark went home and started to go up to his room. When he did, he noticed his brother and sister running out of his room. His brother was holding something in his hand. Mark could not see it because they were running so fast.

He went in his room anyway. He started training. His room was very big. He looked for his good luck charm but could not find it. It was gone. He started searching through the house panicking. He asked everybody if they had seen it, but they said they had not seen it. He invited John over to help him.

"When was the last time you saw it?" asked John.

"In my room," answered Mark.

They started searching but couldn't find it. They searched the big house two times, but still couldn't find it. They gave up.

Race day came and Mark hoped he would win. He still did not have his charm. Fifteen minutes later, the race began. There were ten runners including him. There were ten laps around the big track. Mark was very tired when the last lap came. He had to pass John for the lead. Right before the race ended he made the pass and won. Even though very tired, he was happy he could win without his charm.

He went home and his family congratulated him. His brother and sister told everybody to sit on the couch. They ran upstairs, laughing. They came back with Mark's good luck charm. They told Mark that his mom and dad wanted to take the charm away as a joke. Everybody, even Mark, laughed. And Mark learned he didn't need a good luck charm to win a race.

Braden Prater
Age: 10

"Okay!" Kim said to the manager. She had to be in tomorrow at 7:00 a.m. instead of 9:00 a.m. because she was late this morning -- but she was happy to work overtime for her manager -- anything to keep her job. He had already gotten angry with her five times today.

At the end of every workday, there was one thing that made Kim happy -- going to Mr. Lindon's library.

Kim walked through the glass door and was a little less than happy to find that Mr. Lindon was not at his desk. He was always there to greet her. Maybe she was just having a bad day at work and at the library.

There is pretty much nothing to say about Mr. Lindon, the librarian. He had a pleasant personality except when his helper Alex, who was constantly asking questions, made him a little angry.

Kim looked around at the shelves of books for a while. Then one caught her eye and she pulled it out. At that moment she knew there was something about that book that she just couldn't let go of. She made her way to the counter, checked out the book, and left silently.

Kim had a simple life. She was fourteen. After school on Fridays (and Saturday and Sunday) she went to work at a restaurant called The Food Source. On her way home she would stop at Mr. Lindon's library, and then she would go home to read the books that she had checked out.

Kim opened the door to her house.

"I'm home!" she called.

She put the book on the kitchen table and went upstairs to change out of her work clothes.

As soon as Kim went upstairs the book started growing...

When Kim came back down she stared at the book on the table. It seemed bigger to her.

"Maybe I'm losing my mind," Kim decided.

She grabbed the book and she sat down with a can of soda. She started reading and continued until she fell asleep. She woke up for school late the next morning. When she found herself on the couch, she realized that she never went to her bed and slept. She had slept on the couch the whole night.

Her older brother, dad and mom had already gone to work, but nobody woke her up. She was all alone.

Kim glared at the book. She was not losing her mind. The book was about twice the size of a huge dictionary. Kim screamed. Then she heard a voice. It sounded like it was coming from the book.

It said, "Kim, I shall keep growing until I get big enough to reach out and pull you in, I need you Kim."

Kim was so scared, she ran all the way to Mr. Lindon's with the book. What she found made her burst into tears. Lying on the ground there was a pile of ashes where Mr. Lindon's library had been.

She put the book on top of the pile and ran all the way home. She unlocked her door and ran in to get ready for school. Then she ran to school hoping that she wasn't late, but she was.

When she got out of school she walked past the library. The ruins were being cleaned up. When she saw the book she ran.

She got home safely but found a note on the kitchen table saying the family went shopping and would be back at 9:00. It was only 5:30. She decided to read in her room, but when she got there she heard the same voice calling:

"Kim this is me, Mr. Lindon. How could you do this to me?"

When Kim's family got home she wasn't there. All they found was an oversized book laying on the dresser in Kim's room. Nobody but those who read this story knows what happened to her.

Taylor Williams

THE DAY I SET MY CLUBHOUSE ON FIRE

It was the day of February 23, 2004 and I was up at my clubhouse working on it. I went down to get my brother and forgot about the fire. I came back out and saw smoke going everywhere. So I went up and saw that the door had caught on fire, and all I had was tea and creek water. So I used the tea but it didn't work. So I used the creek water and it worked. Then my mom came out and came up and looked at it and thank goodness the smoke was gone or I would have been grounded.

Katlyn A. E. Beavers

A crackle came across the speakers. The thumping of Sarah's heart reminded her of Scout, the horse she used to ride every summer at Grandma Josie's house when she had her two-week break from her rigorous ice-skating training. Sarah feared the noise would be audible to anyone near her. Thank goodness the only person around was her beloved ice-skating coach Marla Dean. The sweat began to cascade from her brow like the beautiful Horseshoe Falls she enjoyed as she trotted along riding Scout.

On the inside, nervousness penetrated through her entire body. The feeling was like the touch of a monster's fingers she used to have nightmares about before important ice-skating competitions. This deceitful beast now decided to haunt her on the most important day of her amateur figure skating career. Sarah had always hoped she would tame this monster that intruded on her confidence before she reached the pinnacle of amateur figure skating, but she would have no such luck today.

This creepy monster made her leg twitch as she shivered. Sarah heard the crinkle of the plastic covering the numerous bouquets of beautiful red roses and fresh-cut daisies as her leg bumped the pile sitting next to her. The ice attendant retrieved a few soft, fluffy bears thrown by adoring fans. Sarah reached for a large white bear. Sarah clenched the bear for support. More than anything Sarah longed for a hug from her mother, but she was sitting in the stands with her other adoring fans.

Sarah's mother had sacrificed so much to allow Sarah to have private coaching. Sarah's mother had worked overtime at a local factory in addition to her job as a secretary at a law firm. Sarah's mother missed many hours of sleep to drive Sarah to early morning ice-skating practices. Sarah recalled the vivid hues of pinkish-red that glazed the early morning sky when she arrived at the rink for daily practice. At the end of practice, Sarah returned into the brisk weather to find her mother with her head lying on the steering wheel, trying to catch a glimpse of the sandman before heading to work.

She now recalled the years of years of struggling to complete double axles and triple toe loops. Scars and bruises marked her skin reminiscent of the falls she endured. Those were the years of competing with herself struggling to master each move on lonesome and eerie ice rinks.

Sarah prayed that her nearly flawless performance would be enough to place her on the top of the medal stand. She yearned to hear the notes of the national anthem and see the stars and stripes in a prominent place before her eyes. The feeling of the weight hanging close to her heart would be the perfect representation of the joy figure skating never ceased to bring to her heart.

Years of figure skating created the exquisite piece of artwork she skated moments ago. What would her talent amount to if she didn't patch the work together? What good would colored patches be if they weren't sewed tightly to create a pretty quilt? What if her name never amounted to anything but little piece on a television special or a paragraph in a book about all the talented skaters who slipped as they reached the top of the mountain? She poured her entire soul into her performance. Her heart rested in the fate-bearing hands of the judges. They could either squash it or handle it as if they were caring for their own young child. They could break her down to pulverized bits or lift her to the top of the world.

Sarah's dream had been set free like a monarch butterfly she once watched develop in her third grade class. She could no longer foster the butterfly, in the jar, because she was set free to enrich the world. She loved the butterfly, though she could no longer care for her. So many people keep their dreams caged, but Sarah had the courage to set them free. The outcome of her bravery remained in flight. Her skating was like that butterfly waiting to make that perfect landing on the prettiest flower, and not wanting to settle for anything less.

The beat of her song traveled through her pulse. Each note of her music played in her mind while synchronized with the beating of her constantly pounding heart. The final moments of the performance played in Sarah's mind. A crisp clean landing of her double axle-triple toe loop combination and a shower of ice chips as her toe pick struck the cool, smooth ice. She had thrust her arms towards the heavens as a smile emerged on her face. The final crescendo was drowned by the thunderous applause. Speckles of color rose before her eyes as the crowd rewarded her with a standing ovation.

"And the marks for Sarah Moore," stated the announcer.

Everything terrible consumed her inside the monster gripping her stomach and her heart beat at the speed of Scout's canter. Sarah released an ear-shattering gasp.

The faces in the crowd began to blur as her eyes clouded over. Sarah wanted to brush away the drops of water that had already formed a large puddle of water on her red satin outfit. Sarah took her still-shaking hands up to her face to brush away the tears. Now, as Sarah looked at the scoreboard seven straight perfect scores were revealed.

Ann Burkhardt
Age: 18

THE CHRONICLES OF PLAID MAN

Lee Donaldson was an average man, in an average life, he worked from nine to five, and yeah he paid the price. All he wanted was to be left alone, in his average home, but fate didn't want the same for him. One day, while driving his old '86 Mazda 626 to his pathetic desk job, he saw a luminous cloud in the distance, all alone in-between him and a sunny blue sky.

"Hmm, that's strange!" remarked Lee, wondering what this could be.

At that moment, as if the fates were answering his question, a huge meteorite struck the hood of his car, and it burst into flames. Ah, yes. He's not dead yet though, so wipe your tears.

Lee awoke suddenly, surrounded by people in white coats and robotic arms, and everything smelled like ammonia. He blinked, and he heard a trillion buzzing sounds go off, as doctors and nurses rushed to his side.

"Sir, do you know where you are?"

"Uggghhh..."

"Sir, you've been in an incredibly serious car accident, and you have been close to death for a month now, in a coma. It's a miracle you've survived."

"Ugghhh..."

"Well, you may have lived but the bad news is that you look like... well, not good sir... Your skin was burnt worse than KFC chicken and all your appendages were amputated. Basically, all that's left is your head and torso. I am so sorry."

"What? Man, that bites."

"Yes, but we've replaced your appendages with indestructible stainless steel arms and legs, making you stronger and faster, kind of like the show "The Six Million Dollar Man.""

"OK."

"Sir, you will be released tomorrow, but in order to not scare the general public to death, you must wear all-plaid clothes at all times during the day, for it's the only material that will hide your hideous appearance."

"Gee, you're so sensitive, Doc."

"Well, I try. Now get some rest. You will need it for all the appallingly rude comments people will make about your ugly, smelly face."

"Okay."

The next day Lee Donaldson woke up feeling like a million bucks. He looked into the hallway, wondering where it would take him. As he swaggered out of bed, he headed to the bathroom, tripping and stumbling many times. After he was done, he signed all the release papers, and he was off. The medical staff gave him an enormous supply of plaid clothing, in various colors, and then he was released back into the world.

"Let's see what these babies can do!" he exclaimed as he started running on his new stainless steel legs. "Wow! These things really work! I'm really running!" he yelled, feeling on top of the world. In a few minutes, he was winded and stopped to take a break, got a little chilly, and threw on his plaid jogging suit.

"Whoa..." Lee mumbled as a strange blue glow started emitting from his legs. Suddenly a tingly feeling ran up his spine, and into his brain. His fake arms got larger, he sprouted more hair on his head, and his fake legs got as powerful as a donkey's! He felt like The Hulk!

Whoosh! Lee sped by everyone on the sidewalk at 60 mph! He was faster and stronger, and could go to work faster on foot than by car (there are obviously no speed limits when running on foot)! He helped old ladies and beat up criminals, and was feeling pretty good that particular day, but then evil reared its ugly head.

"Ah! Get away from me! Someone help, please! I'm being attacked!" a lady screamed in the distance.

Lee, sensing obvious and immediate danger, rushed to the scene to find something incredibly and horribly gruesome. Some sicko had been stapling people and animals to walls all over the street!

"Muhahaha!" yelled a raspy voice down the street. Lee had heard about this guy in today's newspaper. They had called him "The Iconoclast," and he was supremely evil. He sported an enormous utility belt around his bulky waist, containing evil heavy-duty staples, paper clips, and extra-sticky DOUBLE-SIDED TAPE!

"Growing weak... too many evil office supplies... must... resist..." but it was no use. He started walking towards him in a comatose-like state, just like all the other townspeople. Suddenly a tiny voice popped into his head, saying, "You must resist this evil fiend, and help the townspeople! They need your help! Snap out of it son!"

New life was restored to Plaid Man. He quickly jumped into action by setting his super bionic legs to "karate master" mode, as he yelled, "Heeya!" The showdown had begun (cue old western music). The Iconoclast quickly reached for his supremely evil staples, but our hero reached him before he could fully draw them out. Legs and arms were flailing mercilessly for almost five minutes, and then the dust cleared. The Iconoclast had Plaid Man's hands and feet tightly tied with his extra-sticky double-sided tape! Oh no! But Plaid Man would not be massacred without a decent fight, because otherwise this story would be dumb. So he swung over and used his razor-sharp teeth to sever The Iconoclast's nose! He quickly started biting him all over, with brutal force.

"Ow! Owie! Ouch!" The Iconoclast screamed over and over again, "Stop it! That hurts! I want my teddy bear!"

Immediately after the last comment was uttered from his hate-tinged lips, the entire crowd burst into giggles. The giggles soon became laughter, and the laughter escalated into uncontrollable sobbing fits of complete hysteria! Unfortunately because of this, everyone in town died because they couldn't breathe, so Plaid Man was banished to Siberia. How unfortunate.

"Brrrr...!" Our hero shivered violently out in the cold, harsh climate that enveloped Siberia. He has been walking for miles after his plane had crashed into the hills and he had escaped only because a large man in front of him had broken his fall. No one on the plane had survived but him, and every communication device had been destroyed, severing his link to the outside world.

Reaching a spot of land where the snow was only about fifteen feet deep, our hero decided to make base camp. Fortunately a bunch of really tall trees were just breaking above the crusty snow. Plaid Man turned his legs on "Saw" mode, and quickly turned the dense snow-covered forest into a bountiful pile of firewood that would last him weeks if need be. Pulling out an extra set of matches from his pocket, he lit the fire and was warm in no time. The trouble was, since there was so much snow, and no rocks to make a fire pit, Plaid Man was forced to build the fire on top of the snow (don't worry kids, Smokey says that fire hazard level is very low for today). The snow quickly melted away, and melted, and then melted some more, until Plaid Man was sitting in a hole fifteen feet deep. The good thing was, he had finally found green grass, and there was no longer any wind chilling his body.

"Meow! Meow!" a cat nearby purred contentedly.

"Holy Gravy!" yelped Plaid Man, "it's Magic Kitty Kat! Help Kitty Kat! I'm down here!"

Magic Kitty Kat was a supposedly imaginary beast that lived in the foothills of Siberia, and she rescued stranded hikers and superheroes that had been banished. She quickly dove into the hole without a second thought, and jumped back out with her magic leaping ability. A miracle! She quickly bounded back to good old Homesville, Plaid Man's hometown. She dropped Plaid Man off on his front doorstep, and with a blink of an eye, was bounding off once again.

Plaid Man was safe once again, and the now repopulated town had realized that Plaid Man was trying to help them, so they unbanished him. Everyone was happy once again. So the moral of the story is, don't ever say you want your teddy bear in public. It kills people!

Kevin Aabel

UNDER THE RUG

"Two weeks passed and it happened again."

Amy Collins was an average kid. She went to Columbia Middle School in Texas, and everything was fine until her mom died. Her dad couldn't take care of her, so she was sent to her only other relative, Uncle Joe.

She didn't know much about him, since she had never seen him before, and as the minutes went by she grew nervous. Questions were sprouting up in her mind. Would he be nice? Would he like her? She had so many questions, but came up with no answers at all. The ride seemed to take hours, but yet it was only a few minutes. Suddenly they came to a halt in front of a shabby-looking cottage, and there he was, standing in front of the door, Uncle Joe.

He was a slim-looking man. He wore a dirty pair of glasses, and a worn-out hat on his head. He looked pretty friendly, standing there with a silly grin on his face. Amy said good-bye to her dad, and began to walk up the long, curving driveway. Uncle Joe came to meet her, and with a simple hello they walked into the house.

The first thing she noticed was the large, twisting rug lying out on the floor. It looked old, along with just about everything else in the house. He had antique tables with expensive-looking lamps on them, and unusual paintings on the dark walls. She felt uneasy with the eerie paintings looming over her. Uncle Joe picked up Amy's bags and carried them up the long, musty stairway to her room. Uncle Joe plopped her bags on the dirty floor, opened the curtains, and left Amy to inspect her room. Amy guessed that the room was hardly ever used, by the looks of it. It was covered in thick sheets of dust, and the only blanket on the bed was a foul-smelling quilt. She looked out the window, and was not surprised to see a gloomy forest as her view, but something seemed to catch her eye. A dark shadow was lurking at the edge of the forest, but as soon as it had appeared, it vanished.

As the days passed, the vision of the shadow kept coming back to her. One day she was in her room thinking about the mysterious shape when she heard a yell, and shortly after, a thud. She ran downstairs and was surprised to see Uncle Joe with a chair over his head, swinging at a lump under the rug. The lump was moving forward, and in the process knocking over lamps and tables. Uncle Joe signaled Amy to leap upon the lump, but when she did it vanished instantly. Amy and Uncle Joe thought that it was gone for good, but they were wrong, because two weeks passed and it happened again.

It was a hot day in the middle of August, and Amy had just turned twelve. They were enjoying the afternoon sun, when there came a small stir, but neither one heard it for they were listening to the summer breeze. There was a short scream, a loud shout, and neither one was heard from again.

Sarah Suzanne Zabel
Age: 11

QUEST FOR THE PRINCESS

Long, long ago, in a deep forest, there was a beautiful castle with a young princess. She was like an angel, with long blonde silky hair with braids from head to toe. Her eyes were like crystals in the steaming sun. Her voice was like blue jays swaying on treetops.

One misty, dull day, her voice stopped and an eerie scream echoed through the village. I scampered off the log I was sitting on and headed for the valley in the forest where the castle stood sturdy like knights at war. As I approached the castle, I heard sobbing through the portcullis. I knocked a couple of times and crept in. As I silently padded down the long, royal red carpet, I asked in my most royal and polite voice, "Why does the king cry?"

To my surprise, he mumbled, "Get away, you ol' peasant boy, Jack!"

But I wasn't leaving until I found out what happened to the princess, Elizabeth.

"Where's Elizabeth?" I demanded sternly.

"She... she... she..."

"Tell me!" I insisted, even though you should never talk to someone royal like that!

The king couldn't ignore that, so he finally told me, "Medusa."

Right then and there, I whispered, "Oh." Seconds later, I thought out loud, "I could go rescue Elizabeth, Princess Elizabeth."

The king snickered and then acted like I wasn't good enough and he complained, "I need someone to find my daughter who's royal, for the reward is to marry her."

In my head, I thought, I better go and find Elizabeth. I rushed out the door.

I knew exactly where to start, the dungeons! I decided not to tell the king what I was up to. So, I rushed down the staircase with my hands against the rough wall.

I stopped dead in my tracks as I glared at the big fire-bolting, eye-glaring dragon facing me. Oh, boy! I thought, but I walked forward.

"Hi..." I choked, staring at the dragon.

He coughed and glared at me. I decided to bribe the dragon to tell me where Medusa and Elizabeth were. I knew he had something to do with this!

He cleared his throat and in an old squeaky voice, he told me everything, that Medusa was owned by an evil wizard who wanted to be king so bad that he would do anything. He stole Elizabeth so the king would come out looking for her so he could take over the castle and be king.

I realized the dragon had nothing to do with this, so I let him be free and come on the quest with me.

We snuck out the north tower and were on our way. As we tumbled through the leaves, we heard a rattling behind us. I stopped and turned around. Nothing seemed to be there!

Someone's following us, I thought, but I kept on going. Then, when we were on our way out of the leafy forest, something jumped on my back and started pulling my hair. I twisted and snatched at it. Nothing worked. I fell on the dirt floor and it let go. I rubbed my back a couple of times and turned around.

There was a tiny, little goblin jumping up and down yelling, "Me Glob, me name Glob!"

I knew I had a follower, so all I said was, "Let's go," even though I was as annoyed as a frustrated baby-sitter with two toddlers.

A couple of minutes later, I heard more rustling. I hoped it wasn't another goblin because I already had scratches on my head from Glob, but it wasn't anyone close to a goblin. It was an old man with a long robe, and in his hand there was a leash with Medusa on it! While Glob and the dragon distracted them, I ran!

As I was running, I fell into a ditch and down in the ditch, was Princess Elizabeth! I was so relieved.

As we were walking in the ditch, we fell into a tunnel that led back into the dungeons, but then I remembered Glob and the dragon, so we went back to get them.

When we got back to the castle, I won the reward to marry Elizabeth and we all lived happily ever after.

Lauren Jesch
Age: 8

MY FIRST BIRTHDAY

On my first birthday I was scared because I did not know what was going on. So I stayed with my mom the whole time. When it was time to eat cake, my mom kept telling me to shove my face in it. I would say no and a while after that she shoved my face for me. It was funny!

Later that day we played a game called limbo, but I always cheated on it.

Then my mom yelled, "Come and open your gifts Whitney."

So I ran as fast as I could to get there first but I kept falling down. When I finally got there I got the biggest gift to open it. My mom wanted me to open the smaller ones first. So I opened the smallest one first. It was a box with pink and blue circles on it. When I opened it, there was a card and a purple dog collar. I wondered why I got a dog collar and there was no dog. So I opened more gifts. One was very small and had a dog tag in it, and another gift was a dog bowl. I also got a leash, a dog food bag, and a dog toy. Finally, the last gift was the biggest gift ever. When I opened it, it was a dog house with purple painting on it.

Finally my mom said here's your last gift. It was a box with holes on it. When I opened it a puppy jumped out and started to lick me. My mother asked me what I wanted to name it, and I said Rosey. Then my mom put on her collar with the tag. She even put the leash on Rosey, so I could walk her. She kept pulling me so I gave her to my mom. I said to my mom that this was the best birthday ever! Have you ever had a really good birthday? Well, I have had the best one ever!!!

Whitney Nicole Jenkins
Age: 10

I CAN MAKE IT!

Have you ever lived through an unforgettable experience that would change your life forever? I did, Lana Kecaler is my name and I am willing to tell you about my experience. Although it's not my most favorite thing to talk about. I think some people should know how lucky they are.

I wasn't quite stunning or the best at anything, but I was definitely determined. Determined as I was toward getting good grades, doing my very best, and striving to get to my top standard.

In school I was never the center of attention, but I liked it that way. After all that would mean no one would have any reason to tease me or call me rude names. I'm not saying they did at first because they didn't.

I think of myself as a hardworking, talented, young lady. I was not a selfish wannabe that cares about nothing but fitting in. I don't come from a wealthy, certain family. So it would be hard to get fitted, skintight clothes from places like Gap and American Eagle, that girls wear. However I will admit I was self-conscious of myself, but at that age everyone was. Making sure their teen hair was sleek, their clothes fitted every curve, and to have the latest trends.

Yeah, I had desires and wants as everyone does. But, I kept them to myself. I would not want my parents to feel guilty for not being able to supply me with the big, stuffed horse, or that killer poster of Ty Bersky with his signature.

I tend to wonder what it would be like to have anything I wanted. Then I stop myself and thank God for the things I have, like family and love. Also for allowing me to be strong and overcome my problems.

You see a few years ago when I was twelve years old my parents realized I was acting differently. I never wanted to be bothered, and it seemed my wonderful grades started going down the gutter. Of course, I didn't realize that I was getting bad grades as much. I felt I was just getting challenged more because of my high grades. It was as if my brain was not functioning, or something just continued to get in my way.

Later, all my friends started getting annoyed with my actions. So slowly they began to drift further away. If I would present myself around them they would give me a snarl and strut away. Later, after taking this punishment for a long time I realized they were ignoring me.

The next day I was so frustrated it felt like I was splitting in two different directions. My parents were more aggravated with me in a way that seemed impossible. I was always a good, helpful child showing love everywhere. Every night I would give hugs and kisses to my parents but, wasn't like that anymore. Instead I was completely different from what I once was.

I began cutting my clothes and resewing them so they'd fit tighter. I also started asking people at school for lunch money as if I didn't have any, although I did. When I got money from people I would go out and buy some hairspray, curlers, and anything else I wanted for myself. But my bad deeds were not over. I would spend generous people's money on unneeded clothing. I tried as hard as I could to fit in but nothing helped. I didn't realize that regardless of how much I tried to be cool, I couldn't. It wouldn't fit my laid-back personality.

I started watching television shows that showed people who would get abused or abuse themselves. I would think to myself, who are they kiddin' I got it much worse than them! However I didn't.

After watching those shows I started thinking that I was getting abused. If my parents would send me to my room, I would think that was abusive. I would get continuous headaches that were unbearable. I stocked myself up with pain and stress relievers, my parents took in their hard times. However, they didn't help me much. If the drugs did help the relief would soon be over.

The drugs just weren't enough for me. I decided to try a new stress reliever that people said worked. Wow, I never knew cutting and abusing myself could have been the stress relievers that others have done. There were several teens that would do that.

The next day, my mother seemed to be so angry over the way I've been acting that I didn't want to be around her. Could you blame me though? However, I was lucky and had to go to a doctor's appointment with her. She said it was a regular checkup that I was due for. Yet, I knew the reason was that she really thought I was going crazy!

When we got there the doctor was ready and waiting at his office door. I have a gut feeling that I have the weirdest doctor out of them all. His name is Mr. LeGal or should I say Dr. LeGal to be proper. He's a large, tall, mysterious man, always silent when checking patients. The way his beard shags makes him look like it's been forever since he shaved. His hair combed side to side with a bare line down the middle. Do you know that thing that happens to men when they get older? How they develop long ear and nose hairs that stick out if they're not trimmed? It doesn't look like he's ever trimmed them!

We went into his also dark and spooky room. (When I was younger it was the most horrifying place). I sat on the bed. And he began to check my pulse with his cripply, cold hands. Then, continued to check me normally.

After the normal he went to a different series of checkups. These checkups were strange and tense. Dr. LeGal was extremely serious.

Finally, the checkups were over. I could feel weight lifting off my shoulders. However, I was about to find out news that would put the weight back on. I wasn't prepared for this.

Nurse Gloria appeared with several papers. She motioned my mom to come with her. My mother hesitated then walked unsteadily toward Nurse Gloria.

They were in Dr. LeGal's office forever! When they finally got out they had unsure and troubled faces instead of relieved faces. So I knew at that very sight bad news was about to be delivered, so I did all I could, I ran. Hard and fast as a thunderbolt I was out the door and into our old, ragged, gold Jeep. I locked myself in forgetting my mom had the key.

She got in and we slowly drove back to our bright blue house. In the door and up the stairs I went. My mother went straight to my dad. When she got done with him tears were rolling down her cheek and Dad looked scared. Through the silence they knew it was time to break the news to me.

The process was long and tough but I waited 'til they were ready to spill. After a while my dad took a deep breath and told me I had a serious case of depression. I was shocked! I questioned my parents and they informed me that I had a sadness depression.

The news was tough and hard to take. Why am I depressed? What is so bad in my life? My head was spinning in so many directions.

One day after my diagnosis I woke up hot and sweaty. (My head still spinning.) My parents decided to stock me up with pills and have a talk with me. I was late for school too.

Later I felt better from the pills, but my grades and friendships were still troubling. Suddenly at school it all came to me. My depression was from friends, grades, parents, and much more. Sitting alone at lunch upset me. Understanding made me feel better.

After I got home I had a counselor waiting to talk with me. She showed me the razor with blood and skin on it. She was here to talk to me about that.

I got flustered after knowing my parents snooped in my personal belongings. It never went across my mind that they might have done it to help me.

Now it has though. I am doing so much better in school and I got most my friends back too. I am more of the loving person I once was. I have stopped cutting up my body and am looking at myself in a better way. Even though I have given myself scares and at fourteen I am taking several pills daily, I am surviving and each day becoming more of the person I was and the person I want to be. Now and forever I will live my life to the fullest.

Emily Fishbough

THE PRINCESS PUP

Once upon a time there was a town of dogs. A lonely dog named Lucy lived there, but she didn't have a home. She lived at the dog pound, but it wasn't because she was bad. Some of the other dogs were mean to her and made her do all of their chores. The only dogs who did it were Kailey and Katie. They did this because they were jealous of Lucy. They made her pick up their toys and clean their cages every day, and if Lucy didn't, they made her do more things. Then one nice and sunny day the prince, named Max, was having a ball to find a dog to marry. Every dog went, but Kailey and Katie told Lucy she couldn't go. Lucy really wanted to go but was afraid of what Kailey and Katie might do to her.

The day of the ball Lucy helped Kailey and Katie get ready. She did their hair, ironed their dresses, and picked out their shoes. When they were off to the ball Lucy sat down and rested. Then she heard a "poof," so she looked out the window and saw a dog with wings and a wand shaped like a bone. She went outside and the dog was Lucy's Fairy Dog Mother. She asked Lucy what she wanted most and Lucy said to go to the ball. Her Fairy Dog Mother said she could make that happen. She waved her wand and turned Lucy's cage into a carriage, a cat into a horse, and Lucy's rags into a beautiful yellow and pink diamond collar. She changed a toy into a driver. Her Fairy Dog Mother told Lucy to have a great time, but she had to be back before the clock struck midnight. Lucy's Fairy Dog Mother said good-bye and Lucy was off to the ball. When Lucy got to the ball, Prince Max saw her and asked her to dance, so they did. Just as the clock struck midnight Prince Max was going to crown who he was going to marry. Lucy ran off, but that was who he was going to crown. She lost her diamond collar while she was running. Prince Max found it, but didn't find Lucy. He said he would go to every house until he found Lucy. When Lucy got back to the pound Kailey and Katie weren't there yet. She changed back into herself. The next day Prince Max came to the pound to try the collar on every dog there. When he got to Lucy it fit perfectly!!! He announced that he was going to marry Lucy. The very next day, Prince Max and Princess Lucy were married!! They invited everyone, even Kailey and Katie to the wedding. Prince Max gave Lucy a diamond crown. Lucy finally got a home and they lived happily ever after!!!

Katelyn Parkey
Age: 10

FORMERLY DEAD

Beulah and Tristan stood on the crowded subway. Dusk was upon the city at this time and they were both on their way home.

"You said you spent a year out of school a while back?" Tristan inquired, not putting much emotion into his voice.

"Yeah, it's something I don't usually like to talk about --" Beulah replied. "But you're a nice guy, Tristan; I don't mind telling you." She leaned in close to his ear to whisper her answer. "I was a vampire," she whispered and then returned to where she stood.

Tristan paused. "...You were a what?" he asked, not seeming too alarmed or even that interested.

"A vampire," she said.

"Really?" he acted as if he didn't believe her.

"You don't believe me, I know. That's why I usually don't tell people."

"I think all that Anne Rice stuff's a crock, not that I hold it against you or anything."

"It's true, I was."

"Then tell me, Beulah: how does one go from being a vampire to not?"

The train came to a halt.

"I'd love to tell you, I really would, but this is my stop," she said. "I'll call you sometime this week."

No you won't, Tristan thought. That's what you said last week.

"See ya." She said, exiting through the opening subway door.

"Good-bye."

Tristan was a sophomore at the Saint Peter's Holy Academy; Beulah was a senior. He had only known her for a little less than a year and still knew very little about her. She met him through their former mutual friend, Audra, who, soon after, quit talking to both of them because her boyfriend didn't like either one of them. This didn't bother Tristan in the slightest; he found Audra annoying and hated the way she said just the right thing at the right time to make you feel miserable. Beulah, for some reason, was crushed and mourned the loss for several months. Beulah and Tristan were still only casual acquaintances at this point, as their only means of interaction with each other (Audra) had been eliminated; but they talked on occasions such as this.

On this evening, Tristan was taking a walk by himself through the busy downtown area of the city and happened to run upon Beulah as he cut through the parking lot of a hospital. Beulah happened to be coming out of the hospital at that time and, having nothing better to do, Tristan offered to walk with her to the subway, where he knew he would be going sooner or later, anyway. On their way there, they talked of many things that normal (and not-so-normal) teenage-type people talk about. The subject of her absence from school for an entire year came up at one point. This was something Tristan had only heard rumors about, rumors that ranged from her joining a cult, to her eloping with her then-boyfriend, Zel, to her joining a convent and, in turn, becoming a nun. Tristan didn't care what she was doing, much like he did with everything else, as he took everything at face value and didn't bother to read into anything. The thought of her becoming a vampire, however, had never crossed his mind, though; surely, it had crossed vivid imaginations of some of the other, more gossipy students of SPHA.

Pft... Vampire my foot, he thought to himself as the subway began to take off again. She should become an author, with an imagination like that.

"Hello?" Tristan answered the phone, groggily and agitated; it was 4:32 a.m.

"I told you I would call you." It was Beulah. "You should have a little more faith."

"Beulah? What the...?"

"I've decided to tell you about my experience as a vampire, seeing as you showed some interest in what I was doing last year, today."

"What?"

"Don't tell me you've forgotten already? We were on the train and you asked about my absence but I couldn't tell you about it because we were arriving at my stop, remember?"

"Beulah, it's 4:30 in the morning."

"I know; I've been stewing on it since I got home at six."

This didn't make him any happier. "Really, Beulah, I'd love to hear this story, because I'm sure I would get something of a better understanding of you if I did, but I'm thoroughly exhausted and it's now officially Saturday, thus giving me the right to sleep from whenever I choose to go to bed (in this case, two a.m.) until at least a quarter 'til eleven, so I'm just going to have to ask you to call back then."

"All right, but I can't guarantee that it will be as enthralling tomorrow, after I've slept on it."

"Fine, good-bye." And on that note, he hung up the phone.

Beulah clicked the power button on her phone and tossed it down to the foot of her neatly made bed, on which she lay. The images of her escapade as a creature of the night ran like a slideshow through her mind, more poignantly than they had since they had happened; she wasn't about to let this sudden inspiration to tell her story go to waste. She glanced over at her old, dark wood desk and began to ponder. She arose from her bed, straightened up her sloppy, light brown ponytail, walked over to it and took a seat at the chair. From a drawer at her right, she pulled out an unused notebook she had once bought for school and then never used. She opened it up, sat it in front of her, took a pencil out of the spent coffee can she used to keep her office supplies in and began to write, in detail, the story of her disappearance.

The next day, once he had finally woken up, Tristan took a walk to the bookstore in the downtown region. By now he had forgotten all about his late-night call from Beulah and was more intent on getting back to his house so he could sit in the solitude of his room and read for the rest of the weekend. Carrying several paperback novels in a plastic bag, he walked out of the bookstore and was nearly plowed over by a blonde woman in a black shirt and her brunette companion.

"Hey! Why don't cha watch where you're goin'!" the blonde bellowed, and then took off in great strides with her companion. He mumbled several profanities at her as she marched up the street, as if in a hurry to get somewhere.

Within only seconds of his collision a taxi pulled up on the curb right beside him and from it, leaped Beulah, who paid the driver with a twenty. She looked haggard and drained, like she'd stayed up all night.

"Tristan!" she greeted, running up to meet him. "I called your house and your mother told me you'd come here. I wrote the story of me becoming a vampire last night after I got off the phone with you, so now you can read it at any ungodly hour that you want."

He was still glaring at the angry blonde who had nearly wiped him into the pavement, though he glanced at her when she came up to greet him.

"Beulah, have you been up all night?" he inquired, still glowering up the street.

"Yes," she said perkily before taking notice to what he was looking at. "Oh my goodness! That's Lolita and... some woman I've never seen before in my life!"

Tristan finally looked straight at her. "Who's Lolita?" he asked in his usual, apathetic manner.

"Lolita is my seer!"

"And a seer is...?"

"The person who made me a vampire!"

"Oh no, not more of this baloney," he mumbled, weary of the subject.

"I thought she left the country a long time ago..." Beulah mused. "C'mon Tristan; we've gotta follow her!"

She grabbed his wrist and dragged him, full speed, up the street after the easily-angered, golden-haired Lolita and her... friend.

Brad Walker
Age: 15

THE PARTICULAR PUPPY

Hi, my name is Emily and I love dogs, cats and other animals. One day I went to Sicsa and I found a really cool dog, but it had a problem. She wet herself when someone would play or pet her. Her name was Abigail. I was really sad when the shelter said she wouldn't make a good pet for children.

I was still looking when I found this small puppy. My mom thought about it. My dad said that it was a very big responsibility. Then I begged my dad for a really long time and then he finally agreed.

We picked up the adorable puppy from Sicsa. I love her so much. I named her Sandy because she is a yellow Labrador. I even took her to school and everybody loved her too. But when I took her home, she ate my homework. My parents thought that it was just a way to get out of turning it in. But it wasn't this time. My teacher was going to be REALLY mad at me!!

So I bet you want to know what happens next. Okay, okay... my teacher gave me after school detention but I still loved my dog. The next day I quickly woke up because my mom was screaming. I ran down the stairs and Sandy had broken my mom's new china.

She said, "Sandy and you have to go take dog training."

Now we have to go to dog school every afternoon.

The next day when I was walking my dog, we saw my friend Kassidy who had her new dog. She brought her new puppy, Cleo, to puppy school too. She told me that Cleo chews on the couch all the time and that's why she was there. Every day we brought them to Miss Finney's school for dogs.

I was so glad that Sandy and I can be a good dog and master. Kassidy and Cleo were happy together too. So that was the end of chewing up couches, breaking china and eating my homework. I will always love my puppy. I wonder what she will do next?

Lexi Muller

A NEW BEGINNING

The year is 3051, and the planet is dying. Many people are in fear for their lives and the lives of their loved ones. Above all that, I am told that the sun is running out of its main gas source and will soon explode. I'm worried. Not for me, but for what will happen. The government is calling for all the people twenty-five years and younger to be sent to the planet Loi. This planet has everything we need to survive, lush forests, plenty of fresh water, and a good atmosphere. We will be sent there to populate and colonize this new world.

My name is Jessica Ann James, and I am sixteen years old. My mom and dad encourage me to go to Loi and not worry about them. They say they'll be fine. I do worry, though, and don't want to go. Tomorrow everyone is going to the station. We will be leaving that night. Everyone tells me that everything will be okay. I won't admit it, but I'm scared.

I woke up the next morning to the light of the sun shining in my window. After I got dressed and packed my suitcase, I called for my little Pomeranian, Lucy. We are supposed to bring our animals with us so they can populate too.

During the ride to the station, we all sat quietly. My brother, who is twenty-six, told a few jokes. We all laughed, but nothing could stop the sinking feeling in the pit of my stomach. When we arrived, I was close to tears. A mixture of emotions was coursing through my body. Sadness and pain from having to leave my family and never see them again were the strongest. There was also anger and a twinge of pride.

I boarded the rocket after many good-byes and kisses. Sitting in a seat next to the window, I held Lucy securely and gently wiped the tears of immense sorrow from my eyes. I took my last look out the little circle window at what used to be my home as the rocket flew into the sky. That was the last time I would ever see my family.

I was sitting next to a small boy around seven years old. He was crying and kept asking where his mom was. I told him everything would be okay and that I would take care of him. We got along really well, and he told me his name was Aaron. I held him to my side. After a few moments, he was asleep.

Gazing fixedly into the endless nothingness, I stared out the window for what had to be at least an hour. While staring into space, I suddenly saw a great, bright flash of light out of the corner of my eye. Dreading what I might see, I looked in the direction it came from. The sun had exploded, and the Earth disintegrated before my very eyes. Everything I had ever known or ever loved was gone.

As I sat there staring at the empty space where my planet used to be, I felt myself hold on tighter to Lucy and Aaron, and I began to cry. Hot tears splashed down my cheek. Everything was so loud because everyone was talking about what had just happened. I tried to think of what I was going to do now. It was just Aaron and I now. He and Lucy were all I had left. Nothing seemed right anymore.

I sat up straight and wiped the tears from my eyes as I looked down at Aaron sleeping on my arm and Lucy in my lap. I decided then that I'd have to be strong. I am part of something now that needs me. It is my obligation to help the human race. I am Jessica Ann James and am now Aaron's protector. He needs me now more than anything. I have to look after him and Lucy to ensure their futures. My journey in life, I realize, is just beginning.

Stephanie Nichole Parker
Age: 14

WHEN I WAS THREE

When I was three years old, I was playing with my sister Tiffany. We played in our room, our room was covered with toys. Tiffany got in the box. Then we saw a snake. The snake was trying to get Tiffany when she was in the box.

So I ran to the living room and said, Mommy Mommy snake going to eat Tiff.

Mommy said, there is no snake in the room.

So I went back to the room. The snake was still trying to get Tiff.

So I went to the living room and said, Mommy Mommy snake going to eat Tiff.

So Mommy came in the room and saw the snake and got Tiffany out of the box. We got out of the house to get our papaw to kill the snakes that were in the house. Papaw killed three snakes from our bedroom.

Krystal Michelle Justice
Age: 12

TIKE'S HIDDEN SECRET

Back in the time period of 2000 B.C. There was a man of the name Tike. Tike lived in a small town of the name Asbod (as-boo-d). Tike had never seen anything but Asbod his whole life. But the tides were about to change, Tike was born to a widow of the name Corly (K-or-ly). But when Tike was but of the age of three months, Corly died of a rare disease.

So a family of elves adopted Tike into their family as if he were their own. Liris (Lie-r-is), the father raised Tike up as any other elvish family would. Tike learned to shoot a bow and arrow, learned to protect himself from danger with a sword, and learned to be loving and caring.

Trouble's shadow fell upon Asbod. Asbod was a little peasant town ruled by a sorcerer Sharlar (Sh-are-l-are). Sharlar sent his followers out to destroy Asbod.

At this point in time Tike was of the age of fifteen. Already all of the town had known about Tike's life story. The people of the town had always looked to Tike when trouble came along. One day Tike had gone for a walk and it was Sharlar who had cast a spell on Tike to leave the town. For Sharlar knew his people couldn't withstand the power of Tike, for Sharlar knew something Tike never knew.

Tike's father was a very well-known, highly respected wizard of the council. Members of the council are able to take on Sharlar one-on-one in a duel, and win.

For his father's blood runs in his veins.

Tike was out in the woods taking a walk, when he had heard the sound of thunder, yet the sky was as clear as natural spring water. But it wasn't a thunder in the sky, it was a thunder on the ground, and heading right for him.

Tike had jumped behind a fallen tree. Then four men rode up on a creature, that looks like a tiger, with the head of a dragon. The men were dressed in a red armor, with a silver shield in hand.

Tike now knew what was going on, and Tike knew exactly where Sharlar's fortress was, and knew what its weakness was.

Tike had waited for the four men to leave, then Tike took off for Worton (war-ton), for it was about a day-long ride on horseback but about a two-day travel by foot.

When Tike had finally reached Worton, Sharlar was awaiting him at the southern gate (the southern entrance to Worton). Sharlar had expected Tike to fight without any hesitation, yet he guessed wrong.

Tike had believed that there were ways to solve problems than to fight. When Tike was about to turn his back Sharlar had showed him what was happening in a ball of fire. Sharlar had on a stand, Tike's town was being destroyed.

Just then Tike felt an enormous run of power, and anger he had never seen or felt in himself before. Then all of a sudden a white staff had appeared in his hand, and a red and white cloak had appeared over his body.

Tike turned and looked straight at Sharlar. He saw a great force of anger coming off him. Tike took one last look at the ball of fire, the soldier had stopped with his torment to the people.

Tike drew his sword in hand (which had started to glow), took with one smooth slice cut a piece of thick rope. Then the southern gates all closed.

Tike started to run off and Sharlar said to him, "They will all die before you reach them."

Tike turned and said back, "I'm not running to try to save them, I'm backing up so I won't die of the blast."

Tike picked his staff up in hand spoke in some sort of elvish voice and said, "Gogona pleto foraia."

Then his staff began to glow and a big bright beam of purple smoke hit Sharlar and he died.

Tike ran back to Asbod, just in time to save the remaining survivors. The town looked up to Tike when trouble would occur from there on out. The people of Asbod had started calling Tike, Barsti (Bar-st-e), which was his father's name. The people of the village also said that when he showed up at Asbod, they thought it was his father resurrected.

After Tike's accident he never could turn back to normal. His power stayed with him the rest of his life.

Christopher Lipovich
Age: 14

THE EVIL BIP

"The toys are all gone!" cried the elves. The head elf Crayola went to go tell Santa.

"Santa! Santa!" cried Crayola. "The toys are all gone!"

"What do you mean all gone," said Santa.

"There's not a single teddy bear or fire truck in the shop," said Crayola.

Santa thought about it really hard and said, "That will be all."

"But! But! We only have one day 'til Christmas."

"It's the 24th."

"GO," yelled Santa.

"All right! All right! Don't get pushy."

Crayola went out of the room and all of a sudden Santa's room turned into a big metal room with all these high-tech computers, gadgets, and nice red suits. Santa picked up the phone and called THE EASTER BUNNY! "We have a code magenta I repeat a code magenta!"

The Easter bunny came hopping in with his Eggedystinker gun (that he loads with rotten eggs). Santa called a meeting with all the elves in the lollipop patch. Every elf was there except one, Bip. He was with his evil pencil sharpener full of toys. He was really sneaky and mean. Once he stole some money from Tom Brokaw and was always getting in trouble at school. Now back to Santa. Santa started to take roll call and when he got to Bip's name and no one answered so Santa and all the elves went to Bip's house but no one was there so they went to his mother's house (he's a momma's boy) and he was sitting there having tea with his mother. His mother got up and ran off.

"Bip, where are the toys?"

Bip just sat there staring at Santa.

"Huh!" yelled Santa.

Santa went over and shook Bip 'til his head fell off.

"Gasp," went the elves.

"It's a dummy!" yelled Santa.

"Ha! Ha! Ha! Ha! Haaaah!" laughed a voice. "I will smash you all! Ha! Ha! Ha! Ha!"

"BIIIIIP!!!" Santa yelled.

WHOOSH the house was being lifted over the side of the mountain.

"You are trapped!" yelled Bip. "I will let you fall over the mountain but I will give them gifts this year but next year instead of me giving them gifts they will give me gifts (I'll send the note to them with their gifts this year)."

All of a sudden the Easter bunny broke through the window and shot his Eggedystinker gun five times at Bip and he fell to the floor.

Santa said, "Elves, book 'em. Get us on the ground! Get us on the ground! Hurry! Hurry Easter bunny! Hurry!" cried Santa.

"All right! All right! Don't get your undies in a bunch."

He shot one of his eggs at the lever and they were lifted back to the ground and the toys were hauled back to the shop and put on the sleigh ready for takeoff. Everybody went back and started to look for Bip's mother. They looked everywhere for her. They looked at the candy cane forest, the lollipop patch, the shop, and everyone's house. Where could she be? The last place they didn't look was under Santa's hat and there she was so they put them in jail and got Santa ready for takeoff. Everybody's at where Santa is getting ready to take off and no one is watching Bip and his mother. Wait a minute! There's Bip and his mother getting in the toy bag! UH-OH! P.S. Christmas is saved for now!!!

Lawrence Wedemeyer
Age: 11

MY NEW BIKE

When I woke up at 10:00 a.m. my mommy told me and my brother to get clean and dressed. Then my mommy told us to put on our shoes and our coats. We went outside and we saw our grandma's car.

We got in the car and she drove us to Wal-Mart. When we got to the store we went in the bike section. We picked out a bike. I rode the bike all the way to the cash register. Then we went back home.

I'll never forget that day.

Tyiona D. Allen

SAVE THE LEPRECHAUNS

Bzzzzzzzzz.

Peter's alarm went off just as his mom's voice said, "Time to get up for school."

"Coming," said Peter sleepily.

He glanced at the clock; it was 7:01. He jumped up. He had to catch the bus by 7:15. He rushed down, ate breakfast, went upstairs to brush his teeth and comb his hair, packed his backpack as fast as he could and arrived outside three minutes after the bus had gone. His mom had already left for work. He would have to walk to school instead. He didn't know the way to school very well because he never looked out of the window on the bus. Instead, he read about snakes all the time.

Peter was so interested in snakes that he managed to convince his parents to let him order the biggest snake in the world from another country. He had two of them. One was a male and the other one was female. The snakes laid eggs and had baby snakes already. He kept them in a cage as big as a small house in his backyard.

On the way to school, he saw something that looked like a small man. He kneeled down to examine the creature more closely. It turned around and jumped when it saw Peter.

"What are you?" Peter asked.

"I'm a leprechaun," the creature said. "My name is Sam."

"You couldn't be a leprechaun for two reasons," said Peter. "Number one, leprechauns live in the forest. Number two, leprechauns don't even exist."

"If I am not a leprechaun then what am I?" asked the leprechaun. "And I'm not in the forest because your baby snakes have scared all the leprechauns away. The snakes can easily catch us. They won't let us go even if we give them gold. They just eat us."

"How could my snakes be in the forest? And why are they so hard to escape from?" asked Peter. "Most snakes are slow and I've heard leprechauns are really fast."

"Snakes don't ever close their eyes because they don't have any eyelids so we can't escape. They just stare and then eat us. The snakes are in the forest because a rabbit dug a hole under the cage and the snakes are escaping through it," replied Sam.

"Is there any way I could help?" asked Peter.

"You could kill the rabbit or get rid of the snakes," said Sam.

"I don't want to get rid of the snakes or kill the rabbit. There's no way I can do anything now because I need to go to school. Why don't you come with me, then after school I'll see what I can do," said Peter.

School didn't go very well for Peter that day. First, he had to go see the principal about being late for school again. Then he had to go without lunch because he got to school too late to order his lunch. Next, he missed recess because he was too late to school to do the morning work and had to catch up to the rest of the class. Finally, he ended the day with the most boring one-hour test. He couldn't concentrate because he couldn't stop thinking about Sam.

After school, Peter wrote a note to each of his friends asking them for help. The notes said:

Dear Ben, Kyle, Stephan, and Matthew,
I need help. A rabbit has dug a hole under the snake cage, and the baby snakes are escaping into the forest and eating leprechauns. If you don't believe me, meet me after school in my backyard.
Sincerely,
Peter

Peter folded the papers into airplanes to throw to his friends in school. Then he reset the alarm to go off at 6:15.

The next day, Peter got up on time and ran to breakfast and then to school. At the end of the day, Peter threw the paper airplanes to his friends while his teacher was writing on the blackboard. He watched them open the letters and start to read. Then the bell rang, and everyone rushed out the door.

Peter waited outside after school ended and after about seven minutes he saw his friends coming. When they arrived, Peter pulled out the leprechaun from a small pocket in his book bag.

"This is Sam the leprechaun. First, we need to get the rabbit away. Then someone will need to catch the snakes and put them in their cages. Then we'll need to plug up the rabbit's hole so no more snakes can get out," said Peter. "I'll scare the bunny away by putting a baby snake from inside the snake cage through the bunny hole. Then Ben and Kyle should go into the forest and catch the snakes. There are twenty of them. Sam will be going around telling the other leprechauns it's safe to go back into the forest. Once all the snakes are back in the cage, I'll keep the snakes from going back into the forest. Then Matthew can plug up the rabbit hole. Then we can go home," finished Peter.

They decided to "Save the Leprechauns" on Saturday so it wouldn't keep them from doing any homework. They also decided to do it at night so no one would see or notice them.

On Saturday, Ben, Kyle, Stephan, and Matthew played together the whole day until their parents made them come inside for supper and bed. At ten o'clock, they all crept outside and met at the snake cage.

Peter pulled out a checklist he had made that day and said, "Say check if you have one of these items. Do we have a net to put the captured snakes in and two flashlights so I can see in the snake cage and so that Ben and Kyle can see in the dark?"

"Check," said Ben and Kyle.

Peter reached out to get the flashlight that was for him. Kyle handed Peter's flashlight to Peter.

"Do we have a shovel and a clump of dirt to clog up the bunny hole?"

"Check," said Matthew.

"Do we have a tiny flashlight so Sam can see to tell the other leprechauns it's safe to go back into the forest?"

"Check," said Stephan.

He handed his light-up watch to Sam. Sam took it and fastened it around himself like a belt.

"We are ready then. Let's go," said Peter.

They all split up. Ben and Kyle ran towards the forest. Stephan went to look for the rabbit hole. Peter got out fifteen enormous, different keys that all went to the gigantic locks on the snake cage door. He quietly opened the door from the outside, took some of the five-pound locks and locked the door from the inside with them. Then he got out a hook from the backpack he had packed to hold equipment he and his friends might need and tried to pick up one of the baby snakes with it. The snake hissed and started trying to strangle Peter. He quickly got out a sharp, metal stick and poked the snake harder and harder until it fell off him. He used the hook again and dropped the snake next to the rabbit hole and scared it into going through. He aimed the flashlight out of the cage to see if the snake had gone completely through the hole and if the rabbit was away.

Someone knocked on the cage door. He looked over. He saw two people outside the cage holding a net with creatures in it that were hissing.

It's Ben and Kyle with the net full of snakes, Peter thought. He unlocked the door. Ben and Kyle dumped out the net. Peter counted the snakes. There were twenty snakes slithering around on the floor.

Peter passed the sharp, metal stick to Ben and told him to tell Stephan to put the snake back through the hole before clogging the hole up. He stepped out of the cage and put the locks back on the outside of the door. Stephan and Ben came running and said they were done.

"We did it!" said Peter.

"We can celebrate tomorrow. I think we should go to bed now," said Stephan.

The next day, Peter was walking in the forest. He kept meeting leprechauns who said, "Thank you." Then Peter saw his friends. When they were arguing about what to do, a big leprechaun appeared and gave them five hundred tons of gold. They agreed to bury it and get it out when they were older because it would be hard to explain where they'd gotten it, plus no one would believe them anyway.

They had many other adventures before they were grown up. When they were grown up, they had a few children. They also each bought a swimming pool, a football field, and a huge playground using the five hundred tons of gold they got. All because they met Sam, the leprechaun, and because Peter missed his bus.

Matthew Brockman
Age: 9

92

CHEER FOR FEAR

On February, Friday 13th, there was a group of cheerleaders. Their names are Hannah Brewster, Jennifer Smith, Jennifer Stone, Amber Richmond, and Sara Hunt. Their cheerleader advisor is Amber Silcott. They were at a competition. They were staying at the Days Inn hotel in Chillicothe for three weeks. Hannah was getting ready to put in a scary movie when Amber Silcott heard the floor creak and she screamed.

Amber said, "All right that is enough. Let's just go to bed. Maybe it will be gone by tomorrow night."

When they woke up the window was open. Nobody noticed for a long time that there was a bloody knife laying in the window. Then the two girls named Jennifer went to go get clothes from the closet and there they found their leader Amber Silcott.

They all ate breakfast and tried to forget about the terrible thing that had happened.

Then Hannah came running and screaming, "There is someone dead in the bathroom!!!"

Everyone rushed back to the bathroom just as fast as they could. It was Jennifer Stone. Finally they decided they couldn't stay at this hotel anymore. So they got out of their bedclothes and got dressed. They went out and told the hotel manager about it.

He said, "I'm sorry I didn't mean to give you that room."

Jennifer Smith said, "Why? What happened?"

The manager said, "Well, it is quite a long story. It all happened when there was a family here on February, Friday 13th many years ago. Someone killed the entire family. So ever since then, on every February, Friday 13th, their ghosts come back and kill everyone staying in that room. You must get out and get out fast. Every year they will come back with the others until they have gotten revenge for their cruel deaths."

Alexandria Marie Molen

MEMORIES

International espionage. A fancy politician's term for what I used to do every day. I am a former KGB agent. What is the KGB you ask? You ignorant American. Please try to learn about the world around you before you set foot out of your expensive house and drive in your expensive, big car. The KGB is the former and glorious Soviet Union's international intelligence agency, much like your CIA. We did the same "friendly snooping" that your country did to us, but, of course, we got blamed for the entire "Cold War." So typical of the Americans to blame everyone else.

I take pride in the work I did. In the intelligence world, Mother Russia was equivalent to what Israel is today, and that is because of top agents, like myself, who risked their lives for the spreading of communism. Not only do I take pride in my work, I also enjoyed it. I was physically doing something for my country, which is more than I can say for the politicians of that time.

I remember one particularly enjoyable assignment. I don't use the word "fun" because risking your life is never "fun," but it can definitely be enjoyable. Regardless, I received this assignment from Comrade Nikoslov, my superior. He told me, as usual, that not only is this assignment dangerous, but should I be caught, I would be expected to swallow the pill sewn into my sleeve cuff. It went without saying that should I be captured, and not take the pill, every known relative of mine would be deleted. My assignment was to pose as a police intern at a police station in Washington, D.C. that worked closely with the American Federal Bureau of Investigation. I was to first meet up with a contact named "Mongoose," and I would receive instructions from him describing how to effectively be of service to the homeland.

I pride myself in making some of the best disguises in the KGB, so knowing that I would be going into an important mission in the heart of the enemy country, I went all out on my identity. I made a fake nose with a large mole out of latex and plaster. I also made a wig that made my head look like it had a very bad comb-over. I used a bodysuit to make me look slightly obese. Within a day and a half of working on my costume, I now effectively looked like a middle-aged American cop, who had eaten one too many doughnuts.

During my flight to Washington, I noticed a snooty Brit staring at me from the corner of his eye. He had a standard MI-6 revolver, so I knew who he was working for. The MI-6, being the excellent British intelligence service that it is, must have a mole in the KGB, for there was no other way they could have known I was on this flight. Of course, it could have been my imagination, but I had not come to be one of the best Soviet agents by ignoring my intuition. I would have to order a sweep of any double agents possibly working for the MI-6 when I got back.

I arrived in Washington under the name of Ronald Weston. As I stepped out of the terminal, I saw the man described to me as Mongoose leaning against a wall. He greeted me in the standard, "Hello, Tobapnw," and I returned, "Hello comrade."

He informed me that we should move to a safe place to talk, such as a public park. I agreed and we walked to a park. It was a cold day, and I could see my breath as I asked him how to effectively complete my assignment. He informed me that he had been assessing the situation for weeks and knew exactly what to do, but that he did not have the field experience to get any closer to the problem than he already was. He then proceeded to outline my mission for me. Mongoose told me that he already had a job set up for me at the station, and for now at least, act normal and just do the job.

After a week had gone by and I was thoroughly disgusted with the American disciplinary system, Mongoose arrived at my temporary apartment, and let me know on what to do next. All week, I had been informing him on the doings of the American police sergeant Mark Haldin and an FBI agent known only as Damon. These two men were obviously covering up something damaging to the Soviets. Whatever the secret was, it was contained between these two men. Mongoose explained that these two men needed to be exterminated and their offices searched.

It took me all of twelve seconds to figure out how this would be accomplished. I would need to arrange a mock car crash. Seeing as how foreign relations between the motherland and the Americans hadn't been warm of late, it would be better for these well-respected men to die in a crash than to be shot. Already my mind was spinning with ways for this to be done, so I grabbed a piece of paper, and started writing down the various ideas flooding my brain.

Posing as a worker for a towing company, I picked up Sergeant Haldin's squad car and installed a special Soviet device used in rigging auto accidents. I then returned to the parking lot where both cars were parked. Dressed as a young, rebellious teen, I left a note at the sergeant's parking spot telling him where his car can be found. Next, I went over to where Damon's jet-black sedan was parked. To get the attention of the police, I slashed all of the tires, smashed the windshield, and applied graffiti to the rest of the car as loudly and slowly as possible. As you can imagine, I got the attention fast. Knowing I was much faster than any of these gluttonous cops, I let them chase after me.

After I knew they had no idea where I was, I returned to my apartment to change into my final costume. I emerged from my apartment as a biker. I "borrowed" a bike, and then drove back to the parking lot. Knowing that Damon would have to ride with Sgt. Haldin, I waited until they drove away, then followed them. I smiled to myself as I saw them taking the scenic route. That was the biggest gamble of the plan; whether they would take the scenic route or the short cut. Now I knew that the rest of the plan should unfold flawlessly. I pulled the remote of the Russian car device out of my pocket. This device, when activated, would immediately immobilize the brakes and the steering wheel.

On the country road that we were driving, there was a very sharp turn. It was supposed to be taken slowly because the only thing separating the fifty-something-foot drop and the thin stretch of road was a poorly built guard rail. I saw that the squad car was going about fifty and was fairly close to the turn, so I pressed the button to activate the device. The car didn't slow down when it hit the turn. When it hit the guard rail, it didn't even slow down. It vanished from my view for about nine seconds, then a giant fireball shot up from where the car had landed. I smiled. It had worked.

After searching the appropriate offices and giving the Mongoose what he needed, I was allowed to go back to the land of the Kremlin. I never found out what that pompous sergeant's secret was, but I didn't expect to find out anytime soon. That's just how it worked in those days. Most of the public didn't even know who was in charge.

Yes, I loved my job. Those days when I was flying around the world, meeting new people, that is how I want to remember my life. I was younger, and the Soviet dream was glorious to me. Frankly, it still is. Today, while it is richer, Russia is not what it used to be. Almost all of Europe had been Russia's. Now we are a puny country, spit on by bigger countries. Someone needs to return us back to the glory days. It isn't all about the money. It is all about honor, respect, and dignity. Something needs to be done to replace us as the super-powerhouse we once were.

Curtis Dickerson
Age: 14

TRIGGER AND I

One August afternoon my dad was trying to catch my horse Trigger for a 4-H meeting. My horse is so stubborn and hard to catch. My dad got me so maybe I could catch him. His pasture is the hill behind our house. The garden takes up half of the top of the hill. Last summer it rained a lot and where he had walked so much in the mud. Later when it dried up it was too rough and hard to walk on. I had some grain so I fed him and then it was so much easier to catch him. We loaded him up in the old brown trailer that was hooked up to my dad's jade glow green truck. When we got there Ruchel and her horse Bow were at the Meigs Fairgrounds. The rest of the 4-H club was there, too. I always practice showmanship first.

So I got on my horse and went around the ring with my dad. The rest of the club was practicing speed and control. My dad turned my horse. Trigger was so calm. We turned again and right about at the gate a girl came running on her horse and scared my horse.

My horse started running and bucking. After I felt him starting to run everything was a blur until I hit the ground. I was gasping for air. I was spitting out dirt. When I got up Ruchel said as a joke that I should join the rodeo. Everyone asked if I wanted to get back on him.

He was startled too so he was not in the mood to be antsy and worked up. The girl that scared him offered to ride him because she is a more experienced rider. She said that if he had another buck she would get it out of him. When I got more stable I got back on him. So hopefully when I went the next time I would not be as scared. It would be good for him so he would know that he could not get away with anything like that again.

The next day, I had a huge bruise on my leg and I was really sore. I went outside and spent a lot of time of the day with Trigger. I would pet and hug him so he knew I was not mad at him. I gave him some grain and just paid a lot of attention to him. That day I asked Dad if I stayed on the horse for a buck. He said I stayed on for three bucks.

Miranda Grueser
Age: 11

THE MYSTERIOUS MURDERER

BOOM! This is what I heard on my way home from school on the fourteenth of September in the year 2003. I will always remember this day, it was the day that changed my life forever.

I was walking home from school when something caught my attention. It was flashing lights from a cop car. I looked over to the car and saw an elderly man, about fifty years of age, pointing a gun at the police officer! I was so scared that I immediately dove behind a bush.

"Put the gun down and your hands in the air!" the officer wailed.

At that very moment the strange man pulled the trigger, he had shot the police officer! I screamed, the man had heard me! At the exact time I screamed my head was above the bush, the murderer had also seen me!

"I'm going to get you if it is the last thing I do! You won't know how and you won't know when but I will get you!" the murderer bellowed right before he scurried away frantically.

About ten minutes after the trigger had been pulled the police were swarming the crime scene. Everyone was asking me questions.

"What did he look like, was he fat or thin, short or tall? Tell us!" the investigators yelled.

I was in so much shock that I could only answer the simplest of questions. I told the investigators what the murderer looked like and the threat he yelled at me. This was all I told them, I couldn't remember anything else, it all went by so fast.

"He said he would k...kil...kill me!" I whispered while crying.

"Don't worry sweetie, I work with the Witness Protection Program and we will make sure you are safe. We will get you a new family, a new home and a new identity, it will be OK," the lady assured me.

One day later I was safe in Boisy, Arizona, a small town right outside of Phoenix. I had been put in the Oleson's home, I had been "adopted" by them. The Oleson's were pretty nice but not nearly as nice as my own family I had to leave behind. The little Oleson girl, about my age, was way too bossy, I could already tell she hated me and wasn't used to not being an only child. My name has been changed to Ginger Oleson. I don't really know anybody in Boisy, not even the people I'm living with, so I don't have very many friends. Hopefully I will fit in and the mysterious murderer will be caught and he won't find me. This is one thing, to my surprise, that doesn't happen.

It was exactly one month after I moved to Boisy and I still didn't have any friends. The only person I could trust, who really wasn't a person, was the family dog Bozo. Bozo liked everything that I did. Today I was waiting for a package that I had ordered from PetsMart. I had got a new toy for my favorite little dog, Bozo. The doorbell soon rang and I figured it was just the delivery man so I looked through the curtain to make sure it was just him. It wasn't the delivery at all, it was the mysterious murderer. He was standing there like it wasn't a big deal. I screamed, he yelled something at me that sounded something like, I'm going to get you. It was so freaky!

"I'm calling the police!" I yelled, this was a mistake because at this very moment he ran. I knew I had to call the Witness Protection Program but I just didn't know how I could tell them that the murderer had found me. How could he have found me, only employees have the information of where the people in the Witness Protection Program are safely placed. Then I thought to myself, what if the murderer works in the Witness Protection Program. As this thought crossed my mind I also thought I should call the Witness Protection Program and tell them that the murderer had figured out where I was. While I was on the phone with the secretary of the Witness Protection Program I asked them if it was possible that the murderer worked at the Witness Protection Program. The secretary said that it was possible but not very likely. Even after I heard this I asked for the pictures of all of the employees, just in case. The secretary agreed and also told me I would be safely placed in another city and my file would be placed in a safe place. The secretary assured me I would be safe but I just didn't know, hopefully it will be true.

I am now on a plane to a city in Minnesota. The city is in a nice area, lots of beautiful landscapes, lots of hills and farms. This was one of the most beautiful places I had ever been to, it was a perfect place for me. A nice and calm place where I could stay and be safe.

I got to my new home at about 10:00 p.m. The town I was in had a perfect name, Angel. While I was on the plane a lady who worked for the Witness Protection Program told me that the pictures of the employees was safely put in my suitcase and I could look at it when I got to my new home. I worried the whole way to Angel, Minnesota, what if the mysterious murderer did work at the Witness Protection Program. What could I do, the mysterious murderer might be on to me and he might have already gotten my file, what would I do then?

Finally I had a chance to unpack. I saw the manila-colored folder, I knew the pictures had to be in there. I opened it up slowly. The pictures were soon spread out in front of me, I slowly looked through them looking for the right picture. I looked through all of the pictures, but I found no murderer. So I went back to put the pictures back in the folder when I saw I had left a single sheet of pictures in the folder. I carefully pulled the sheet out of the folder making sure not to smear any of the pictures. Next I carefully skimmed the page, I saw him, it was the murderer! I immediately picked up the phone and called the Witness Protection Program.

"Hello this is Laura Thesing," I said calmly, "I have looked through the picture files you gave me and I have figured out who the murderer is. His name is Jimmy Host."

"Laura, that can't be right, Jimmy is our janitor, he can't be the murderer he's such a sweet man. Are you positive it's him?" the secretary asked politely.

Just to make sure I glanced at the photo of the murderer.

"Yes, I'm positive it's him. I remember a face when I see one," I replied.

"Well we'll take your word on it. We will call you when we arrest Jimmy to tell you that you are safe and he won't try to come after you." At this note the secretary hung up.

I was so nervous, what if I was wrong about this, what if Jimmy was just a look-alike to the murderer. I worried all day, it had already been three hours after my original call to the Witness Protection Program and I was so nervous. Suddenly the phone rang, I hesitated to answer it in case it was the Witness Protection Program calling to tell me I was wrong about the murderer, but after four long rings I picked up.

"He... Hello," I answered cautiously.

"Hi, this is the Witness Protection Program, is this Ashleigh Anderson (this is what my name had been changed to after I moved to Angel, Minnesota)?" a nice lady asked me.

"Yes it is," I responded politely.

"Well you were right. The mysterious murderer turned out to be the nice old janitor, Jimmy Host. When we arrested him he cracked under the pressure and confessed the whole thing. Jimmy told us that he got the files of where you were staying while he was cleaning. He used to stay until everyone was gone and when he emptied the trash cans and vacuumed he looked in the file drawers. Old Jimmy could do this without anyone suspecting anything because no one was there to see it. You are a great detective, we would have never even thought that the nice janitor Jimmy Host would be behind this whole thing, thanks for your help!" the secretary told me excitedly.

"It was no problem, it's always the nice and quiet people you have to worry about. Well, I'm just glad I'm safe."

At this I hung up. This little town called Angel was perfect for me, it was like I had my own little guardian angel looking down on me. I was finally safe, safe at last.

Laura Thesing

SARAH WILDALLS

Hi my name is Sarah Wildalls. I was born on September 20, 1860 in Findlay, Ohio. Now on to my story.

When my parents first brought me home I was so gentle with animals a bear would never attack us! When I was three months I started walking and when I was five months I started talking. For my first birthday I got a dog and I named her Dolly. When I was two I ran away from home to help animals and I took Dolly with me and we set off. In that year I lived with bears, wolves, and other animals. When I was three I was so smart about animals I went to college to be a vet. I graduated when I was six and I took an animal first-aid kit with me wherever we went. We went so fast around the country we went faster than a jack rabbit. When I was sixteen Dolly died. I cried so long that when I stopped I was like in an ocean. When I was nineteen I moved back home. While I was home I met a boy named Jonathon Migelin. When he saw me he said my eyes were as blue as the sky. We fell in love and when I was almost twenty we got married. He traveled around the U. S. with me and he loved it. When I was twenty-three we had a baby and we named her Carrie Elizabeth Migelin. After she was born I made the decision to settle down in a nice little house in Findlay. Jonathon thought it was a good idea and off we went. When we got to Findlay my parents had a nice little house built for us and they said, "Carrie was so cute she looked like a chipmunk." About one year later there was a fire so all our stuff was gone, it was really gone. So we built another house. It was a nice house but it was not the same. Three years passed and Carrie was old enough to go to school. And Jonathon had to do the farm work, so it was a little lonely in the house. But one day when Carrie was in 1st grade she didn't come home from school. We were so worried we went to town to look for her and we found out she had fallen in the town well. A couple men got her out and she was OK.

One year passed and I didn't feel well. I went to the doctor and I found out I was going to have another baby. Nine months later on July 4, 1885 I had a baby boy and I named him Jonathon Mathew Migelin Jr., we called him Junior.

When Junior was four and Carrie was ten I got sick with pneumonia. About one week later on February 13, 1890 I died. Jonathon, Carrie, Junior, and the rest of my family buried me in St. Michael cemetery. I know they will all miss me but we will all be together again someday.

And that is the end of my story.

Katie Logsdon

SUPERHERO

It was a sunny hot Malibu morning, when Theodore Stanford III woke up semi-rested. He leisurely strolled around in his five-hundred-thousand-dollar luxurious penthouse suite, which overlooked the beautiful blue Pacific Ocean, and he knew something just wasn't right. Now maybe it was because he woke up on the wrong side of the bed because he usually woke on the left side of bed nevertheless, for today he woke up on the right side. But that couldn't be the only problem. So Theodore went around his penthouse looking for what he thought was the problem. He searched high, low, near, far and wide but still couldn't seem to find the problem. He even searched through his underwear drawer (which was filled with tighty whities). And then his shoe-shaped black phone rang. Theodore briskly walked to the phone because he never got many calls because he was a nerd. He picked up the phone and it was his boss Professor Renaldo. Professor Renaldo told him to come over to the laboratory as fast as he could because there was a problem that needed his immediate attention. So Theodore quickly jumped in the shower. After quickly cleaning himself up he changed into some crisp khaki pants held up by starched suspenders, a white broadcloth long-sleeved shirt, a polka-dot green tie and his favorite rainbow socks and a pocket protector. He ran as fast as his toothpick legs and nerdy stature could run to his three-car garage. Without wasting any time he hopped into his black Lamborghini and sped out of the garage. When he got to the Nerdy Bayside Laboratory he went to his boss' office he opened the door and his chubby, short, bald boss showed him a red and black spider.

His boss said, "Be careful it's venomous."

Theodore didn't know how to handle spiders because he only worked with beakers that had blue and red liquids in it so he could make purple liquid, this made him look fancy. His boss Professor Renaldo thought Theodore had a doctor's degree in biology and physics so Professor Renaldo thought Theodore would be the man for the job. But Theodore had lied to get his job. Theodore never had a doctor's degree he just had a bachelor's degree in physics. Even though Theodore didn't know too much about spiders he still picked up the spider. Theodore noticed it wasn't so bad holding the spider so he began tossing it from one hand to the next. Then he threw the spider up into the air and to his surprise it landed in his mouth.

Professor Renaldo said, " Noooo!" and slapped Theodore on his bony, weak, asthmatic chest. Which made him pass out, and because Theodore suddenly passed out Professor Renaldo was so startled and confused he passed out also.

When Theodore woke up he was in his luxurious penthouse with a note on the very top of his massive forehead. The note said,

> You have swallowed an extremely special spider which lets you have superpowers that no one else has. Here are your powers: You can fly over humongous buildings and see through the thickest walls. You have incredible strength. You now have an extremely fast black car with an evil villain detecting radar. You can also shoot extremely sticky strings.

With those spectacular powers comes the responsibility of fending off bad guys. There is a guy who swallowed a fly who is your main enemy. His name is the Comedian. He has two sidekicks, one swallowed a bee and the other one swallowed a flea. The Comedian tells the worst jokes, and he can jump from building to building. The guy who swallowed the bee is known as the Ace of Diamonds. He shoots cards that have razors on the end and loves money. The guy who swallowed the flea is called Mr. Unbreakable he has a force field around him but it can only be broken when he sees bare skin.

    Signed,

    An Eerie Psychic.

Theodore didn't believe it but he looked over to the couch and saw a spandex suit that was red, black, blue, and green. He tried it on and he felt himself getting bigger and stronger than ever before. He went outside and tried his powers out. He shot a dog with his sticky string and he flew amazingly high up into the sky. Then he went to his garage and hopped into his new car he put the top down and flexed his new bulging muscles. He tested the power of his new ride and by the count of one hundred he had already circled his neighborhood sixty times.

After all of the fun was over Theodore went up to his house to take a nap because he was still a little tired from all the thrills that he had today. When he woke up he heard the phone so he picked it up. The voice on the phone was an old-sounding voice.

It was a man he said, "Hello my name is Charlie Angelo because of your superpowers I'm now your new boss and you now have a new job."

Theodore confusedly answered, "What?"

Charlie replied, "That's right you are now a good crime-fighting superhero."

Theodore said, "All right," and let Charlie talk some more.

Charlie said, "Your enemies have robbed five banks and it's up to you to stop them."

Theodore said, "I'm on it," and left out of his oceanfront penthouse and leaped into his shiny black car.

He used the evil villain detecting radar to find out where they went and zoomed to their hideout. The enemies were in a tall old factory that used to make drinking cups. The door was nailed shut so The Incredible Genius a.k.a. Theodore Stanford III ripped open the door and he began his search for the evil villains. First he looked through the walls on the first floor. Then, he looked around but saw nothing, so he tried to see through the walls on the second floor but still saw nothing. When he went to the third floor he saw Mr. Unbreakable and quickly showed him his skin so the force field would break. He quickly shot string around Mr. Unbreakable's legs but that didn't stop Mr. Unbreakable who suddenly dropped and bit the string and it fell off his legs. So the Incredible Genius went after Mr. Unbreakable and picked up Mr. Unbreakable and then threw him out the window of the huge building. It looked like he was knocked out or dead so the Incredible Genius started to look around on the fourth floor where he saw the Ace of Diamonds. He tried his best to sneak up on the Ace of Diamonds but since he had become bigger and stronger the floor creaked and it was easier for him to be heard when he was tiptoeing. The Ace of Diamonds turned around and threw ten different cards at the Incredible Genius. The Incredible Genius dodged every one of the cards and picked up a card and threw it at the Ace of Diamonds and the Ace of Diamonds fell out of the window. Two down one to go. This time the Incredible Genius didn't use his amazing see-through vision to catch The Comedian all he had to do was follow the continuous laughing. The Incredible Genius searched all over the floors until he heard an extremely large chuckle coming from above him. The Comedian was on the roof. Instead of taking the stairs the Incredible Genius flew through the remaining floors. Then the Comedian turned around in surprise and screamed.

The Incredible Genius said, "Are you ready to tango?" and all of a sudden tango music started playing.

The two arch nemeses started dancing until they saw two shadows.

It was Mr. Unbreakable and Ace of Diamonds while they both had gone down by the Incredible Genius they were still alive. Although, the Ace of Diamonds had been hit with the card, he had a pack of cards protecting him where he got hit. All three enemies surrounded the Incredible Genius. The Ace of Diamonds took the first move by throwing his cards at him. The Incredible Genius flew up in the air to dodge the cards and the Comedian jumped up to take a shot at the Incredible Genius.

The Comedian said, "Why did the chicken cross the road? To get to the other side."

Then the Comedian fell back down laughing at his own corny joke. This gave the opening the Incredible Genius wanted and he shot his sticky string and made it turn into a lasso that went around all three criminals. He shook them like a Polaroid picture and then he threw them to the nearest cop station he could see. The authorities were very pleased to have these bad guys in custody. His new boss Charlie Angelo was proud of him. And our hero went back to his house and slept for the rest of the day.

Adrian Warfield

DISAPPEARING SMILE

A smile is priceless if it is given to you by a friend, a family member, or a schoolmate. But one given by James is truly unforgettable.

Every day at school, I see James, a normal healthy kid. But what isn't so normal about him is that whenever he smiles, he always makes someone or something disappear. Something that I have always wondered, where did my dog run off to?

Anyway, when I was over at James' house to work on a science project, I had to watch my back. We walked into the kitchen and we sat down at the table. He, very cunningly, placed a whoopee cushion on my chair before I sat down. The sound of this whoopee cushion was amazing; so amazing, that a dog started howling outside.

James started cracking up and smiling at the same time. I thought to myself, Oh boy, this isn't good. This isn't good at all. Just then, I heard a loud POOF sound. I was suddenly floating in this tornado of swirls that were many different colors. Blue, black, green, red, yellow, all swirling around me. I look down at my watch and the minute hand is speeding counterclockwise and the hour hand is just trailing behind it. It was like something that you would see in the "Twilight Zone."

In the distance, I could scarcely see a black hole that was getting bigger and bigger. Now I know what happens to the things that James smiles at.

I could see that the black hole was humongous. I was gently set down on my feet. I looked behind me and saw total darkness. I started to walk toward the black hole. "Forward and forward I go. Where I'll wind up, nobody knows," I sang out. I repeated the little tune in my head until I reached a white wall. On that white wall was a picture of James, smiling at me. I let out an ear-piercing scream.

All of a sudden, it was a bright and shiny day outside and I am in my room, sitting up in my bed. "Hey Barky," I said to my dog, who was lying right next to me in my bed. "Oh thank goodness it was just a dream," I said to myself. I laid down to go back to sleep, with a huge smile on my face.

Jaqueline L. Storer
Age: 13

ALWAYS IN MY HEART

I looked out toward the horizon and watched the last streaks of color from the sun fade into the darkness of the sky. The gentle breeze caressed my face and the leaves floated off of their branches. A distant rumble of thunder made my heartbeat quicken, as if there were some mysterious force beckoning my moment of silence. I rose up off of the swinging bench and rubbed my warm hands over my arms, which were now starting to grow cold. I hesitated and sat down again. I missed Justin...

I was lying out in the grass, doing my homework, when I gazed up at the sky above. It was clear and there were big puffy clouds scattered across the blue dome. The sun shone brightly and the breeze was just right. I said to myself, "I wish I was with Justin right now."

I heard a soft voice saying, "I'm right here. I'll always be here."

I smiled as I jumped up and wrapped my arms around Justin's neck. He pulled back and asked, "How's my Sweet Sixteen today? She's looking gorgeous as ever."

I closed my eyes and kissed him sweetly on the cheek. I felt like I was the luckiest girl alive and nothing could go wrong. Justin's auburn hair blew in the breeze and revealed his deep blue-green eyes. They danced with my hazel ones as he tucked my blonde hair behind my ear.

Justin took my hand in his and he walked me out to his Jeep. I climbed in and fastened my seat belt. He drove me down to the pier so we could watch the sunset together. It was beautiful; and the best part was, I was sharing this moment with Justin.

Have you ever noticed that some of the most significant moments in your life are shared with the ones that you never would have suspected? It's in these moments that you see the real person in you and the other individual, the good and maybe sometimes the bad. And it's these moments that make life even more worth living for. I loved sharing these moments with Justin and I hoped he felt the same.

A few hours later, Justin drove me home. I kissed him good-bye, even though I was reluctant to let him go. Something just didn't feel right.

About two hours after Justin left, the phone rang. I ambled over to my dresser and picked up the receiver, "Hello?" I answered.

"Yes. Is this Miss Scott?"

I had never heard this voice on the phone, but I answered, "Yes. This is she."

"Hello, I am from Skylark Hospital. Miss Scott, Justin Morgan has just been in a car accident..."

My heart stopped. I dropped the phone and sank to the floor. I buried my face in my hands and started to cry. My parents came up and I told them what happened. They offered to take me to the hospital. A few minutes later, we were off to the hospital.

I rushed into through the double doors and peered through the window where Justin was being looked after. I couldn't stand it. I ran into the room and sank to Justin's side.

The doctor looked at me in horror and said, "Miss, I'm sorry but you can't be in here."

"Please let me stay. I love him, please?"

I cried out to Justin as my parents led me out of the room. My world was falling apart and I felt as if all hope had faded. What would become of me? What would become of Justin?

That night, I lay in bed at the Ronald McDonald House and thoughts of Justin floated throughout my head. I remembered the day he asked me out, our first kiss, all of those special times when we were alone or out with friends. I didn't know what I would do without Justin. I started to dampen my pillow with my tears. What if something happens? What if tonight was the last night I would ever get to hold him in my arms, hear him say 'I love you,' or see him smile? What if I lose him?

The next few days seemed to go fast and Justin was looking better and better with passing time. We would take walks around the hospital, his hand clasped in mine. He would tell me not to worry about him and that he was doing fine but he said the only bad thing was the food. I would laugh every time he would joke about it. Every time I saw Justin, I would think about all of the things that we would do together after he was released.

Every night before I had to leave, I would sit on the side of Justin's bed and lean my head against his chest. He would whisper, "Who's my best girl?"

I would smile and say, "Me."

Then I would ruffle his hair and give him a soft kiss. Our eyes stayed glued as I stood up. I didn't want to leave him even though I knew I had to.

The next day, I went to see Justin earlier than I usually did. I walked into the wing, but Justin's room was empty. Everything was gone. The walls were bare; the nightstand no longer balanced the picture of Justin and me.

I ran up to the desk and asked the receptionist what happened.

She looked up at me and said, "I'm sorry Miss Scott..." My heartbeat quickened. "Mr. Morgan has been moved to the upper wing. He's in Room 39."

I breathed a deep sigh of relief and entered the elevator. I finally got to Room 39. Justin looked weary and weak. I didn't understand. What had happened to my Justin? The Justin that just yesterday was dancing with me in the hallway?

I ran over to him and he managed to give me an innocent smile. I looked into his eyes. The blue-green gems that had once been dancing with laughter, were now fading with the beat of the EKG monitor. I kissed him and his lips didn't hold the same warmness to them that refreshed me every time they met with my own.

I grabbed his hand and laced my fingers with his. Even though I denied it in my mind, my heart told me that Justin was dying. Tears welled in my eyes as Justin started to speak.

He caressed my cheek with his strong hand and said, "Taylor, you know that I love you, right?"

"Yes, and I love you too Justin," I struggled to say with a lump in my throat.

"I want to thank you for all the times that we've spent together. You've been so good to me."

I shook my head and said, "Justin, we can still have more time together. Don't let go Justin. Please."

Justin smiled, "I'm trying. I just want you to know that I'll always be shining down on you from Heaven."

"Justin, don't say that. You can make it. Don't give up on me, on us."

"I really love you but you have to say good-bye. I don't think I can hold on much longer."

"Justin, I can't say good-bye. I love you, please don't leave me."

"You have to say good-bye. I don't want you to suffer. I want to stay here with you but I can hear God calling my name. Taylor, I want to go home."

"Justin please. Stay here."

"Taylor, say good-bye to me. It's okay, don't cry. We'll meet again someday. I promise."

I wiped the tears from my eyes, although they kept coming. "Good-bye, Justin."

"Who's my best girl?"

"Me."

"I love you."

"I love you too."

Justin's grip started to loosen as he said, "Good-bye, Sweet Sixteen. I'll always love you... forever."

Those last few words were a whisper and he let go of my hand. The room was silent and the monitor's resonating tone finally came to its endless sound. I couldn't control it any longer. I cried heavily and managed to say as I rested my head on his chest, "I'll love you, always and forever..."

The next morning, I went down to the pier to watch the sunset. I looked down upon the glistening sand and saw Justin and I walking along the beach, hand in hand. I walked down to the ocean's edge and let the water refresh me. Suddenly, everyone around me disappeared and I was alone. I gazed out toward the sparkling ocean and saw a figure. It was coming towards me. I squinted and ran into the water. I embraced Justin. I looked up at him and saw those luminous blue-green eyes. I ran my fingers through his hair and started to cry.

To stare into those eyes, to feel his touch again; made me miss him more. Justin smiled and faded away.

I looked to the sky and smiled. I knew he was shining down upon me. A soft breeze blew and I knew it was him, telling me everything was all right.

Jasmine Johnson

THE HOPE OF STARLIGHT

A couple of years ago this girl named Mandie was sitting on her porch enjoying the view of her big farm. She was enjoying everything until her neighbor Joe came out. Joe wasn't very friendly at all. Mandie noticed that he had some stakes and some wire in his hand. So Mandie was looking through the old wooden fence that separated his house from her house to see what he was doing. She couldn't see very well, so when she went to see it up closer she could then tell what he was building was an electric fence. Mandie couldn't figure out why he needed it though, because he didn't have any animals.

Then a few days later Joe came up the driveway in a big truck with a trailer on it. So when Joe parked his truck he pulled out a big beautiful horse named Starlight. It had been a week since Starlight was in his new home. Joe hadn't fed Starlight at all, but Mandie did. Starlight hadn't been groomed in a while and his hooves needed to be trimmed badly. Luckily Mandie had a bunch of horses of her own, so she had all of the equipment to trim Starlight's hooves. He needed to be washed and brushed out too.

So one day while Mandie was feeding Starlight, she noticed that every time she went to pet him he would flinch. Then she was worried that he might not be able to see very good. Mandie told Joe to turn the fence off so Starlight wouldn't walk into it and get shocked. Joe didn't listen, he kept the fence on anyway. Starlight seemed to be doing fine.

Late that night Mandie got up to get a glass of water and noticed the fence was crooked. So she turned on the other sets of lights and saw Starlight. He was being shocked. It was horrible. Mandie threw her boots on and ran to turn the fence off. Then she ran for Starlight. He was laying on the ground as if he had no more life in him.

Her parents called the vet and he said that Starlight probably wasn't going to make it through the night. Mandie was determined not to let that happen. She stayed with him all night, then she fell asleep. Then suddenly, in the middle of the night, she was awakened by this beautiful woman dressed in a golden robe and she was touching Starlight's wound. So when she went to get a closer look the woman disappeared. Mandie thought it was strange, but then thought she was just seeing things. Then, in the morning, Starlight woke her up and he was just as perky as he could be. He was doing great.

Then when Mandie went to see his wound it was completely gone. She wondered if it had something to do with that woman last night, but she thought it couldn't have. So when she went to turn Starlight out of his stall she heard something behind her. When she turned around to see what it was she saw that woman again and Mandie knew she wasn't just seeing things, she knew that her prayers really did come true.

Morgan Danielle Howard
Age: 10

THE JOURNEY OF THE DONKEY

One day, when Jack woke up, he didn't recognize where he was. He was in a dim room and the only light that was showing was from the ceiling. The light shined onto the staircase. Jack saw the staircase and walked up cautiously, because he didn't know what was up there.

When Jack took a peek, he saw a lot of people. They were all working and they seemed like they haven't taken a shower in months. One of the workers saw Jack, so Jack sprinted to the edge of the massive structure that he was on trying to find a way out, but all he could see was water.

Now Jack knew that he was on a ship and the people working are sailors. "What am I doing on this ship?" Jack asked himself. "Where is this ship taking me?"

Suddenly Jack felt something grasp his back. It was one of the sailors.

"Gotcha you smelly donkey!" and the sailor threw Jack back into the cellar. Then he closed the lid. "Well that should hold him off until we get to America," said the sailor.

"So I'm going to America," Jack said after he heard the sailor. "Why do they want me there?" Jack decided to go to sleep and pretend that this is all a dream. He would wake up back in Asia with his friend. Jack drifted into sleep and did not wake up for a long time.

When Jack woke up he was already in America. Four men came down into the cellar and picked Jack up by his front and hind legs. They carried him out into a small boat and floated to land.

Jack stepped out of the puny boat and onto the soft ground, which was when the same four men picked Jack up again and shoved him into a cage. They locked it up and put the cage in the back of a truck. Jack knew that he was in North Carolina because he heard someone say something about it.

The truck ride was long and boring. Jack was about to go to sleep but the truck slowed down and came to a halt. When the truck driver took Jack out, Jack saw a farm with a lot of animals. Then the truck driver took Jack to the farmer.

The farmer's name was Farmer Dan. Farmer Dan took Jack into the farm and put him in a stable with a lot of hay. Jack was glad there was hay because he hasn't eaten since he woke up on the ship. Jack munched on the hay until Farmer Dan came.

He tied a heavy pile of hay on Jack's back. Then he tied a long cord on Jack's neck and started walking him around the farm like Jack was a dog. Farmer Dan walked Jack from one horse to the next. The horses were eating the hay off of Jack's back. Jack felt like a slave.

It took Jack about thirty minutes to feed all of the horses. Then Farmer Dan put Jack back into his stable and left. As minutes passed, Jack hated this place more and more.

It was getting dark outside, so Jack decided to go to sleep. He slept on a pile of hay and it was comfortable. It was the first night since two days that Jack had a good rest.

COCK-A-DOODLE-DOO!!! Jack woke up astounded. It was the rooster that woke him up.

Farmer Dan came in and did the same thing he did yesterday, except he didn't tie the cord on Jack's neck. Instead he held it in his hand. Jack didn't move so Farmer Dan whipped him with the cord.

Now Jack was bolting towards the horses' stables. He fed the horses breakfast and then went back into his stable. But Farmer Dan forgot to close the door.

Jack decided to go out and talk to the animals to make a plan for Jack to run away. First he went to the cows. He told them that he was going to use them to jump over the fence and run away. Then he went to a pig and a spider.

"Hello. I'm Jack," Jack greeted them.

"Hello Jack," said the spider, "my name is Charlotte. This is my friend."

"Hi Mr. Donkey," the pig said.

Jack started to tell them about the plan. He told them that they needed to make a distraction so Jack could run away. Charlotte and the pig agreed to make a distraction.

When Farmer Dan came, Jack got ready. Jack fed the horses lunch quickly and went back into the stable. Farmer Dan was about to close the door, but the pig started acting crazy. He slid in the mud and did everything he could to distract Farmer Dan. This was Jack's chance to get away. Jack ran towards the fence. He saw that the cows were in position so he jumped on the calf, then he jumped on the cow and leaped over the fence. He was free!

Jack was galloping along until he heard someone yell, "Christopher Robins! Come out to play!"

Jack recognized that saying, but couldn't remember who said that so he went to see who it was. To his surprise, it was Winnie the Pooh and his friends. Then he saw Christopher Robins.

"Hello everyone," Jack said in a friendly way. "When I was little I watched your show. But now I think it is just boring!"

Suddenly Winnie-the-Pooh and all of his friends turned red and looked furious. That was a signal for Jack to run so he dashed in the opposite direction with Pooh right behind him. They chased Jack from North Carolina to Virginia and to Washington, D.C.

It was the longest chase ever, but Jack managed to lose them. It was windy in Washington, D.C. and a newspaper blew right into his face. Jack read it and it was talking about President Bush going to Asia!

Jack had to find President Bush. He searched and searched and finally found the White House. Then he saw three limousines pulling out, and Bush was in one of them. Jack grabbed onto the back of one of the limousines and used his hoofs to slide along the street.

The limousines stopped next to Bush's private plane. When everyone was putting their luggage into the plane, Jack snuck on and hid. A few minutes later he was flying to Asia. They flew smoothly until something went wrong. The pilot couldn't control the plane. They were going to crash! The ground got closer and closer to the plane, but something stopped them from crashing. The plane landed perfectly on the ground. Jack went to see what it was that saved them and he saw Superman! Superman saved them.

"Thanks Superman," Jack said with gratitude and appreciation.

"Anytime," Superman replied and then flew off. Jack was now on the coast of Africa. Asia was on the other side of the ocean!

Jack couldn't think of anything to do but to swim to Asia, so he did. He couldn't swim well so he drowned.

Surprisingly, Jack was still alive. He woke up and smelled pineapple. Then a yellow sponge walked into the room. It was SpongeBob!

"Hello there, friend," said SpongeBob.

"Hi," Jack said. "My name is Jack. What am I doing here?"

"You drowned so I saved you by putting that oxygen mask on you," SpongeBob said pointing to the mask. "Why were you in the big blue anyways?"

"I was trying to get to Asia. But now I'm lost."

"Well you're in luck," said SpongeBob. "I can help you. Just follow my instructions carefully. All you have to do is keep swimming in this direction until you see a big water current. Then you swim into it and it should take you to Asia!"

"Thanks," said Jack and he swam in the direction that SpongeBob told him to. It took Jack a long time to swim to the current, but he made it because he was determined to get to Asia.

The current was very large. It looked like it moved as fast as the wind. But Jack didn't care. He swam straight into the current and was instantly washed into the direction that the current was flowing. It felt like Jack was flying like a rocket. His belly had the butterflies because it was so exciting. In the current, Jack could see many sea turtles, big and small.

All of a sudden the current got extremely fast and then the current just blew Jack out. Jack saw the coast so he swam towards it, but for some reason his legs were numb.

Once Jack made it to the coast, he took off his mask and breathed the fresh air of Asia.

Right away, Jack started towards his home. When he finally got there, he knocked on the door. The door opened and his friend Shrek was there. They both were shocked and happy at the same time.

Jack told Shrek everything that happened and Shrek seemed interested. Both friends rejoiced and they became better friends then they already were.

Sonny Ha

SMOKING IS HARMFUL TO YOUR BODY

You should not smoke, because it is bad for your heart, lungs, and your brain. It is bad for your heart, because it speeds up real easy when you just start playing sports. It is bad for your lungs, because cigarettes have carbon monoxide in them and you take in that carbon monoxide and your lungs don't need carbon monoxide so they can't really get any air. Smoking is also bad for your brain, because it kills your brain cells as well as alcohol can.

When you see someone smoking and you think in your head HEY THAT LOOKS COOL SO I'M GOING TO TRY ONE, BECAUSE THAT PERSON MAKES IT LOOK LIKE IT WON'T HARM THEM SO THAT MEANS IT WOULD NOT HARM ME. Well if you think that then think again, because smoking can really harm you badly. Even if you go to a family member's house and you go to live there, because something happened to your house and the members you are staying with smokes you can get sick by SECONDHAND SMOKE!

You can get really sick by SECONDHAND SMOKE, because you breathe in tar, carbon monoxide, and nicotine. TAR is a thick black material that sticks to your lungs and can cause cancer. CARBON MONOXIDE is a poisonous gas that replaces oxygen in the bloodstream. NICOTINE is an addictive (habit-forming) drug. Nicotine makes the heart work faster.

If you start to smoke this is what would happen to you smoking slows your gums' ability to heal. It can cause gum disease and eventually cancer. Smoking damages tiny hairs that keep the throat and lungs clean. Tar, dirt, and germs get into the throat and lungs. Tar, dirt, and germs collect in the lungs, turning the lungs from a healthy pink to black. The tiny air sacs that pass oxygen to the bloodstream are damaged. Nicotine makes blood vessels smaller. This makes it harder for the body to get the oxygen it needs. Narrowed blood vessels make the heart work harder.

Now you know that SMOKING HURTS EVERYONE, SMOKING IS ADDICTIVE, AND MOST OF ALL SMOKING KILLS PEOPLE!!!

SO CHANGE YOUR MIND BEFORE IT IS TOO LATE!!!

SMOKE FREE IS THE ONLY WAY TO BE!!!

Ashley Ryan

THE CHILD PRODIGY

"Gather 'round children and let me tell you an amazing story," said BillyBob.

"Oh boy, I love stories Grandpa!" Johnny said enthusiastically.

All of BillyBob's grandchildren came running to his feet to listen to this story. "This story is very long. I warn you, but there is no ending because William is still here among us," warned BillyBob.

"It all started when, well when should I start? Um, oh yes I will begin when William was born. When William was born his parents looked at him funny because he didn't look like a Bob. Bob was going to be his name, but then they looked at the doctor and complained. 'William, this does not look like a Bob,' his parents said. 'Really, he doesn't look like a Bob at all,' replied the doctor. Then the father said, 'I like that name, William.' The mother said, 'Yes, William will be his name, William Food.'"

"This boy," continued BillyBob, "this boy was very, very special. Right away in preschool, he knew division, subtraction, multiplication, addition, social studies, science, all the languages in the world, language arts and English better than I know it now. He right away got put up five grades to put him in the fourth grade," BillyBob said enthusiastically.

"He wasn't just all brains, but could beat anyone in anything. Anything from soccer, football, baseball, track, swimming, any game system too. He could beat you in pool, air hockey, or foosball. Colleges were already reserving a spot for him to play any sport he wanted to. As William reached seventh grade he already had problems. His schedules were colliding with each other so he had to decide which sport he liked the best. William loved all the sports he could do so he thought and thought. He decided to quit all sports but soccer, because his dad loved soccer and William wanted to make his dad happy. Every day when William got home from school he went outside to practice. His dad watched with a grin from his window. Another problem was that he was short, so smart, and stronger than the other seventh graders that they picked on him. Sometimes he couldn't take it and went to the restroom and cried. Everyone picked on him until one day when he..." expressed BillyBob.

"What," said Johnny, "what happened to William to make the other seventh graders stop picking on him?"

"Oh yes, William was very upset but there was going to be something to change all that. He overheard some other students that were in his class talking. They said there was going to be a new student and they thought it was a girl coming. William thought in his head, oh a little competition. They also mentioned she was going to come in the fourth period. All that day he thought whom the new student would look like. When he got home he couldn't practice right. He was thinking about the new student. He couldn't even get a full night's sleep because he was thinking about the new student. He waited anxiously for fourth period. When the door opened to reveal the new student, he froze. When she looked in he turned bright red and looked away. The teacher said this is the foreign exchange student, Cindy. The teacher told Cindy to tell a little about her. She cleared her throat and started talking about herself. William just gawked at her and all he heard was hi William, hi William until she was finished. Then the teacher told Rich, the boy sitting next to William, to move to the front of the room so Cindy could sit there. William was now drooling. Then Cindy put her hand on her chin and closed her mouth and said, 'Hi I am Cindy what's your name?' William stuttered and said, 'Wi, Wi, Wal-Mart.' William went as red as a rose.

"Since every guy in the class knew that he liked her they always teased him when they saw him. He always was afraid to talk to her because he was too afraid to say something wrong. He loved fourth period because they always had to work with the person next to them. He always was as red as a rose. They had to do these worksheets and Cindy just sat there and smiled at him while he worked it out. Then when they got out of fourth period she noticed that he tried to avoid her so she followed him and asked him if he liked her more than a friend. He answered with a yes. Cindy said, 'OK I was wondering because my friend said you do.' When he got home he skipped practice and called Cindy," BillyBob said intensely.

"The next day at school," BillyBob continued, "William told everyone that Cindy was his girlfriend. No one believed him until they asked Cindy and she said yes. Then something nobody thought would be possible happened. The teacher came up and asked that William might move up to college if he gets a hundred on the test called THE HARD TEST. The teacher said 'No high school student has passed this test and if you get a hundred percent then you will be the youngest child ever to be in college.' William agreed and studied every chance he got. He had to skip his daily practice just to study for this test, it covered everything that he would learn in high school. The high school coaches were asking him to get a ninety-nine percent just to help their teams to get to state. He said no viciously. The day finally came when he had to take THE HARD TEST. When he entered the room to take the test he noticed mirrors everywhere, on the ceiling, and walls. There were no windows and they checked him to see if he had any papers. They supplied him with his own pen also. When he asked why all this stuff was here they answered so you don't cheat. 'If you cheat you will be sent back to kindergarten,' threatened the teacher. He answered back, 'Sir, I wouldn't go back to kindergarten I would be sent back to preschool.' The teacher said, 'Be quiet and sit down.' He gave William the paper that had one hundred multiple-choice questions," BillyBob intensely said. "The teacher just sat down in the chair to watch and screamed to see William standing in front of him with the test finished." BillyBob went on, "'there are no questions. I know I am finished with THE HARD TEST. Actually I don't really think it was really hard sir,' William said that sarcastically. OK it's time for a break," BillyBob said.

When BillyBob returned he said, "Let's continue kids."

"William stood staring at the teacher grading the test until he was done. Then handed it back and screamed 'Here I come college.' Once William said his good-bye to Cindy, because he couldn't say good-bye's because he only has one friend, he left," BillyBob said with a tear in his eye.

"When William got to the college the first person to talk to him was his soccer coach. The coach begged him to play and William agreed. When he got to class he had to pay attention to the professor because this was a thing he didn't even know. After a year of being at college he had as many friends as he wanted and the soccer team went to state. Cindy secretly was studying and planning to take THE HARD TEST. She got a hundred percent and packed her bags for college. When she arrived she noticed his name everywhere, on bulletin boards, posters, walls, ceilings, and on people's shirts," BillyBob expressed.

"She asked people where William was and they answered 'on the field,'" said BillyBob. "She walked on the field and saw him. She said 'hello' and hugged him and said 'what have you been up to? He replied, 'just going to go and try out for the Brazilian team.' 'The country Brazil' screamed Cindy. 'Yes' answered William," BillyBob said.

BillyBob continued by saying, "He went to Brazil and made the team. I say he played very good."

Johnny yelled, "Hey wait a minute, how could you know and plus you said this story never ends."

"Yes Ponnie, Johnny, Donnie, Connie, and Ronnie."

BillyBob bent down and whispered, "Because I am William." Then they all went outside and played soccer until bedtime. BillyBob tucked them all in and when he got to Johnny, Johnny said, "You never did finish that story."

"Oh, you're right I didn't, William became a professional soccer player and is now called the world's greatest soccer player. They also say his grandson will be as great as him," BillyBob answered.

"And Cindy?" said Johnny.

"Well, Cindy and William stayed girlfriend and boyfriend until he was twenty-two and she was thirty-five, and then proposed. They got married and then that week later watched him play soccer. When William retired he moved away and settled down in California. They lived happily ever after until they had kids.

Joe Day

TURTLEFOOT

Oh yes, the mark. The mark on the bottom of my left foot. The mark that looks like a turtle. The mark that gives me the name "Turtlefoot." Honestly, I don't like to talk about it.

My real name is Jonny Bigfeet. And yes, I get made fun of because of my last name.

The turtle mark has been on the bottom of my foot since I was four years old. I don't exactly remember how I got it, but this is the best I can do.

It all started when my family went on a camping trip without me. Well, they forgot me, really. I was found two days later behind some trash cans by the next-door neighbor, Miss Wink. Miss Wink had just graduated from Blink University. At Blink University, they taught you how to mark people by their personality, literally.

Miss Wink took me to her house and looked after me for a few days. Then things started to get weird.

Miss Wink started to chant things around me saying stuff like, "Jonny Bigfeet. Hmmm, Jonny Bigfeet. Interesting character. His personality is slow. A Turtlefoot." That really freaked me out, but my family came home three days later and Miss Wink let me go back to them.

After that, my left foot constantly itched causing my mother to take me to the vet thinking that I had fleas. Unfortunately, the veterinarian told her that since I wasn't one of his regular patients, he couldn't see me. The doctor then told her to feed me well and give me a bath when we got home.

During the bath, my mother noticed my foot. "My goodness boy! You're turnin' into a turtle!" she yelped.

I knew that it was impossible for a four-year-old kid to turn into a turtle. I was just too young. That was one of those things you did when you grew up. I wanted to be a fire truck, not a turtle.

Unconvinced by my fire-truck theory, my family sent me to a place called, "Ribly's Believe it or Don't." I was put on display as the "Turtle Man (well kid)."

No one came to see me because no one could believe it, or so Ribly said.

I tried to explain to Ribly himself that I was only four and it was impossible for me to be "Turtle Man" because he was just on a show called "Ripley's Believe it or Not." Ribly yelled at me for bringing up his more successful brother. He also called me a bunch of names that I called my sister when I got home, which I eventually did. Ribly decided that he didn't want an annoying kid around anymore. When I called my sister those names, by the way, my mom made me sit on my bed.

Nowadays I catch myself staring at my unusual turtle mark. I sometimes wonder why Miss Wink gave me that particular mark. Why not a snail? Or an inchworm? I like inchworms.

Since then, I have learned of Miss Wink's power that can mark people. It's very simple and easy to remember. Now what was it again...?

Also, I ponder on why I can hold my breath for half an hour.

Today, I live all alone. I am Jonny Bigfeet.

Felicia Noel Berger
Age: 13

"Faster, faster," James told himself while running in a track race. James had asthma and was the only one in his family that had it. James loved track, but this time he thought his heart was going to give up. He heard his sister, Hope, his mom, and his four brothers cheering for him in the crowd. His dad had passed away two years ago.

James felt horrible. Then he immediately stopped. He fell to his knees, then laid there on the track thinking, "What a failure." Hope rushed down to see what was so wrong that he would stop in a race.

Hope said in a worried voice, "What's wrong?"

There was no answer. Hope kneeled right by his face. His forehead was getting hotter by the second. James' mom went to go get his four brothers and her cell phone to call the ambulance. Hope was not letting her brother go to the hospital without her. Hope heard the howling of the sirens and saw the ambulance and fire truck pull up one by one. The medics rushed out! Hope did not think that they could fit so many men in such a little truck!

A guy named Mike with green eyes and thick brown hair put a breathing mask on James. He looked down at Hope and smiled.

"Get him to the hospital as fast as you can," Hope cried. "He is my brother!"

As soon as she said that, they were gone. She hurried to the car with her mom and brothers and they quietly drove to the hospital.

Once inside the emergency room, the nurse advised them that James was on oxygen and had suffered a severe asthma attack. The nurse told their mother only one visitor at a time could go in and see James. After his mother returned from his hospital room, Hope walked down the hallway, opened the door quietly to his room, and there James lay. He looked tired and weak.

"James?" Hope said in the softest voice possible.

"Yeah," he answered even softer than hers. "The doctor said that I am going to live," James whispered.

"I am so glad!" cried Hope.

After a week had passed, James got to go home from the hospital. James was still sad thinking he was failure. He tried out for the tennis team, and did not make it. The coach said he would not accept a player with a condition like his. James really did not care. Hope was right by his side all the time.

James tried out for the basketball team, too. But the coach said the same thing as the tennis coach.

James thought he was a failure. Nobody agreed. They thought he was perfect! James felt all torn up inside. Hope said to him, "All's well, ends well." James thought it over and realized he is not a failure.

The next morning, he got dressed fast and skipped breakfast and headed to the tennis coach's house.

James said to him, "I am now perfectly fine. Just because I have asthma doesn't mean I can't join the team! The doctor said I was just running on an empty stomach and was full of water. I know better now!"

He wanted a chance. A chance to feel good about himself, and to prove he was not a failure.

The coach looked at James with approval. "Well, young man, I really didn't mean to hurt your feelings, but when I heard you had asthma, I didn't want you to get hurt."

The coach and James had a long talk and agreed he could be on the team.

James rushed home to his mom. Hope was there, too. His mom said she would buy him a new tennis racket. He was so excited! He was so excited about the whole thing that he didn't have an appetite for dinner. James ate a big dinner anyway and jumped from the table to go and practice.

There at the court he met his team. James felt good about himself. He was not a failure! He was a winner! His dad would be so proud! His dad had taught him how to play tennis when James was just a little boy.

It was finally the big day! His first tennis tournament. "I will win!" he said. Five seconds left in the game and it was all up to James to win it.

Five... four... three... two... HIT!! James hit the tennis ball with all his might. He scored!! He won!! His dad would be so proud of him because he died of asthma.

Marissa Galaviz
Age: 9

THE STORY

The young writer sat down at her desk. She took a piece of college-lined notebook paper and began to write. She wrote furiously, letting the words fill all the available space on the page. Her mind raced with a thousand ideas, each of them colliding into one another. Each of them sparking a new idea in her brain.

"No good! None of this is any good!" she said in frustration as she crumpled the paper up and tossed it in with the medium-sized pile at her feet. She had already been writing for days on end, trying to find an idea she liked. Slowly, she picked up another piece out of the already thin packet of papers and began to write again.

The writer wrote quicker now, hardly pausing to even catch a breath. A great idea had just struck her. Her pen flew across the paper at an incredible speed. Words fell across the paper like droplets of rain. Soon they had filled one side of the page and darted down half of the other. Suddenly, as quick as the idea came, it had vanished.

"So much of that idea," she said in complete frustration. She felt defeated and tired. Why couldn't she think of anything? Why couldn't she write anything good?

She sighed in frustration and got up from the computer and headed toward one of the file cabinets by her desk. She pulled open the fifth drawer on the file cabinet to the left. The drawer was filled with at least twenty notebooks. Each notebook was a different color. She pulled out the blue, purple, green, and orange notebooks and shut the drawer. It shut with a loud clang as it hit the metal body of the cabinet.

The young writer sat back down at the desk and opened the green notebook. These notebooks were full of old stories she had been working on. Most of the notebook's pages were filled except for the last section. She looked over the pages carefully, looking for anything that would give her a page-worthy idea. The green, purple, and orange notebook held nothing. She sighed, not even bothering to open the blue notebook. It too would probably have nothing to help her either.

The writer turned back and stared at the wood of the desk. No ideas had come from her old stories. Her thoughts didn't help her much either.

"I got nothing," she said to the air. Suddenly another idea popped into her head. She grabbed a piece of notebook paper and began to write again. Her hand flew quickly across the page. This one showed promise.

She quickly filled page after page. This idea was fast transforming into something grand. The young writer's pen was flying. It filled line after line. There seemed to be no limit to the depths of the idea. Suddenly, the idea disintegrated in her mind. She laid the pen down and resumed staring at the wooden desk in frustration.

She sighed again, letting the stress and fatigue out of her mind. She looked over at the packet of paper. It was already depleted of its contents. She sighed again and threw the empty plastic container in the trash can beside her. The writer stood up and threw away her large pile of crumpled paper into the trash can. She couldn't believe that she had gone through the entire packet in four days.

The young writer headed to the kitchen and opened the fridge. She took out a can of soda pop and some leftover pepperoni pizza. She took her lunch and sat back down at her desk. Before she began to eat, she turned on the computer. She quickly ate her food while she waited for the computer to turn on. Once the computer was booted up, she double-clicked on Microsoft Word and waited for it to pop up on the screen.

"This computer is slow," she said in annoyance. Finally, after a few minutes, it had fully loaded onto the screen. The young writer leaned back into her chair. She had no ideas. What could she write anyway? Her idea bank was dry as a bone.

Slowly, she placed her hands on the keys. Her fingers fumbled at the keyboard at first. She didn't move her hands for a while. Slowly, an idea flowed into her head. The young writer sighed again; it probably was a dead end. She hoped it really wasn't.

The morning sunlight shone brightly. The sky was cloudless blue. It was a perfect day for... she keyed in slowly. Bells suddenly went off in her head. Her hands moved faster across the keyboard. She had almost filled up half a page.

"I need to name the characters. Hmm... their names could be Autumn, Liz, Cassandra, and Bridget. Yeah, those are perfect names for them," she said with renewed energy. Finally she had an idea that was worthwhile. She kept on writing, filling page after page. Soon she had come to the beginning of chapter three.

"Ugh!" she said disgustedly as she stepped over a pair of men fighting. The writer keyed. The story was on a roll, it seemed like it had no end in sight. She kept on typing as a smile played on her lips. Finally she had found the perfect idea for her. Something she thought was worthwhile. Something she thought was good.

"Finally, a good idea," she said happily as she continued to write the many adventures of Autumn, Cassandra, Liz, and Bridget in the imaginary world she had created for them.

Sara Nicole Knox
Age: 14

ONE FOR THE TEAM

I held my breath. All I could think about was the gun and I only had about two minutes left before it would explode. I stood with the other boys, watching the man who would shoot the small pistol. My eyes never left his gaze. He raised the gun; I thought I was about to die. BOOM! It sounded like the devil's laughter taunting me. I shot off like a bullet ahead of all the other boys. I moved my legs praying to God that I wouldn't slip on the moss-carpeted ground. I was easily ahead and my spirits lifted. I began to slow my pace a little. What was I so nervous about? I had this thing in the bag. So I continued following the arrows and enjoying the serene scenery. That is except for hundreds of people scampering around the course trying to get a glimpse of one of us. I was actually having fun, and then I heard it. The thumping that sounded a lot like war drums coming up behind me. My diverting run was over. I had to kick myself and lift my legs like bouncy balls in fear of the runner who was gaining on me like a target missile. Soon I could hear him heaving in vast amounts of air. I could feel the hot breath breathing down my neck. I moved my speed up a notch. But he stayed right with me, like a magnet sticking to metal. My face crinkled with frustration of the kid not falling back with the rest of the guys who were too far behind to care about. I knew the race basically consisted of this gaining stranger and me.

We were right next to each other now. I could see his face. He had black curly hair and eyes that matched the moss on the ground. His skin was a sandy color. His muscles bulged at his every step. He smirked at me and took off with what seemed like an uncatchable speed. Well, that's not cool, I thought. I tried to put my mind in another place. I started humming my favorite songs and prayed the whole time. I continued striving at top speed for the whole mile. I had finally caught up with him, but that was just in time, for I couldn't take another step at this speed. I slowed for a minute and kicked myself back into speed. My heart was racing and I was gagging with being parched. I had an excruciating cramp in my side, but I wasn't about to give up. The only thing I could think about was that runner and the finish line.

Now I was pretty close with two of the three miles done. I was in so much pain that every time I took my focus off running, I felt pain reach its fingers up through my body and squeezing every ounce of strength out of me. I was so close, so I couldn't give up now.

I've got to keep breathing. In and out, in and out, this is helping a bit. I closed my eyes. I was in so much pain, I couldn't figure out how I was still running at a pace that was gaining on the guy in front of me. I opened my eyes to see that he was right next to me now, and we were running up the final stretch. He glared over at me. But I kept my eyes on the finish line. I was biting my lip so I could focus on that pain other than the vexation that had now spread like a disease through my entire body. I had no idea how I was going to win this race, but it was my destiny, my life, I had to win this race. Not just for myself but for my team.

I came back to reality after being in what felt like a daze. The crowd was screaming and clapping. There was an equal ratio of people cheering for us. I had to beat this guy! I couldn't stand the fact that after all this pain that I'd come out second best. No way! I'm doing one for the team! I then shot off. Somehow I was sprinting down the last hundred yards. The crowd roared.

But I could barely hear it, I was too focused on the line that would make me the best runner in my state, in my school, at this race. I heard the other boy trying to keep up with me, but as the finish line grew closer, he grew further away. A smile crept across my face as I soared across the finish line. I stopped and walked, hands on my head. I was done. I had finished the all-state meet, and I'd won it! I did it for the team.

As my fellow members came in I screamed ignoring the pain tugging throughout my limbs. Someone tapped my shoulder; it was the guy that I'd almost lost to.

"Good job. It was cool running with ya," he said shaking my hand.

"Thanks, you too." I smiled and turned back to cheering for my team.

We ended up winning the all-state meet. I couldn't have been more proud of our team.

"Hey, let's hear it for the guy who won first place!" one of my teammates shouted.

"No, let's hear it for the team!" I answered.

Amanda Schmunk
Age: 13

WINNING ISN'T EVERYTHING

Her mottoes were "Take calculated risks" and "Don't be afraid to go for the gold." So, she didn't hold back a thing. The saying winning isn't everything had long ago flew out of the window. Why, because to her winning was everything. There just was no other option. Failure? Ha! Never would you hear failure and Kristen Hennings in the same sentence.

When you ask anyone to describe her, they'd say smart, beautiful, perfect and definitely successful.

So, you may now be wondering, why would anyone want to hear a story about some girl who is perfect in every way? I'll tell you why because there happens to be a lesson amidst all of these words. A valuable one that sooner or later you'll have to figure out. And so it begins...

Kristen stood, admiring her thousands of trophies, medals, ribbons, and awards. All of them seemed to be sparkling as the morning sun shone against them. She sighed and smiled at the thought of all of the memories each of them contained. Just thinking about her many many moments of success made her tingle.

She glanced at her biggest and most favorite trophy resting on the top shelf. It was about three feet tall and had a huge gold cup on the top of it. She remembered that dance contest like it was yesterday. Gosh was she nervous that day, peeking out through the curtains at the enormous crowd. Her stomach was nothing but butterflies. After her stupendous performance, she was handed that gorgeous trophy. She smiled up there on stage while people crowded around her to take pictures. Suddenly she remembered that she had never been all that proud or excited to win. Her parents had been ecstatic, but to her there was no feeling.

"Must have been great, huh?" Her thoughts were interrupted by her best friend's voice. When Kristen didn't answer right away, Amy went on. "I mean to be up on stage winning in front of all of America. I remember watching you on television thinking gosh it must be a great feeling to know you're the best." Amy stood staring at a glistening crown and pure white sash that read Miss Teen America. "You must have been so happy!"

All Kristen could do though was smile weakly and answer yeah. Really though in her heart she knew she hadn't felt any different than she normally did. In fact, she had expected to win. So, it ended up being no big surprise when she did.

As her life continued, winning became an obsession. So, that she would do almost anything to get it. Hey why quit when you get it all, right! Wrong! You see sooner or later, there will come a breaking point in everyone's life. Like when you mature and learn you are not the best. You never will be. For Kristen, it came later than sooner.

During her winning streak, as you may call it, she began to win more than just ribbons and trophies. She began to win the sorrow that no one else wanted. She began to win the feeling of having no friends and the pain that goes along with it. She couldn't understand what was going wrong. She figured it must be a problem with her friends because it by all means wasn't her. No one could change her mind.

She finally hit her breaking point when she walked into her history class just seconds before the bell rang. In the top, left-hand corner of the board was the quote of the day. As she read it the lessons her friends had been trying to tell her all along finally sank in. This is because the board read "It's not about being the best, it's about trying your best." Under this quote, a second one read "Success is the ability to go from failure to failure without losing confidence or momentum."

Inside Kristen's heart nearly burst, she gleamed with happiness. So maybe she didn't have to be the best at everything. Now she knew she could never truly be called successful until she had tried, but ended up failing at least once, and somehow managed to continue!

Stephanie Moeller
Age: 13

AN AGELESS LETTER

"Thank you, I was worried I was never going to sell that thing," the kind-faced, elderly woman said as I handed her the money for the flag I purchased at her yard sale.

"No problem, I collect old war relics and this will help complete my collection."

I went over and got into my car. I put the faded and torn boxed flag on the seat next to me and started for home.

When I reached my destination I went inside to my "restoring center," or otherwise known as my kitchen sink and started scrubbing the front glass panel of the box holding the flag. It had enough dust on it to start a small desert and it took a while to even start to see the faded blue and red of the flag.

I'll probably have to restore this wood paneling around the edges but I think this could be a real treasure! I thought to myself. I retrieved a small screwdriver from my tool box and began to pry the wood off. Before I was halfway done a piece of yellowed and crinkled paper fell to my floor. I bent over and picked up the frail paper and began to throw it away but something caught my eye, a date, 1939. Then a heading, "My Dearest Love," I began to read and as on I went I realized this was a love letter, from the war! The letter read:

> My Dearest Love,
>   If you are reading this letter then our life together has ended. I put this in "my belongings to be sent to you" in the case that I might die before returning home. It tears my heart in two knowing that I will never hear your voice again but I want you to remember I died for what we believe in. I hope you never have to witness the horror I have seen over here in Germany. So many lives lost for no reason. I now increase this number but do not cry for I am happy to give my life for this cause. I love you with every molecule of my being and I hope that our daughter is raised to be as wonderful and as beautiful as you are. You have been in my thoughts and prayers every day for the past two years as I am sure I have been in yours. There is no more that I can say other than I will love you forever even as death do us part. Tell my family and Gracie that I love them so much and that now I am in a better place.
>   Forever and always yours,
>   Jimmy

I wiped my misty eyes with my shirt sleeve and placed the flag and the letter in the box and went out to my car. I drove straight to the women's house that sold me the flag to tell her what I had discovered.

When I had arrived I found the woman still packing away things she had not sold. I got out of my car and slowly carried the letter over to her.

"Well hello," she said as she recognized me, "are you here to buy more stuff for your collection?"

"No, I am here to give you back something," I said as I handed the letter to her.

Her frail hands almost matched the delicacy of the paper and I almost wondered if she was, "My Dearest Love." As I watched her read the letter her pale eyes filled to the brim with tears that slowly carved wrinkled streams on her cheeks.

"Oh Jim," she whispered as she read on.

This had to be the woman that Jimmy addressed so fondly. Who else would show the passion this woman held in her eyes as she read this ageless letter?

"Thank you so much. I would never have sold this had I known... I have wondered about my husband for sixty years and now my heart can rest."

There were no words to say to that so I hugged her and went to my car and started for home. As I drove I realized that true love and treasures like that will be ageless.

Lauren Williams
Age: 13

LOVE AT FIRST SIGHT

Adam Scott was twenty-four years old, when he decided to enter a chance to meet twenty-five girls and in the end marry one of them. Adam is six foot two inches and has blonde hair. He lives in California and is an actor. He has been in five famous movies. He has blue eyes and every girl wishes that she could have the chance to date him. Soon, every girl's dream will come true...

Adam signed up to win a chance to meet twenty-five girls, get to know them, and in the end, pick one girl to marry. When the advertisements got out to the world that Adam was trying to settle down with someone, all the women entered this contest. Two thousand entries came in and only twenty-five girls were allowed to be picked. This made the decision very hard for Adam to watch the tapes that these women sent in and pick twenty-five of them. As he began to watch the tapes, he limited them down to twenty-five in one week. There was one particular woman that caught his eye. Her name was Emily and she was twenty-three years old. He thought she was the one without even meeting her, but he had to go on with the show.

The castle that the twenty-five women were staying in was called The Rose. It was the nicest castle in London, where the show would be filmed. They called the show, The One. On the first night, Adam and the twenty-five girls were all put in a room just to socialize and get to know everyone. It was the first chance to get Adam to get to know the girls, and the girls to know Adam. When Adam first walked into the room, he saw Emily right away. By the end of the first night, Adam limited it down to fifteen girls. When he made his decision, he asked each girl if they would accept a flower to his heart, and Emily was the first girl that he picked to accept a flower to his heart.

The women had one week to have fun in London. They saw all the sights and everything there was to know about London. The second night came around. This week, Adam was to go on group dates with all of the fifteen women. There were three groups with five women in each group. The three dates that Adam was going on was, boating on a wonderful river that had the most beautiful scenery you had ever seen. The next date was a big carriage ride around the city at night. The last date was a picnic at one of the most famous parks in all of London. At the end of all the dates, he was to pick ten women. This was very hard for Adam to do because all of the women had something about them that just meant so much to him. Once again he asked ten of the women that he thought could be his wife, to accept a flower and Emily was still the first woman picked.

The next week, Adam's best friends, Greg and Kelli picked three of the women that they thought could be Adam's wife. With these three women, he was to go on single dates with them, but the other women had to go on a group date. This was very hard for the women because they all started feeling extremely jealous of anyone that was getting in their way of marrying Adam.

Adam went on the three single dates, which Emily was one of them. They had a great time, and learned a lot about each other and their families. Emily was beginning to have very strong feelings for Adam and Adam had feelings for Emily. At this point, Adam did not care about anyone but Emily. He still went on his other dates and acted like he did care for them. When Adam went on all of his dates, he limited it down to four women. The four women were Emily, Ashley, Laura and Carolyn.

For the next four weeks, Adam would visit all of the four women's families. From getting to know each family, he can only pick two women to move on to the next round. After he met each family, the decision was even harder to make. All he knew was that he was falling in love with Emily and did not care about anyone else. Since he did not care, at the next ceremony, he chose Emily and Laura.

For the next week, Adam would take Emily and Laura to his home and let them meet his family. This was the challenge for Emily and Laura. This meant that they had to make his family like them. After Emily and Laura met Adam's family, they liked both of the women, but they thought that Emily was in love with Adam more than Laura was in love with Adam. With his family's decision behind him, Adam asked Emily to marry him. She said yes without even hesitating. Laura got very upset, and started crying because she had big feelings for him and she did not know that he only picked her because he did not care about anyone but Emily. He knew that when he first saw Emily on the video that she sent him, that it was love at first sight, and they both believed in fate.

Michelle Pence

THE DARKNESS INSIDE

Revenge, loneliness, despair, hope; these feelings run through me day by day, night after night. I long for the day when I'll be ready to leave this place and seek out the murderous villains. The people, if you can call them people, eleven years ago sought out a small ship on its way to the sixth planet past Pluto. They were looking for data that the ship was carrying that held the evidence against them on a mass robbery in the capital of Terium on the planet Mars. These thieves had managed to steal enough money and secret data to get them anywhere and to make them disappear from any law enforcement in the galaxy. Unfortunately for them, they forgot to clear the records from when they broke into the Terium Bank Complex. These records were being stored on the Bentan 3, a ship owned by a simple man who, at the time, was the security manger at the TBC. By the time they had gone back to Terium to find the records and destroy them, the ship had already set off. The crime was committed on March 4th in the year 3327, thirteen years ago to this day.

Security manager, Ron Vincent, had left the TBC, with his wife, three boys and his two-month-old daughter to spend the rest of their lives on Balzai, the sixth planet outside of Pluto. They were to stay with friends who had lived with them on Mars for quite some time. It was about a four-year journey to reach the planet. The family bonded strongly on the small one-acre ship and researched stars and planets they were going to pass on the way there. They exercised twice a day to keep their muscles and the rest of their bodies healthy on the long trip. They had a section of the ship where they grew plants for nutrients and used hydrogen machines to create enough water to last them the trip. It was two years, three months and two days into the trip when it happened. The men who had been searching the solar system looking for this ship had finally discovered the ship's course and had now caught up.

The screaming of my father, crouched over my sister, and the look of horror from my brothers' and mother's faces are the last memories I have of my family. The Bentan 3 was my father's ship. I had been cleaning the circuit boxes when the first explosion hit. I ran to find my family, but another explosion hit the rear right side of the Bentan and the emergency locking doors had shut and I could only see the dreadfulness on the other side of the door through a small window. It haunts my every waking moment. I was the only one who had access to the three escape pods, so as impossible as it was, I jettisoned my father's ship without being detected by the vile enemies. I didn't look back. I had to contain myself and stay alive before I went insane with the shroud of emotion that had suddenly fallen upon me.

The pod set me on course for Renbest, three sectors short of our set course. I had somehow, with extreme luck, landed in the center of a large city on the northeast face of the small planet. Here I stayed. I worked hard, trying to track the ship that had changed my life, and ruined everything that was me. I lived with a small family originally from Earth for the duration after the accident until now. With much support from these generous people, I had gotten myself onto a transporting ship that came only once every fifteen years and was headed to Earth. Something in my gut told me that I would find my answers there.

It is the warm period here on Renbest, and I leave today. Today is the day I will feel a new hope. Today I will begin my long voyage of vengeance. The range inside of me all these years is finally letting itself loose and guiding me to what I should, what I must, do to avenge the innocent deaths of my two brothers, darling sister, and loving parents. The growing fear and hatred that have built up from the endless nights of thoughts of that tragic day will propel me through this final struggle of revenge.

As I glare out my window, waiting for the ship to finish its checks and take off, I notice a ship docked on the opposite side of the transport. It's dark, and it gives me a rushing feeling to just look at it. It has the markings of the port where my family had blasted away from those many years ago. I quickly rush to the men fueling the ship, with an intense feeling of satisfaction for what is about to occur.

Scott Fenner

BLOODLINES

A rush of nervousness shot through my body like a stampede of horses. I couldn't balance my musket steady because of uncontrolled shakiness. The words of our outstanding leader Abraham Lincoln vibrated through my ears. "Now we are engaged in a great civil war, testing whether that nation or any nation so conceived and so dedicated can long endure... that this nation under God shall have a new birth of freedom."

My knees ached, my shoulders throbbed, and the awareness level of my senses was in high gear as my body lay still on the dewy hillside. Our regiment was preparing to charge as soon as we were called upon. Thoughts drifted in and out of me like a swift wind. Turning back wasn't an option now. I didn't know if I was in the middle of living my last day on the planet Earth. Why do I have to be here? I'm eighteen years old, and I could be carousing with my friends right now instead of risking my life on the plains of Gettysburg. Then I thought of my duty to America, and I was convinced to keep moving. I made up my mind. I was going to fight for what I believed in the most, which was freedom.

June 2, 1863 was the final day of my best friend George's life. I'll never forget such a sociable companion like George. He had been my mentor in battle, showing me how to use firearms and how to apply tactics and strategies. Two days ago we were marching into opposing territory when we encountered a band of southerners. It was during that encounter that brave George was killed by the burning metal of a Confederate shell. I remember his last words as if they were lifesaving directions. "Stay strong," he said while clutching his heart and slowly taking in his last deep breaths. "Be tough, fight for what you believe in, and remember all that I taught you." He was my master, and I was his apprentice. Now I have a better reason to charge, which is vengeance.

"Soldiers!" barked the colonel, "mount your positions!"

I shivered at the sound, but in vengeance I was poised to attack upon those cowardly Confederates. As I stood my position next to my partners in the second row, the colonel ordered us to start marching. We had about fifteen thousand men, and our spies had told us we were going up against about the same number. I continued marching until suddenly I heard a shot and saw a man fall in the first row. The battle was on.

"Charge!" screamed the colonel. The supreme moment had come. I saw the gray flannel of the Confederate uniforms as I was running towards them alongside others in the Union. As we trudged over the hill, we fell into the lap of the enemy, and artillery combat broke out like never before. I reflexly shot down two Confederates as I first entered the threshold of hell's gates.

"Aaagghh!" I yelled as a bullet grazed through the flesh on my left shoulder. I spun around and barely held onto my musket. I was lucky, but the bullet only scraped me. The blood oozed out of the fresh wound and bled through two layers of shirts. I threw myself on the ground to protect myself from the outburst of bullets. My left arm was weaker, but I was motivated to keep going, as if George was guiding my way. I reloaded and shot, reloaded and shot, doing that over and over again as fearless fighters from both sides were sinking to the ground. We fired and fired until we came to the point where we no longer saw any Confederate gray standing. I peered around and saw comrades that I knew were lying helplessly dead. The most unfortunate ones were some of the northerners that got shot in the leg or somewhere else and were writhing to a slow, excruciating and antagonizing death. I could feel their pain burning up inside me as I watched them squirm helplessly on the ground.

I rose quickly and followed the northerners across the valley of death and through the once silvery stream that was transformed into a red river. Only half of our men remained. As soon as we reached Cemetery Hill, I saw that the open range had perfect fitness for a great battlefield. Drooping valleys and winding streams made me feel like I was involved in a complex game of Stratego. Little did I know that this magnificent view would soon be covered by flurries of blood. Every inch of air seemed to be covered with some death-dealing missile. Bullets were buzzing back and forth and men were slumping down simultaneously. If I said it was like a summer storm with the crash of thunder, the glare of lightning, and the shrieking of wind, I would have made an understatement.

After a long period of rapid, bloody fire, both sides realized they were out of ammunition and the hand-to-hand combat began. The two sides went on fearlessly until the last of the rebels crumbled from the exhaustion of fighting for two days. Their leaders were dead as they fell to the hail of artillery fire. Only a remnant of the Union army remained. The flags, which had once floated over Cemetery Hill, lay on the ground along with the prostrate forms of men who had so bravely fought to the verge of victory.

Robert Thomas Burger
Age: 15

FAITH

Faith Cambell, she must be the brightest and happiest six-year-old in all of Jerold, Minnesota. She's always smiling, on rainy days, sunny days, and sad days. She's always got that same smile, with her front tooth carefully wrapped up under her pillow, waiting for the tooth fairy to drop by. Faith is always shining like the sun, nothing can get this little girl down, not even the diagnosis of cancer.

You see, last week Faith was diagnosed with leukemia, a type of cancer. She went to the doctor for her yearly checkup. When the doctor was checking her out, he noticed her ears were beet-red. He asked her if they bothered her, but she said they didn't. Just to make sure, Dr. Cline scheduled an appointment at Children's Hospital so they could take some tests.

A week later, still with her smiling face, Faith took a trip to Children's Hospital. After taking some tests, Dr. Alberts told Faith and her mom they could go home because it would take a few days for the results to come back. So Faith and her family carried on as usual.

Three days later, the doctor from Children's called back about the results. Faith's mom answered the phone.

"Mrs. Cambell? Hi, this is Dr. Alberts from the Children's Hospital. The results from Faith's tests and I'm sorry to say that she has leukemia all throughout her abdomen. There isn't much we can do because it is a fast-growing cancer. Chemotherapy won't make a difference because it is too late. I'm sorry. The only way we found it is because of her red ears. That is the only symptom of this type of cancer. Spend as much time as you can with her; she has six months to live."

"Faith honey?" her mama said in a quivering voice, "you know your Aunt Sandy who had cancer?"

"Yes Mommy, why?"

"Well, honey, Dr. Alberts called back from the Children's and -- and -- you have cancer." She couldn't hold it back any longer. Sobs broke out uncontrollably.

But Faith's only response was, "It's OK Mommy, don't cry. I'm a child of God. He will protect me."

Faith's diagnosis was very hard for her family, friends, and all of Jerold. Faith's older brother, Jacob, couldn't just stand by and watch his baby sister suffer. He thought he had to do something; take a part in Faith's cancer. So Jacob got all these people in Jerold to come to St. Joe's Church every Saturday night and take part in a prayer service for Faith.

"Everybody's prayer counts," said Jacob. "If it's God's will for Faith to go, then she'll go and we won't be mad at God. God has a reason for every choice He makes. Even if we don't understand it now, we have to have faith in Him, just like our Faith does. Faith's time here with us is growing short. So let's pray that if Faith goes, that she will not be frightened into what lies ahead of her. Pray that God will comfort her and take her by the hand. Pray that she can stay with us, but if she can't, that's OK too. God will do what's best for Faith, even if we don't think it's the best. So, while Faith is still here with us, let's make it the happiest time that she will always remember on earth and in Heaven!"

Six Months Later

All you could hear that October night was the whine of the ambulance siren as they came and took Faith away to the emergency room. Neighbors came out of their houses and could only watch their little sunshine that lit up all of Jerold be driven away.

In the emergency room, doctors and nurses did all they could to keep Jerold's sunshine alive but it just seemed they couldn't. Faith always loved life. She loved butterflies and flowers and every form of spring, but most of all she loved God. Faith promised God would protect her and He did. He protected Jerold's little sunshine from all the evil in the world and brought her to live in everlasting happiness with Him.

In a way, Faith's death made Jerold stronger. It made the whole world stronger. It taught us a lesson to appreciate life and all it gives because someday it will be your turn to join Faith and God in everlasting happiness. Even though Faith's body is gone, she shines brighter than ever in all of Jerold's hearts.

Jamie Berling
Age: 12

THE CASE OF THE MISSING BACKPACK

Chapter One: The Case

It started September twelfth at St. Sarah School when a girl named Karen Zarco lost her backpack.

Karen says, "It's sky-blue with KMZ in black block letters, it's also new and it doesn't have much in it except for some textbooks and notebooks. (Oh yeah, and also the key to my house)"

When Karen found out about her backpack she told her friends Elizabeth Horner and Lindsey Hacker. She also told her two teachers Ms. Marissa Byrne and Ms. Kat Shappelle and her principal Ms. Sarah Sharbell.

Chapter Two: Missy Mystery

Karen hired famous detective Missy Mystery to help solve her mystery. Missy told Karen that she overheard someone who sounded very much like Elizabeth say, "I found this backpack in the hall, isn't it cool? At first I thought it was Karen's but I thought her middle name was Rose."

Chapter Three: The Talk

Missy and Karen saw Elizabeth walking down the hall and Karen said, "Have you seen my backpack?"

"I might have but I don't think it's yours it had KMZ on it but I thought your middle name was Rose," Elizabeth told her.

"My middle name isn't Rose, it's Melissa, and what did you do with the backpack that you found?" Karen asked.

"I put it in the lost and found," Elizabeth told her.

The three girls went to the lost and found, but her backpack wasn't there!

Chapter Four: Thinking

"I wonder where my backpack could be," Karen said.

"Hmm... I wonder if anyone else in this school has the same backpack as you do," Elizabeth said.

"You could be right," Missy told her.

Chapter Five: Posters

"Maybe we could make posters," Elizabeth suggested.

"What would they look like?" Karen asked.

"Like this...

LOST
Backpack
if found see
Karen Zarco
Room 207
Ms. Marissa Byrne

The next day a girl named Clarissa Mucker came to see Karen and said, "I found a backpack and I think it's yours!"

"Where?" Karen asked.

"I saw it in the janitor's closet!"

"Let's go!"

Chapter Six: Found It!

"There it is!" they said together.

"Well, I'm glad you found it but it's time for me to go," Missy said.

"Bye, thank you, Missy!" Karen, Elizabeth and Clarissa said together.

"Maybe I'll come back to help you some other time," Missy said.

"Okay," Karen said. "Come on, Elizabeth, we need to get back to class."

"Bye Missy," the girls said again as they walked back to class.

Sarah Tapogna

THAT ONE NIGHT

Chapter One

That one night my uncle and two cousins were called into a wager. My mom and dad started the wager. The wager was worth ten thousand dollars. The wager was to stay in the McAlister's house for a month. It was surely haunted. They say that McAlister died because he hung himself. It was a sad day. The house had a graveyard that was the size of a super big mall! My uncle was in awe. He had never seen a graveyard that big before.

"A sign says to come in and don't come out," said my cousin Michelle.

"I guess we should go in," said my other cousin Karen. (She's not so smart!)

"They say that there were murders that went on here a long time ago. Those who are dead haunt this place now," said Michelle. Obviously she had done research on this place.

"Hauntings or no hauntings, I am going in there! Wait a minute. It's locked. There is a note on the door," said my uncle.

"It says the key is in the grave," said my cousin Michelle.

"OK, Michelle, what is his first name?" asked Karen.

"It's Troy McAlister," said Michelle.

"OK, let's go look," said Uncle bob. "Here is Neil, John, Nik, Alliso, Tori, Sami, Antonio, Zak, Morgan, Jeff. Man! How many can there be dead???" said my uncle.

"Hey look, I found the key," said Karen lying on top of the grave.

"Come on, hurry up, let's go look," said Michelle.

So they went to the door and went to unlock it but it was already unlocked!!

"Wait a minute! First it was locked and now it's unlocked. Freaky!" said my uncle.

"Well, let's go in," said Karen.

Chapter Two

It was a big house but not a mansion. They went inside and it was bigger than they thought. They had to split up so that they could look around, adventure it.

"Go away!! Get out," said a weird ghost.

"All right Karen, cut it out," shouted Michelle.

"Hey! It's not me so stop shouting!!" said Karen.

"I am the ghost of Troy McAlister," said the ghost.

"Very funny, Uncle Bob. I know it's you," said Karen.

Then behind the wall came Uncle Bob with his cloth ghost. He had a reputation for spooking everybody at the wrong time. "Ha! Ha! You should have seen the look on your face," said Uncle Bob.

"Uncle Bob, not again," said everyone.

"Come on and let's get unpacked," said Michelle with a brave voice.

They went to their own separate rooms. I, the narrator doubt they will ever find each other again.

"Wow! These rooms are huge," said Michelle.

"I love food!!" said Karen with amazement at the sight of the dining room table filled with food.

I need my camera in case I discover some clues, thought Uncle Bob.

They went back to the corridor to talk about who is going which direction. Karen took a camera and went to the attic. Then Michelle took another camera and stayed there and looked around. Then Uncle Bob took the digital camera and went to the basement. Karen walked up the stairs and she saw a hideous monster with four eyes, five hands and two feet. That was thirty feet tall. My cousin Karen ran down those stairs so fast she left burn marks on the carpet behind her. Luckily the monster was made of wax. While Karen was doing that, Michelle had found a secret entrance. She opened it and saw a vampire. She quickly touched it and saw that it too was made of wax. Then down in the basement there was my uncle and in the dark he could see a mad monkey with glowing eyes and drool running down his face. My uncle ran upstairs while the digital camera was still rolling. When he reached the main floor he had told Michelle and Karen about his experience. They also told him about their experiences.

Chapter Three

It had been a month now and it was time to pack up. They would finally get their ten thousand dollars. They packed up and left to go home to Indiana. After they collected their money, Karen was able to go to college and get a degree in engineering. Michelle was also able to go to college and get a degree in teaching. My Uncle Bob was a lawyer and was able to finally retire. Finally, my mom and dad understood what betting was all about.

Kortni Young
Age: 10

BOOM!

After one hour in the huge ship, I heard the engine start. My first space journey was about to begin.

"This is gonna be a lot more exciting than you think!" exclaimed Tom, the man sitting next to me.

"Shhhh," I said.

A few seconds later I heard a loud booming voice say, "All astronauts prepare for takeoff." Then I heard the sound of numbers counting down. Ten, nine, eight, seven, six, five, four, three, two, one TAKEOFF!   SSSSHH CCCCHHH SSSCCCC the engine roared as we blasted upward through the clouds. Soon we were in space. I took off my spacesuit. I was floating.

"Is everybody OK?" asked Tom.

"Yes!" we shouted with excitement.

There were four people aboard the ship. There was Bill. That's me, of course. There was Tom, Calvin, and Dexter. We call Dexter "Dex."

"Man, we're on our way to the moon," said Tom.

"Yaaah!" we all yelled with excitement.

"Hey Dex, turn on the engine for a second or two," said Tom.

"Sure will," said Dex.

As his fingers touched the buttons, I heard a BOOM BAM CRASH BANG!

"AAAAAAA!" everybody shouted as the whole ship shook around and bumped from side to side.

"This is the NASA space crew. We have a problem," shouted Tom to the NASA Space Center on Earth.

"What's wrong, what's wrong?" someone yelled from the NASA Space Center.

As Tom yelled, "There's been an explosion," the power was out like a flash. "This is the NASA space crew, can you hear us?" yelled Tom. There was no answer. "Men, we're on our own," said Tom.

"What's gonna happen to us?" I asked.

"I don't know, but we might not make it back to Earth," replied Calvin.

"If that was a shooting star we'd be dead by now," said Dex.

"Put on your spacesuits, men," said Tom. I put on my spacesuit and went into space. I looked around at the ship. "Bill, Bill, come quick!" yelled Tom, Calvin, and Dexter. I floated to them and saw what was wrong. One of the engines had exploded. "We only have one engine left," said Tom. "Get back in the ship," said Tom. We floated back into the ship and took off our spacesuits. Tom hit a button. BOOM! The power was on.

Two days later, we floated by the moon. Everyone looked at the moon. "Too bad we couldn't land on the moon," said Tom. As we floated away from the moon, I heard Tom say, "Everybody get ready to go back to Earth." Everyone put on their spacesuits.

We floated down to earth. Faster and faster we went. We went so fast that fire shot up from the bottom of our ship. Soon we had reached Earth. The ship had landed! We all yelled with joy.

"Next time we go up to space, we aren't gonna crash!" said Tom.

Neill Jones
Age: 11

THE DETECTIVE HORSE

Once upon a time there lived a horse named Tiffany. Tiffany is a detective. She had a magic rope. If she stepped on it she could call a friend. She stepped on the rope. She called her friend Tommy. Tommy is a detective too.

"I think my owner is a robber!"

"A robber! He's always so kind when I'm over at your house.

"I know but I saw him stealing money from his mom and dad. He stole his mom's jewels and his dad's fossils. That stuff's expensive. I've got to go."

One day Tommy came to play with Tiffany. No one was home except Tiffany. They stayed to play alone. They listened to their owners talk so much that they could speak English. They decided not to tell on Tiffany's owner. But that night they found out that Tommy's owner was the stealer. I knew it had to be him. But how could he have done it. He always sneaks out of the house. They told Tiffany's owner's mom and dad. Tiffany's owner's told Tommy's owners. Tommy's owners got in big trouble.

Holly Shively
Age: 8

A HAUNTING PAST

"Mommy do we gotta move?" cries a little girl from the backseat of a pick-up truck.

The Merandos were moving up north because Mr. Merando had received a promotion. Mr. Merando's promotion meant that he and his family must move. The family consisted of Mr. Merando, Mrs. Merando and their nine-year-old daughter named Beth. Beth was a plain, ordinary girl with brown eyes but the ordinary part about her was about to change.

"I have told you a billion times, Beth. We need to move but we have a nice, old house out in the country so you can always go out to play," replied Mrs. Merando.

The entire journey from Georgia to Pennsylvania passed in the same fashion. Every five minutes Beth would ask the same question and her mother would give the same response.

Eventually after many questions asked and many answers given the family finally arrived at their new home. The home was made in 1862. It had a white exterior and wooden shudders.

While the family was investigating their new home a knock came from the front door. Mr. Merando went downstairs to open the door while his wife and child followed close behind. Mr. Merando opened the door and on the doorstep stood a middle-aged man in a gray suit. The strange man whispered something to Mr. and Mrs. Merando. Mrs. Merando told Beth to run along and finish exploring the rest of the house. Mommy and Daddy had to talk business to the nice man.

Beth ran off to look into the attic. The attic was the only room the family had not looked in. In the attic, Beth found a room full of clutter that the prior owner had left behind. There was a sewing dummy, a tricycle with a bent wheel and many other things. Beth wanted to touch everything but the item that Beth wanted to look at the most was a dollhouse set along the far wall. Beth walked over to the exquisitely built dollhouse. She knelt down in front of the house and undid the latch that held the two fronts of the dollhouse together. The two halves sprung apart smoothly and easily. The inside of the dollhouse was an exact replica of the house she and her parents had just moved into, down to the grain on the wooden floor in the dining room. There was an old man doll, an old woman doll, and two children dolls. One of the children was a teenage girl and the other was a boy that looked about Beth's own age.

Pulling Beth out of her dream world came a call from downstairs, it was time for lunch. As Beth stood up to go downstairs, the room became as cold as ice. Beth felt a creepy sensation as she went downstairs she tried to shake off the strange feeling.

Beth slid into her chair at the kitchen table. Mrs. Merando put a plate of food down in the middle of the table and Mr. and Mrs. Merando took their seats. As the family started to eat their meal of grilled cheese, Mrs. Merando asked her daughter if everything was all right. Beth assured her mother that she was fine. Beth did not know why she was lying to her mother they had always been close, yet something stopped the girl from telling her mother about the dollhouse and the cold feeling.

After lunch, the family started to unpack everything from their old home. After half an hour, Beth became bored of lifting heavy boxes to the rooms they were needed in. Beth slipped away from her parents and the movers and went up to the attic. She walked across the cluttered room which now was as warm as the midsummer day outside. Beth undid the latch on the front of the house and two halves slid open. Inside there was a flurry of activity going on. There was the old woman doll cooking on the stove, the old man doll sitting in the living room reading the paper, and the children running around chasing each other. Beth couldn't believe her eyes. She closed the front of the dollhouse and opened it again. Inside everything was still nothing moved, none of the dolls twitched. Fooling herself that she had imagined dolls coming to life, Beth went downstairs to finish helping her parents.

That evening Beth went up to her new bedroom and climbed in bed. She did not go to sleep; she had too much to think about. Around midnight Beth couldn't take it anymore; she got up and went up to the attic. She crossed the cluttered room, knelt down in front of the dollhouse and undid the latch. Inside there was no movement from the dolls but a pair of unseen feet was moving up the stairs quietly and quickly as though they knew what they were doing. The girl doll was laying outside the house to show that she was not home at this moment, the boy doll was nowhere to be seen and the old dolls were upstairs in their bedroom. Silently the door to the old doll's room swung open. Beth was transfixed by the entire scene. The girl doll started to walk toward the house. Meanwhile in the old doll's bedroom the quiet footsteps of the unseen feet went to the old woman doll first and then to the old man doll's side of the bed. The footsteps stopped at both points briefly and then they ran down the stairs in the dollhouse and out the back door. A few seconds later, the girl doll walked into the house through the front door. She walked over to a little door by the fireplace and opened it. Inside she found the little boy tied up with a piece of rope. The boy doll quickly whispered something to the girl doll and she flew up to the old doll's bedroom. When the girl doll got into the room, she stopped running and stopped moving altogether. Then she started to cry. It was apparent to Beth that both the old woman doll and the old man doll were dead.

After the scene had replayed itself several times, Beth quietly closed the front of the dollhouse, walked solemnly down to her bedroom and got into bed.

The next morning, Beth was sitting at the kitchen table thinking about what she had seen last night when an idea dawned on her. She asked her parents if anybody had ever died in this house. Mr. and Mrs. Merando promised to look in the library records and newspapers after breakfast.

After breakfast Mr. and Mrs. Merando went to the library, leaving Beth behind at the house.

Beth decided that while her parents were gone she would go outside and walk around in the garden and so she did. Beth spent the entire morning looking at the beautiful flowers in the garden that the previous owners of the house had planted.

When Beth's parents came home they informed the girl that a hundred years ago an elderly couple had been killed by their granddaughter while they were sleeping. The elderly couple's grandson had testified at her trial.

After several days of pondering what she could do to help the elderly couple be put to rest. What would she tell anyone, she saw dolls come to life and explain to her that the granddaughter was not the murderer? No one would ever believe that she saw a dollhouse and all its contents become a miniature of the house her parents and her had just moved into.

Beth could do nothing, the murderer knew he was guilty and the granddaughter knew she was innocent and was wrongly convicted.

Beth lived to be ninety-three and she never told another soul person about the haunted dollhouse in her attic except for me. Now I am telling you. I am not totally convinced all that was the truth but now it is your turn to be the judge. The story might have been an old woman's rambling or it might have been a miraculous truth retold through an old dollhouse and its old dolls.

I have done some digging myself and have discovered the true murderer was the gardener. He committed the crime because he had just been fired from his job working for the elderly couple, and that the granddaughter was not allowed to be out at night. I think the granddaughter felt guilty that she left and so she admitted to committing the crimes.

Beth sadly passed away last year while she was sleeping. She died from a heart attack. She died still not able to do anything about the death of two people one night over a hundred years ago.

Jennifer A. Beasley

THE LEGEND OF HWANG

Once upon a time there was a man named Hwang. When he was a boy he began to learn about the art of fighting. First he took karate to learn how to use his kicks and punches. When he got older he took sword classes to learn how to use his advanced sword that he got a few weeks before. It took him three years to get through his sword classes. Year after year he got much better, and on his third year he was a professional. When he passed his final test he went to take magic classes where he would learn to disappear behind someone. He took Japanese after so he could hide his identity.

He got his wife Katie to sew him an outfit to fight in. When his outfit was done he tried it on immediately! When he looked in the mirror he saw himself in light brown pants with a blue sweatband, and a weapon sash on. He really liked his outfit so much in fact he wore it every time he left the house.

One day he went to a sword shop located just around the corner. He found a deal where he could get two swords for one, even though one sword was ten thousand dollars! He got his swords and set off on his journey.

It took him hours to find what he was looking for and a few minutes later he saw a bunch of fighting arenas in a line together each one different. Then he saw the proving grounds where his old friend hung out at. His name was Kilic. He was a good fighter, but instead of using a sword he used a big wooden pole. Next to him was Edge Master, the one who trained him in sword class. Edge Master was a nice guy to be with. He would practice with you and all kinds of stuff, so Hwang went to meet up with them. When he got there they greeted him with kind, pleasant remarks, and told him with their mission was. It seemed that Kilic had the same mission he did. Hwang's mission was to steal the souls from evil people and turn them good so he can use them when he's fighting, so Hwang set off to find his first opponent. A few minutes later he saw a port hole that would take him to his first arena. He stepped into the port hole and found himself in an arena with lava surrounding it. He was against Astroth, a very strange slow guy. He would have to be quick on this guy, so he pulled out his sword and prepared to fight. When the battle started Astroth already had a hold on him. Hwang managed to break free just before Astroth's ax hit him. When he broke free he had enough time to get up and stuck Astroth's blade. When he got up he launched himself into the air and dug his sword into Astroth's foot. Astroth immediately surrendered after having his foot sliced by a sword. When the match ended the ground started to shake in front of Hwang, and a giant sword split out of the ground along with a man made of fire. Then they lifted off the ground and into space. They were set on a small arena where they would fight. This man's name was Inferno a big fire-like man. He wasn't easy, he had to bounce back and forth to confuse him and then he had to charge straight at him, stab him in the leg. He waited for his moment to strike. When Inferno ran towards him Hwang jumped out of the way and stuck the sword on the ground blade up and cut Inferno's foot. Inferno stopped immediately and surrendered to Hwang. After all of that Hwang went home and told his family what had happened. His legend will never die!

David A. Owens
Age: 10

THE BEGINNING

In the beginning: nothing, emptiness, not even a thought. Yet there was Jünshai, and he was lonely. Then in the Void there became a vision, an idea, a dream, and the dream became reality. From the Void there came forth spirits with the attitude and praise of Jünshai in their hearts. The spirits each brought with them a song of praise to Jünshai, and a sound like this had never been heard, nor would such a triumphant and perfect tune be played in which mortals may partake. Yet this worship was not satisfying to Jünshai, and it was not enough for him. The songs of the spirits was not equal to what he needed and deserved. So from the Void he made a world and let the spirits have free reign over the world. The spirits took the world and created mountains and valleys, planted trees, dug canals for rivers, and being together in mind with Jünshai, built a paradise parallel to his thoughts.

When the work had been finished, the spirits were banned from any contact with the world until Jünshai was done with the job only he was able to accomplish. He created life: small creatures that ran along the ground, fowl of the air filled the skies, water-dwellers danced in the seas, and the creatures that prefer the underworld came into existence. Then Jünshai made a form of his own image, then another beside it, taller than the first, and then yet another, larger than either of the first two. Into these bodies he breathed his life and his will. The three stood and hearkened to the sultry song of the spirits and joined the jubilee, becoming the first physical beings capable of being in the presence of their creator. There was much rejoicing in the Heavenly Dwellings, and almost all were joyful, but there was one who wanted more than what he was given.

Colrisáith was the most beautiful of all the spirits, over whom he was second in command only to Jünshai. He had been given control over almost half of the spirits, directing the course of their song, and though he was placed higher than everyone else in the Heavenly Dwellings save Jünshai himself, he thought he should be and was better than every being in existence. He began to lead his choir in a different direction, in a song with the words of self-glorification.

Jünshai heard this and rose from his rest to question this clash of songs. Colrisáith perceived Jünshai's movement, for he was of similar mind such as were all of the spirits, and in attempt to possibly intimidate Jünshai brought the song to an even louder and more chaotic level. Jünshai arrived at Colrisáith's quarters in his full ominous glory such as word on paper cannot justly describe and confronted this rebellious spirit. Colrisáith cowered in the sheer presence of his master and forgot of his uprising; the spirit voices ceased.

Jünshai spoke. "I gave you this lofty position because you were trusted, your command is my gift, and this is how I am thanked. I cannot share company with the corrupt, and for your pride you must be eternally condemned to dwell in the Void from whence you came." Then he was cast from the heavens and into the Void and was seen no more as a spirit; no more would he be known as Colrisáith, for in the Void he rotted and fumed his anger toward Jünshai, and his anger permeated the nothingness that surrounded him. His angry spirit overtook the Void and became one with it and from then on was only given the name of Üblisada, The Emptiness, and dwelt in the Void until his time had arrived.

Jünshai returned to his rest and the spirit voices trickled back into full song. The Three that had been formed sensed complete satisfaction in the spirits and longed for something more than a song to fill the loneliness in their souls. Their voices stopped and they approached Jünshai. They said to him, "We have spent our entire existence praising you and our voices grow weary. Give us companions that may aid us in our labor."

Jünshai smiled upon them and replied, "This is good, for I created you to want mates and I have been waiting for you to ask me. I shall grant your request, but I must warn you that you shall not let these partners of yours to get in the way of the task you were made to complete or else you shall be cast from my presence such as Colrisáith."

"Oh, there is no need to worry, master. These companions shall be to us a help and not a hindrance."

"Very well. Then let it be done. I shall create them like you yet unlike you, for they shall be from you," and with that he took from each of them a bit of flesh and laid it in the dirt of the earth. The soil gathered around the flesh and cultivated until there were three forms such as the first three, only different, as Jünshai said they would be. Then he breathed into each of them the same as he had with the others, and they stood and went to the one whose flesh had been used to make each of them. So it became that there were two of each kind, and Jünshai saw that it was good. The Six then burst out in the most glorious song yet heard in the Heavenly Dwellings.

Time passed and never was a note repeated in that glorious song, for it was always new. But after time dissatisfaction again began to grow in the souls of the Formed. They each looked to their similarities and saw the goodness in their own eyes. Their focus shifted from their song and onto pleasing themselves, just as Jünshai had warned them not to do. He saw this and was grieved.

To them he said, "I gave you freedom to spend your entire existence free of troubles. Yet you'd rather look for enjoyment in your companions that I gave you. You dishonor me with your actions. Now be gone, and let me see you no more."

The Six hid their faces from Junshai as they fled his presence. They found refuge in the World Created among the lower creatures. There they wept, for they were cold, unclothed, tired, starving, and worst of all separated from their master's presence, and forever shall be apart from him so long as the door to the Heavenly Dwellings remained shut. But there was another among who had been cast from Jünshai's presence, and he took notice of these new beings. He went over to them, and the Emptiness took their hearts.

The Six longed for something to fill the void now left in their hearts and to replace the joy once brought by the praise of Jünshai, but when they opened their mouths, no glorious sound exited their lips. They again turned to their similarities, looking for some form of satisfaction and saw the pleasure that could be enjoyed. They forgot Jünshai and spent their time with their mates. They multiplied and therefore began the civilizations on earth known to us today.

Ages went by, and the Six now had made more of their own kind so that they numbered in the hundreds. As the generations passed by, less and less did any think of Jünshai and the happiness once in their possession. They completely forgot about him. He looked down from the Heavenly Dwellings and had pity on them, for this was not what they had been made for. He wept at their ignorance, and he knew in his heart that something must be done to return them to his side.

He called for his most beloved creation: a spirit that was not merely a copy of him but actually a part of him. This spirit was sent down to the World Created to renew the passion that once burned in the hearts of the Formed. Nothing could hinder him from completing his task, not even death. For this was Rhinuar, Prince of the Flame Kingdom and the one being capable of defeating the Emptiness that dwells in the hearts of the Formed. Hope was reborn.

Gabriel Pyle
Age: 13

THE WEIRD KID WHO RULES

He has big pointy ears, four arms, weird hands, four legs, two noses, and two mouths. The dude is a fifth grader from Goofy Elementary, and his name is Himig. He gets his homework done quickly. He is best at soccer, dodge ball, and basketball. He is a great student.

One day some kids called Himig a loser.

Himig got real mad and said, "Surrender and no one will get homework."

The kids ran to the principal.

The principal said, "We surrender."

Now Himig is the ruler of the school. The kids got out homework passes. Now homework won't harm them. So the principal gave Himig detention for the rest of the year.

Timmy Daum
Age: 11

TUNNELS

It was one big blur -- like a dream; floating down a dark tunnel. Or maybe it wasn't moving at all... It was hard to tell. And there may have been colors, but my eyes weren't focused. I had no control. It was like a dream.

Suddenly, without warning, a bright light exploded in my eyes. I screamed, or I thought I did. Maybe I just screamed in my head, like in a dream... I hope it is a dream... I hope I wake up soon. I hope I see my mom's face looking down at me saying, "It's all right honey, I'm here..." But I know that won't happen -- ever again.

The light vanished as quickly as it came. My eyes heaved a sigh of relief. Around me, walls started materializing before me. The tall, dark sides closed in around me, making the hallway more like a tunnel. But I wasn't afraid, I wasn't even surprised. It was like it was supposed to happen this way, like hallways always materialized out of nowhere like that; like in a dream...

I was lost. It had been easy at first, just following the path the hallway made for me. But now I'd come to a split in the path, a choice. Left or right? Did it matter? There was no sign that said "This way to Heaven," or, "Take a right to Happiness." So I stood there a long time, debating which path to take. Not long later, I caught a glimpse of a light at the end of the left tunnel, and my choice was made.

No sooner had I taken two steps, when I smacked promptly into a door. I stumbled back, rubbing my forehead. In peeling gold letters on the door (in many different languages), I made out the title:

GOD'S OFFICE

I looked uncertainly up at the door. Then, taking a deep breath, I knocked. No one answered. Impatiently I knocked again. This time, there was a soft click and the door opened. Hesitantly, I stepped through the doorway.

Inside was a room with a desk, a small table lamp on a small table, and a large collection of doodads from all over the world. A big, green chair behind the desk swiveled around to reveal... Absolutely nothing! There was no one in the chair!

"Welcome! Welcome! Please sit down! Make yourself at home!" boomed a bodiless voice. I was puzzled at this request because I distinctly remembered there not being any other chairs. However, I turned around and found a perfectly good chair to sit in waiting behind me -- so I sat.

"Um... It may not have occurred to you... But it's very unnerving talking to someone who isn't there..." I pointed out tentatively.

"Ah yes... But it's rather hard to take a shape that will please everyone at once..." the voice said rather regretfully.

I nodded.

"So... Do you golf?" the voice asked, breaking the awkward silence.

I looked up. "I've just died and gone through quite a lot to get here... and you ask 'do you golf?'?!?!? Don't you think I have questions? I mean, I left a perfectly good life behind... Well, er, um... I mean -- I didn't even get to say good-bye to anyone!" I cried. "I don't even know where I'm going yet!"

"Where you're going? I'm afraid I don't know what you mean..." the voice said.

"Aren't you God?!" I hollered. "I assumed you were -- the sign on the door SAID so!"

"The door... the painters STILL haven't come yet? Yes, it confuses many a-people. Oh well... to answer your question, no. I'm actually God's personal shrink, Gad. God went on a little vacation."

"Oh, OK Gad, what about the whole heaven or hell thing? I was good; really!" I insisted.

"Heaven or hell... A lot of people come in here asking about it... Is that some kind of joke? Because I don't like jokes..." Gad commented.

I opened my mouth and some not too nice words were there and ready to pop out at this Gad person, but I was cut off.

"Tell me something, Elizabeth J. Walters..."

I winced at the use of my whole name, one I hadn't heard in a long time.

"I prefer Beth..." I muttered through gritted teeth.

"...Right, of course... So Beth, just what kind of person are you?"

I frown. This guy asked weird questions... Was it even a guy? For all I knew, it could be a computer, or a trained parrot!

"I dunno..." I stated uncertainly, "I guess I'm nice, kinda pretty -- but not glamorous..."

"No, no... I mean WHO ARE YOU really?" Gad interrupted.

"Come on... You know who I am! I'm Beth, we just confirmed that!" I tapped my head, "Remember?"

An exasperated sigh echoed around me. Suddenly my mother began to materialize before my eyes.

"Mom?" I squeaked.

"Correction, me. Your mom is at your death scene, crying. This is me --"

"You possessed her?!!?!" I screeched, cutting the voice off.

"Please hear me through," Gad said patiently. "Here we like to call it imagery -- basically a mirror image. You can see and hear her, but she's not actually in the room or anywhere near the room for that matter."

I looked at the sobbing form of my mother...

"Mom..." I whispered. I jumped up and put my arms around her, only to find there was nothing to put my arms around.

"I never said you could feel her," Gad reminded.

I stepped back and stared at my mom. She leaned forward to smooth something out. Instantly I felt a loose strand of my mousy brown hair being pushed gently away from my face and behind my ear. She smiled sadly. I felt a sudden urge to throw my arms around her whether she was there or not. I just wanted to cry alongside with her. And so I did.

"Mom!" I sobbed, "It was all my fault! I didn't want to make you feel bad! But you looked so sad... You were always so sad... I felt I was the source of your sadness! And I didn't want you to be sad... I wanted you to be happy... So I left..." I trailed off. For a few seconds I forgot Mom wasn't there, that she hadn't heard a word. But I felt better. I felt like she was listening.

"...So you're the regrettable sort, eh?" Gad concluded.

"I'm not regrettable! I don't regret dying!" I retorted. But I stopped.

"...OK, so maybe I do regret it... but not really! I mean... I just wish... I wish my mom knew I was sorry. I never got to say good-bye..."

"Do you really think death separated you from your mother?" Gad asked. "Remember how you felt your hair pushed aside, yet your mother was on earth? And just now... your little breakdown (I hope you didn't stain the carpet -- it's new), it was probably strong enough emotionally to connect with her."

I stared, utterly confused at the chair (assuming that's where Gad was).

"OK," Gad started again, "It's like this... When strong emotions are involved in imagery, the feelings and energy are transported. Your mom may not have heard your speech word for word, but she got a sense of it," I thought this concept through.

"Now I can't have you cluttering up my office, there's been a high death toll in the last minute and that means lots of souls to conference," Gad said.

A door I hadn't remembered being there before opened.

"Take the side door; it'll get you there faster."

"Get me where?" I asked suspiciously.

"Your destination," Gad replied matter-of-factly.

"Oh, YOU'RE a great help..." I muttered, turning to face the open door.

"Thank you, I do my best."

"Sure... So where exactly is this 'destination' of mine?" I asked, starting out into the dark oblivion just past the doorway (and not too keen on going in).

"Just follow the light at the end of the tunnel."

Anna Zabaglio
Age: 13

THE WHALE SONG

On a windy day in late October I sat on the front porch and watched my younger sister, Celeste, play with the dog in the front yard. I had just finished raking leaves for them to jump in. Celeste was the sweetest girl, never hurt a fly. She was ten years old but had the mind of a four-year-old. She still carried around with her a stuffed mouse that she had gotten when she was born, and never left the house without it. When Celeste was born Dr. Randolph had told me and my family that she was Down's syndrome and would never be able to function completely on her own. Dad hated it when she pestered him or threw a temper tantrum. She was his excuse for going out all of the time. But Celeste and me, we stuck together, in a way she looked out for me and I looked out for her. She always made me laugh with the silly faces she could make. I used to take her out a lot, Mommy didn't like going in public with her, she said that when Celeste had fits it was too embarrassing. Mom was normally great to both of us around the house but I guess you could have called her high-maintenance, always going to get her nails or hair done, and talking about stocks to her friends on the cell phone.

I remember everything about those years, the smell of the air, every family event. The way that Celeste hugged me every night before bed and every morning before school. We always loved to go to the aquarium. I had a seat on the back of my bike and we could ride there in about ten minutes. Celeste made me take her every weekend without fail, rain or shine, we were there, and I didn't mind at all. As soon as we got through the entrance Celeste would run to one of the security guards, Jacob, if he was on duty, and give him a huge bear hug.

He'd say, "There's my girl," and then give a low belly chuckle.

Afterwards he would walk us back to the whale viewing area. It was her favorite place, she could lean over the edge and Splash, the beluga whale, would perform for her. We were the aquarium's best and maybe even favorite customers so on days when not many people visited, Jacob would talk to the whale trainers and we would be permitted to put on wet suits and stand on one of the rocks so that Splash and the others would come up and clap their fins at us. We always had to watch out for Celeste, she couldn't swim, but she would laugh and laugh when the whales would get her wet. Her mouse of course went with her and over the years it even acquired a mini wet suit. She loved to hear the beautiful music the whales could make underwater. It always calmed her down.

Then one night, when Dad came home he was madder than normal. Celeste was scared that he would yell at her so she always ran and hid in my closet, this made him furious, especially when he had just been out drinking. He slammed the door behind him when he came in. We were eating supper. I grabbed Celeste's arm before she could get up and hide. If I could rewind time and do everything over again, I never would have stopped her from leaving. She threw up her arms and started screaming, wailing her body around as if she was a palm tree during a hurricane. Then she took her fist and slammed the water glass that was on the table to the floor. Daddy raised his finger and began to yell at her, I screamed back that she doesn't know any better.

"Alex, go to your room," was all he said to me.

I obeyed, not wanting to cause any more trouble, so I'm not completely sure what happened next. That night everything was normal, we ate our nighttime snack and brushed our teeth. Mommy locked up and we said our prayers and fell asleep. Everything was normal that is, except Celeste.

When I woke up the next morning there was a calm, dead feeling in the air. I couldn't put my finger on it but something wasn't right. After a bowl of Frosted Flakes I packed up my backpack for school. Mondays were always the hardest for me to snap out of my sleep. I yelled up the stairs for Celeste to come down. Mom, from her room next to the staircase shushed me and told me to walk up there and get her. I walked up the stairs and when she hadn't met me on my journey up, my heart started racing. Normally she would have galloped towards me with a silly grin on her face. As I inched towards her room and looked in my heart stopped. Celeste wasn't in there. I tried to wake Mommy and she swatted me away.

Finally I screamed, "Celeste is gone."

We searched everywhere around the house and yard and my eyes began to water, I don't cry. But then an idea popped into my mind. I raced to get on my bike; Mom stopped me in her car before I reached the end of our long winding driveway. I jumped in and directed her to the aquarium parking lot. As we got there I began to bawl. There were three ambulances, two fire trucks and a police car sitting out front with their lights flashing. Through my blurred vision I saw someone being carried out on a stretcher, my radiant sister.

November 7th, 1987 my life ended. Celeste was my life. Today, eight years later, as I watch the security camera tape I know that this was my fault. She is in a wonderful place now, living with whales, swimming probably. She led a beautiful life. On camera she had never looked happier. Splash came up to the surface and clapped. She squealed with delight. For no more than five minutes Celeste disappears from camera and then shows up on the rock, wearing a wet suit. I close my eyes knowing what comes next. Her whole life Celeste had wanted to swim with the whales, they unlike man, unconditionally accepted her. Then came the splash and I cringe to myself. She stayed afloat and held onto Splash for all of two minutes until the screaming began, and ended. If I had only been there one hour earlier, or not grabbed her arm that night at dinner, she might still be hugging Jacob and visiting the whales. She might still be playing in the yard or stumbling around with her mouse. If only. At least she heard the whales sing for one last time.

I hit the stop button on my VCR and swallowed the lump in my throat. It was the first time since I moved into my new apartment that I had watched that horrible occurrence. There was a knock at my door. I got up to answer it. Jacob gave me a large grin. We hugged for what seemed like hours. Jacob was old enough to be my grandpa and his wrinkles felt soft on my face. I invited him in and out of a brown paper bag he pulled out Qubie, Celeste's mouse. I began to cry again and I hugged it close to me. I asked him where he had got it. On the day when the world stopped spinning, he told me Celeste had suited him up and they had gone out together to the rock. Celeste had left him on the edge while she leaned over. Jacob had kept it all these years, unsure of what to do with it. He informed me that he had just stopped in to give Qubie to me, and he had to be going. As Jacob got up to leave I thanked him. His exact words filled me with the greatest kind of happiness.

"No Alex, thank you, Celeste made my life complete."

"Me too," I said, "me too."

Rinnie Modzelewski

4 X 4 ADVENTURE

Cody M. Wade and I were driving our trucks. Cody M. was driving a Ford F250 so was Wade. I was driving a Ford F350 Superduty extended cab. They were all four-wheel drive. We were driving in the woods until we came to a river and saw Austin.

I yelled, "Hey Austin, whatcha doin'?"

"Nothing."

"Do you want to ride in the woods with us?"

"Sure."

"Then come on over, we'll meet you at the bridge about five minutes down the trail, OK?"

Cody M., Wade and I hit it to the floor until we got to the bridge, so did Austin. Austin came across the bridge.

I said, "Let's go."

We started up our engines and drove around until dark. Then we made camp. We ate hot dogs and drank Coca-Cola. In the morning we went home and went to bed and slept the rest of the day.

Matt Hughes
Age: 10

MY CONCLUSIONS FOR DOGS

Introduction

Hi! My name is Amy! I solve mysteries about dogs. In this book dogs can talk. But they use their own language. It's like a secret code with your best friend only it's not. Characters in this book cannot understand dogs. Some people want to know what dogs are saying to one another. Find out what happens in... My Conclusions For Dogs!

Chapter One: Finding Out

"Creepy," I said.

My class and I were on a field trip at a museum and I, Amy Barron, was standing right in front of a snake cage.

"Creepy," I said again.

"No it's not," said a voice behind me.

I turned around and saw Jeremy Stewert, the science nut. I quickly walked away to a much more interesting exhibit, the dogs from Africa. My dream job was to have something to do with dogs. I wasn't sure yet what I wanted to do but I knew it was going to be the best experience in a lifetime. I quickly pulled my thoughts in from la-la land. The class moved on to more exhibits. Finally it was time to be bused back to school. Right when we got back, it was time to go home because it was an all-day field trip. I ride the bus! I hate riding the bus because it's hot and stinky and everyone is loud!! Finally I got off and stepped into the fresh air and warm sunlight. I was lucky that it was Friday and I didn't have to go back on for a while. I opened the back door and walked in my house. I am the first one home. I finished my homework. Just then the phone rang. I picked up the phone and listened for a voice.

"Hello," I said.

"Hi, Amy. This is Myra."

Myra is my best friend.

"I have some news for you," said Myra.

"Okay, shoot," I said.

"The science nut, Jeremy Stewert, is doing a really cool... well... uh... investigation," Myra said. "If that's what you wanna call it."

"Well, what is it?" I asked, anxiously.

"It's about dogs and..."

"Awesome!" I said, before she could even finish.

"Slow down," Myra pleaded. "This is what he's doing. He met a man called Kisawayna (KiZ-A-wOn-A) at his church. Kisawayna thought Jeremy looked pretty smart."

"Yeah, right!" I argued.

"So, Kisawayna asked Jeremy to solve a problem," Myra continued. "He wants to know what dogs are saying when they bark."

"What?! He wants Jeremy to solve a problem? No way! I know tons more about dogs than Jeremy Nut does!" I disagreed into the phone.

"Be careful, Amy," Myra warned. "Jeremy also said that Kisawayna is a very powerful and rich man."

"Oh pooh!" I said. "I could beat The Nut any day!"

"You know what?" suggested Myra. "Let's try to solve the problem before The Nut!"

"Yeah!" I spoke.

"Let's get on it right away!" I said.

"Okay!" Myra agreed. "8:00 tomorrow at Sunbeam Drive."

"Sure!" I said excitedly. "8:00 tomorrow!"

Then we hung up. We were in for a very exciting adventure!

Chapter Two: Step One To The Solution

I woke up and stretched. It was Saturday. Suddenly I remembered! Time to solve the mystery! I quickly got up and got dressed. I ran down the stairs as fast as I ride my dirt bike. I opened the door and slammed it behind me. I raced down my driveway and turned onto Lacey Lane. I ran the whole way and turned onto Sunbeam Drive. When I got to the corner, Myra was already there. We did our secret handshake.

"What's up?" Myra asked. "Ready to solve the problem?"

"I am ready!" I said cheerfully. "Now where do we go?" I asked.

"I don't know," said Myra, puzzled.

"Let's think," I said.

So we sat down on the curb of Sunbeam Drive. Finally, a light bulb appeared!

"Maybe Ms. Terri knows something," I said. "We could go to her house and check it out."

"Okay," said Myra. She had agreed.

Ms. Terri lived on Lacey Lane, my street. Ms. Terri is a very smart lady. She'll surely know what to do, I thought. Ms. Terri has long, flowing auburn hair and soft eyes. She lives in what looks like a castle and wears tons of jewelry and awesome clothes. I am lucky she is my neighbor. I have two good neighbors. Ms. Terri lives on one side of Myra and me on the other. When we arrived, we rang the bell, which made a sweet and welcome little tune. Ms. Terri came to the door, bracelets rattling.

"Why hello girls. Come in. You're just in time for milk and cookies," Ms. Terri said kindly.

Chapter Three: A Good Idea From Ms. Terri... So We Think

We sat down at a little round table with three chairs. She placed china plates and cups in front of us. Then she put on a handmade mitt and pulled out a plateful of warm chocolate chip cookies from the oven. I gulped my milk and scarfed my cookies. I had gotten up so fast I didn't have time for breakfast, so I was starving.

Ms. Terri broke the silence. "So what did you gals come here for?"

"We came here for --" I stopped. I had just realized my mouth full of cookie. I swallowed. "We came here because we need to ask you some questions," I started again.

"Well, start asking and I'll try to give you the best answers I can," said Ms. Terri, ready for us to start talking. So I told her the same story Myra told me over the phone.

"Sounds like you don't even need to ask questions," she said.

"But there's another side," I said.

"We need help," said Myra and me together.

"With what?" she asked.

"There's more!" I grumbled. "We're trying to beat this other guy to it. And we need help on where to go to find some sort of answer for this," I declared.

"Well," said Ms. Terri. She was thinking. I could tell she had no idea. But I was wrong.

"I've got it!" Ms. Terri hollered as she snapped her fingers.

"What?!!!!" Myra and me screamed.

"You guys can go to Know-It-All Nina," she suggested. "Just tell her what you want to find out and she'll tell you. Her name is Nina Conceir."

"What a great idea," mumbled Myra sarcastically.

"Myra! That was rude! Do you have any better ideas?" I had just shut Myra out totally.

"Oh, OK!" Myra said grumpily. She had given in.

"Where is the location?" I asked Ms. Terri.

"Right on Wilford Circle," she said, as if we knew every location in the world.

"We'll be on our way then. Thanks for your time and the snack," I said kindly.

Myra said the same.

"Oh no! Anytime!" said Ms. Terri.

So Myra and I walked to Wilford Circle. There we saw it! A sign said:

Know-It-All-Nina...Open Every Day!

Myra and I walked in. We paid Nina Conceir 50¢ and sat down where she commanded us.

"Thank you, Ms. Conceir," I said politely.

"Call me Nina," Nina said. "What do you two gals need to know?"

"We need to know what dogs are saying when they bark or where to find it," were Myra's first words since Ms. Terri's.

Then our hearts sank after we heard what the so-called know-it-all had to say.

Chapter Four: No Good But Good

"I'm sorry you young gals, but I have no idea," said Ms. Conceir.

"Aw, c'mon!!!" I cried.

Nina said, "Now out. You're holding up the line!" she said, even though there was no line.

"We want our money back!" Myra fumed.

She gave us 60¢ back but was I complaining?

"Now where to?" I asked.

"I don't have a clue!" said Myra.

"Face it," I said, "we can't beat Jeremy Stewert. He's the best and everyone knows it."

"Yeah, I guess," said Myra, not wanting to give up.

Ring, Ring. It was my cell phone. It was Lindsey Mitchell, another girl from school.

"Amy?" Lindsey said.

"Yeah. Who is this?" I said

"It's Lindsey," she said.

"Oh, hi!" I said. "What's up?"

"You know how Jeremy Stewert is trying to figure out what dogs are saying when they bark?" she said.

"Yeah."

This was serious business.

"He's making it a contest for everyone," she said.

"We've been working on it all day and we can't find out a thing," I said.

"Well, it's in the school auditorium," Lindsey smirked.

"Okay. Me and Myra will be there." We hung up.

"Come on, Myra! I cried. "We're going to the school auditorium to see who wins the Conclusions for Dogs contest!!!"

Chapter Five: Who Will Win??

We ran all the way there.

When we got there, the host, Kisawayna, was saying, "And now Ms. Terri will step up to the mike to nominate Amy Barron and Myra Cole."

"Oh my!!!" we both screeched!!

We took our seats and waited for Ms. Terri's speech.

This is what she said: "I think Amy and Myra should win because they went place to place asking questions. Jeremy Stewert only uses Websites and the Internet. These girls worked very hard. They had joy and sadness while they were working on this. Amy and Myra used what they had. Jeremy Stewert just uses high-tech equipment. Even though they didn't find conclusions, Amy and Myra worked very hard. That's all. Thank you."

Myra and I just sat there with our mouths hanging open. A few other people went up and nominated for Jeremy and Lindsey. Finally it was award time.

"First place goes to...," cried Kisawayna.

Silence filled the room.

"Amy Barron and Myra Cole!!"

We were amazed!! We ran up and grabbed a big trophy. Second place was... Lindsey Mitchell!! Third was Jeremy Stewert!!! Myra and I just watched and smiled as Jeremy stomped up to get a tiny medal. Then out he ran. As I looked over, Ms. Terri winked at me. I smiled back. Well, it was good to know that we won. All in all, it was a great day!!

Gina Gaerke

Age: 10

Her stomach began to bubble and froth, upsetting her even more. Her legs were weak and trembling from the thoughts racing through her mind. Alyssa slouched over the cool porcelain sink, using all the strength in her arms to support her frail frame. She gazed into the mirror, not recognizing whom she saw. Her eyes were bloodshot, and her tears ran black from her heavy mascara. She bit her lower lip to control its violent shaking and abruptly turned her head away from the mirror. Alyssa looked down upon her once neatly groomed black nails that were now nothing but stubs, with small amounts of the nail polish still intact. Her forehead prickled from anticipation, and slowly she brought her eyes up to see what was in the mirror. Alyssa's pallid complexion gave her a ghostly appearance, a shade of her true self. Her fragile nerves broke at this sight, and she gasped for breath. She tried desperately to suck in oxygen like a vacuum, but it was no use. Her right hand slipped off of the sink, and the hall pass she was holding in it fluttered to the floor. Alyssa's legs gave way, and she crumbled to the floor. Her breathing steadied as she sat on the outdated green-tiled floor.

I just don't know what to do with myself anymore, Alyssa thought. Suddenly, she heard talking in the hallway. To hide from whomever was about to come through the door, Alyssa jumped up and fled to a stall and slammed the door shut, locking it afterwards. The door burst open, and two bubbly voices danced in the air.

"Like, oh my, Bethany, can you believe what Jessica wore to class pictures last week?"

Two loud clunks rang out through the bathroom as the girls sat something on the sink. Alyssa then heard two zips and some ruffling and assumed the girls were looking for makeup in their purses, a teenage girl's most important possession. The girls' strong perfumes invaded Alyssa's lungs to the point that she found it hard to breathe again.

"Oh, I totally know. There were so many things wrong with that outfit, it you could even call it that."

"You are so bad, Beth. And, I know, I was like 'Can you say skank?'"

"L.O.L., anyways, where did you get that color lipstick? I'm like totally in love with it!"

"Um, I don't really know yet..." the girl's voice drifted out of Alyssa's hearing range.

"Oh my goodness, did you steal it?"

"As if!" the girl replied emphatically, "I'm bad, but not that bad."

"Oh, OK then, whatever."

Alyssa heard two little clicks, and she immediately knew that Bethany and her friend were finished applying their makeup.

Bethany's sugary voice shattered the silence. "C'mon Liz, we got to get back to class."

Liz grunted in disagreement but followed her friend out of the room. Alyssa remained in the stall until the sound of the girls' heels clicking against the floor followed them out of the room and down the hall. Alyssa emerged from the stall, her spirits lowered due to her closeup encounter with "popular people." I'll never be like that, Alyssa reflected dejectedly, and I certainly will never be respected in the way that they are. I just; I just don't see any point in trying to live my life anymore. Memories surged in her mind, of times past when people didn't even see her because they chose not to and of times when even teachers took no notice of her being. I've never been a part of the "in crowd." I dress differently, talk differently, and think differently. I wasn't like other kids who dreamed of being an astronaut; I was always more interested in what bark was made of on a tree. The style of my life isn't in accordance with mainstream society's, and I guess I should be punished for that. It's not something I can change, so it must be ended. I can't go on living a life that's looked down upon, and I'm not about to live a life that isn't true to myself. The thoughts coming to Alyssa were like bubbles bursting on the surface of a hot stew.

Tears began to flow again at Alyssa's realization. She understood that the only solution to her problems was to take her life. Her body began to shake uncontrollably and again she looked to the sink to support her failing body. Her stomach felt like it dropped down below her knees, and she was now perspiring. She looked into the mirror again, as a final farewell to her earthly body. She balanced the weight of her body on her left hand, and with her right hand slowly reached into her jeans' pocket to pull out a scarf. She stood upright, her legs wobbly, and fashioned a noose out of the scarf. Alyssa started to wrap the noose around her neck when the girls' bathroom door exploded open and Mr. Hawkings rushed into the room.

"Alyssa! What are you doing? I've been looking all over for you! I gave you that hall pass twenty minutes ago!"

Alyssa found it hard to find words. "I, uh, but, um..."

"What's going on in here, and what is that on your neck?"

Mr. Hawkings' glaring eyes burned through her soul. It was the first time she ever felt uncomfortable in front of her art teacher.

"Mr. Hawkings, I can explain. I..."

"Oh Alyssa," his compassionate voice returned to him, "what were you thinking?"

"I-I," she started to cry again, "you wouldn't understand."

"Try me."

"I've never been cool or popular or anything. And I just don't fit in in this life. It's my only way out."

"Suicide is never a way out, Alyssa. Someone as bright as you should know that. You have a great life, and why would you want to be cool or popular? Those kinds of people don't have half as many skills as you do. You have a future ahead of yourself brighter than anyone else at this school. Look at your life through someone else's eyes."

His love-filled words registered in Alyssa's head. She knew that by the way he spoke that everything he said was true.

"Mr. Hawkings, I, I, don't know what to say. You, you saved my life."

Alyssa's streaming tears were no longer because of her pain, but because of her happiness. She ran to him and hugged him as if he was her father.

"Oh Alyssa. What could have made you do something like this? I'm extremely happy I came in when I did, but what if I hadn't? I'm afraid we're going to have to contact your parents and inform them of this and get you some psychiatric help."

"Anything Mr. Hawkings, anything. I don't ever want to consider this again because I am definitely not ready to leave this world yet!"

Justin Temple

ISABEL AND JACK

Once upon a time, in a faraway land, lived a princess named Isabel. Isabel, a ten-year-old, is a beautiful young princess who is loved very much by her parents. Yet there is one problem, Isabel is only ten and her parents treat her like she is fifteen, they expect a lot out of her.

One day Isabel is tired of it but she does not know how to tell her parents how she feels. So she goes to her enchanted bedroom and prays, "Oh fairy godmother, please help me get the courage to tell my parents how I feel."

This goes on for a couple weeks and still nothing happens, when one day she says, "I will not ask any more if you help me." Then suddenly in pops a glowing boy.

"Who are you?" Isabel asked stunned.

"Well I am the answer to your prayers, Isabel, I am here to help!"

"But, but, you're a boy, fairy godparents are supposed to be girls."

"Well not anymore!"

Isabel is flabbergasted to see a boy who claims to be her fairy godfather standing in her room, yet deep down she is relieved to finally be heard. Suddenly there is a knock on the door and the sweet voice of Isabel's mother is speaking.

"Honey, who are you talking to?"

"Um, uh, no one mother."

Then she hides him in her wardrobe and goes to eat brunch in the garden. When she gets back she finds that his name is Jack. She then asks him to help her tell her mother and father how she feels.

So Jack gives her some advice and it still took her like two weeks to tell them but all this time Jack and Isabel are growing into a relationship.

Finally Isabel gets courage to tell her feelings to her parents. They understand so Jack had to leave, but it all worked out. She is now thought of as a ten-year-old!

Kristin Drees
Age: 13

HANDS

"It is so unbearably hot in here!" I mumbled as the back of my hand wiped the dripping sweat from my forehead. I no longer felt the bliss or excitement of Christmas as I did when I was younger, and my holly jolly spirit -- which I've managed to keep year-round for quite a long while -- had been swept out with the ashes of last night's hearth fire. My patience, as well as my freshest coat of paint, was running thin, and I told myself that if I don't get out of this box soon I'd --

All my worries were abolished when the top of the box was viciously torn apart, and I was hurled against one side of the cardboard walls. The box was dumped upside down, and I came tumbling out engulfed in a sea of tissue paper. Two eager hands grasped me by my neck, and I choked on what was surely my last breath. However, an older pair of hands, wizened with age spots and wrinkles, came to my rescue. The small fingers were reluctantly pried loose, and I was free to breathe once more. I caught a glimpse of the face that belonged to those saving hands, and an eye winked at me. This pair of hands knew me, and for some reason I believed I recognized them also...

"Oh boy! Thanks Grandpa! This is the best Christmas present ever!" What I now gathered to be a little boy squealed. He then proceeded to whiz me around the brightly decorated room, making foreign whirring noises as he hopped up and down to the beat of "The Bumbling Wooden Soldier," which was humming faintly from the radio. I could feel the joy radiating from his fingertips, and an old feeling of content flooded back to me.

The old hands chuckled, "Now, now, Colin. He's not an airplane! Calm down before you knock his head up against the wall!"

The young hands relaxed their hold on me, and I was set upon a brick-laden fireplace. I was submerged to searing heat, and felt like I was trapped in the box for a second time until the ancient hands swiped me out of the reach of the high temperatures of a family fire. I was now in the gentle care of the old hands.

The same eyes I could not help but thinking I had seen before were staring down at me. I could not read the emotions written in his face, but his learned fingers were enough of a book for me. The tender touch of the rough hands told me that a respect of the highest degree was felt toward me, and that he knew how old and brittle I was. The way he cradled me in the palm of his large hand alleged that he had had experience handling those like me before and was returning to memories of the past. However, there was also a hint of reluctance in his touch. It was as if he yearned to hold me and play, but, at the same time, knew that I wasn't his. With a final dust-busting sweep of my wooden cap, the pair of old hands found me a home on an end table next to a cushiony sofa.

"For now," he murmured.

My painted eyes followed him back to his position in the rocking chair next to a tree that soared up to brush the ceiling, and then rested upon the next gift the little child was opening.

The impatient hands of the young boy shredded the colorful wrapping of the next box, and I noticed his plump fingers trembling with excitement. Grasped by the hands of a child spellbound by the Christmas season, a new toy emerged from the depths of the mysterious package.

"Oh boy! Thanks! This is the best Christmas present ever!"

I chuckled softly, and was, for the meantime, forgotten in the boy's newfound enthusiasm.

***

Hours later, when the young hands full of candy canes and cookies were finished making trips up to his gaping mouth, the old hands came and scooped up the child. The aged hands made a journey up the stairs, his arms full of little boy.

"I'll be back," he whispered.

And he was.

When all the paper scraps had been cleaned up and gone, and the only sources of light were the illuminated bulbs on the Christmas tree and the glowing embers resting peacefully in the grate of the fireplace, the old hands stood before me. A smile that crept across his face also spread to his hands, and ten fingers opened up to reveal palms that told endless stories.

"Let's go upstairs, son. Colin will want to see you tomorrow, I reckon."

The hands told me. I now recognized him. Lifting me up off the table, I stared at the hands of my beloved Glenny -- my very first master who guided me through the first six years of my life. Looking down at my own hands, I realized how crudely carved my fingers were, and how more than a few were chipped and cracking. How could he still love me, even when I am almost to the point where any other owner would toss me out with the leftover turkey and uneaten apple pie crusts? Shifting back to Glenny's precious hands, I answered my own question. Though the hands were now shriveled and the skin was papery with the presence of old age, I still adored that stroke, and will always adore that boy. For in my eyes he will never grow old, and I suppose that in his eyes I never will either.

Upstairs, Glenny switched on a light that revealed a room containing a massive collection of teddy bears, soldiers, and nutcrackers. A small bed sat in the center of the room, and beneath layers of blankets and quilts the outline of a little boy squirmed with the piercing light. He drew a quilt over his tender eyes, and disappeared amidst the mounds of cloth, returning to his undisturbed dreams of Santa Claus. Glenny's hands smiled softly, and I was placed on a shelf next to a rather attractive lady teddy bear. My cherry red lips drew up into a grin, and the bear's furry face flushed. Glenny's face was now smiling as well, and he left the light on for a moment longer.

I glanced at the teddy bear's hands, and she looked at mine. My face, like hers, turned crimson with embarrassment, for the obvious imperfections were sure to send her away. However, she took one of my hands in her fuzzy paws and said, "These are the most beautiful hands I've ever seen. All of the other toys who come in here are shiny and new and have never been loved before. Their coats of paint are still fresh, and, despite their wooden bodies, their hearts are still made of stone. You though, in all your simplicity, come in here with a lifetime of cherished memories, and put all of these others to shame. I love your hands."

I was astonished as she pulled out one of her own paws and showed me. Patches of fur were missing, and the claws were disfigured or long gone. To any other toy, these hands would have been revolting, but to me they were signs of the love and affection that fills her past. I smiled, and so did Glenny's hands as he switched off the light.

"Good night, little wooden soldier." He spoke softly, reliving an old dream. "The hands are the true tale of love," he added, gazing down at his own crinkled hands.

He turned and marched out of the room as he used to do when he was young like his grandson, gently humming the melody of "The Bumbling Wooden Soldier."

Leah Todd
Age: 14

THE LOST DOGS

One day I was sitting looking for my dog named Sam Godenschwager in the woods. I was looking in the woods because that is where he ran away trying to chase the deer and I could not keep up with him. I have not seen him for one year.

My dad said, "That dog could not be alive."

But I did not care what people said so I kept looking for him. I get money when I find other dogs because their owners will buy their dogs off of me.

One foggy morning I heard a dog bark and it was brown and white.

I said, "Sam," and he came to me and I was so happy. Every day me and my dog Sam go into the woods exploring for more lost dogs. We give them to their owners, free sometimes, if they are nice.

We found a puppy Jack Russell and I named him Jake Godenschwager. Now I have two dogs to go looking for other lost dogs. That's my job.

Mason Godenschwager
Age: 10

FORGETTING PAIN

Keep it up, after all it's only been about twenty minutes! Her mind said to her but the pain throughout her body told an entirely different story.

How can you be tired from playing the violin? You've never done this before. If Armand were here -- She didn't finish the thought due to a sudden surge of tears.

She was crying because Armand was gone.

Placing the violin inside its case, atop an unmarked envelope, she then fell upon her bed and sobbed fervently. Armand had been gone for a week now, and she was yet to recover from the loss.

Over the last three years, he had been her violin instructor. They became friends almost instantly. However, while she didn't know it, he had been sick the whole time.

There was a soft knock at the door.

"Are you all right chére?" asked Madame Mercier, from the hallway.

She answered yes, and hoped there would be no further questions from Madame. That might be too much for poor Lucie's nerves.

That's the trouble with boarding schools, she thought, there's no one here to help you with your problems.

Not everyone had been as sympathetic as Madame was. Due to the loss of her instructor, she had been forced to take lessons with a group of students.

While she was ahead of the other five students (two boys and three girls) her sorrows had obviously affected her performance.

After class one day, she heard two of the girls saying malicious things about her behind her back. Their words hurt, but not as much as the death of Armand.

He didn't tell her about his illness until the day that he nearly fainted in class. Then he explained everything to her. However it wasn't until he used the words "terminally ill" that she understood the magnitude of what he was saying. Armand wasn't going to get any better, ever.

That was six months ago. From that time Armand's condition increasingly worsened until her lessons had to be moved to the parlor at Armand's house, because he was too weak to be out of bed for extended periods of time or leave home.

Lucie knew he wouldn't let his health put an end to her lessons.

On the day of her last lesson, she was, for the first time, aware of his suffering. She asked him why he kept up with lessons, since he was so very sick.

"The most important lesson I've ever learned is that, no matter what is happening in your life, you have to be able to put aside your problems to receive the full benefit of doing the things you love. If you can't forget your pain even if it's just for a moment in time," Armand had told her.

She then told her fears, and he comforted her. She told him how she felt that he didn't deserve to die. She said that at twenty-five he should have life to look forward to.

He explained to her that he had lived ten years longer than any doctor said he would, and that despite knowing that at any point in time his life could come to an end, the last ten years had been the best ever.

"You can't live in fear of death for when that time comes, you'll find that you've never really lived at all," he said to her, as she prepared to leave.

Armand died that night. She was informed just minutes after he left this earth. Even with six months of preparation for the event, Lucie found that she wasn't at all prepared to say good-bye to her friend.

When her thoughts finally managed to wander back to the present, the present with Armand gone and life seeming absolutely, she happened to glance at the calendar. It was Saturday, April third, Tuesday, April sixth was the day of the spring concert that she was supposed to perform at.

On Monday, Madame informed her that if she didn't feel up to performing the next day, everyone would understand. Lucie told her that she would be at the performance the next day ready for her solo.

She stayed up late that night practicing with very little success. She didn't stop practicing for breakfast or lunch on Tuesday morning. After hours of endless practice with no progress, she finally sat down.

Maybe you can't do this, she thought. Perhaps you're talentless without Armand.

Then she heard Armand's voice again.

"We have to forget our pain and troubles even if it's just for a moment in time." She could almost hear him say this to her again.

Her gaze shifted to the manila envelope sitting inside her violin case. She decided to open it and see what it was.

A paper fluttered out of the envelope and onto the floor as she opened it. When she picked it up, off the floor, she noticed that it was written in Armand's handwriting and addressed to her

> Dear Lucie,
>   I want you to know that, while it might not have seemed like it, I have been very afraid and at times even angry because I did not want to die. However, we cannot control when we have to leave this earth. Cancer is a scary thing.
>   Recently I wrote a piece of music for violin. It's the last thing I'll ever compose. I'd like you to have it.
>   Best Wishes,
>   Armand

After reading this, Lucie knew what to do. She looked at the clock. It read six forty-five. She only had fifteen minutes to get to the concert.

Quickly she dressed for the concert and grabbed her violin and rushed out of the building with her.

Once she reached the performance hall she stopped only to open the door. As soon as she got inside, she headed backstage.

Backstage was filled with pandemonium and chaos. Children of all ages were searching for their music or making last-minute costume repairs.

"Lucie, you're on in two minutes," Madame said after noting her arrival.

Lucie whispered her idea to Madame, and, after gaining her approval, it was time for her solo.

After her name and grade had been announced, Lucie went up to the microphone.

"Most of you are probably unaware of the death of my violin teacher, but he passed away last week. Before he died, he composed a piece of music. That is what I am going to play for you tonight."

Then she started her solo. She started out strong and played flawlessly throughout the piece. The notes became emotions, thoughts, hopes, and fears. For a moment in time everyone forgot their problems, and hung on every note like it was the only thing they ever cared about.

She received a standing ovation, and for a moment she thought she saw Armand in the crowd, standing in amongst the crowd, standing and cheering for her.

When she got backstage she found her parents (who couldn't come for other reasons), had sent her a dozen red roses.

I'll have to make a detour on my way home she thought, so I can share these with a friend.

Victoria Dickman
Age: 15

ALREADY A HERO

The air was crisp, and the moon shone brightly on that tragic Monday night. A small, young boy stood impatiently on the sidewalk next to Wallace Street. He tightly held onto the tattered leash that was attached to his dog, while he waited for his mother. She had run back inside their small town house, adjacent to the sidewalk, to retrieve the new leash she had bought earlier that day. The boy, tired and in a groggy daze, gradually loosened his grip on the large dog's leash. He felt like he had been waiting for his mother for such a long time. Suddenly, an old orange tabby cat darted through the alley across the street. Usually, the boy's old dog doesn't bother the stray cats, but since he hadn't gotten to go for his walk yet, he was quite eager. Unexpectedly, the golden retriever perked his old ears, and jerked away from the boy. The abrupt movement pulled the little boy's attention back to the dog, but he wasn't quick enough to seize the free end of the leash. The dog darted to the street in attempt to chase the cat. As the dog proceeded into the street, the young boy rushed after him, yelling, "Goldie! Stop! Come back!"

The blasts of a shrill car horn and the screeching of tires drowned out the boy's last calls. The image of the blinding beams of the Honda Civic's headlights was a sight that would be imprinted in the young boy's mind forever...

The sun was shining bright, and the warmth from the sunlight made Bakersfield, California seem like such a beautiful place. The gentle breezes made the day feel like paradise to Laura. She would have never thought it was a Monday morning. In her mind, Mondays are usually boring and dull. While Laura was tying her jogging shoes, she realized that this was the first Monday she's been off work for a long time. Her job is just so time consuming, she really can't afford to have a day off. She's always just thought, When you're a doctor, and people's lives are depending on you, you can never have a day off. Now that she did finally have a free day though, Laura decided she could use the break. Things have just been too busy.

With the sun shining and the birds singing, Laura thought an early jog would be the best way to start the day. After she finished tying her shoes, she pulled her medium-length, dark hair back into a ponytail. She looked in the full-length mirror facing her. Inspecting her reflection, Laura looked into her hazel eyes and thought about her life. It had been a long time since she last jogged. She missed it. Laura knew there were rewarding aspects of being a doctor, but sometimes the busy life could just be a bit overwhelming. She pushed aside her thoughts, and left her apartment.

Finally, she was off, and the fresh air felt great. She jogged past lots of people she hadn't seen in a long time, but kept going. After a while, Laura realized she was only a couple blocks away from Maple Elementary School, the school that her sister, Jaime, taught at. Deciding she could use a break, Laura headed towards the school. As she neared, she saw her sister's kindergarten class outside, just as she had expected. Walking up to her younger sister, she saw that Jaime was busy talking to a student.

"...But Miss Hanes, do I have to play on the playground? I kinda wanted to just sit by you and color in my book," Laura heard the little boy say.

"Ethan, it's great that you want to keep me company, but don't you want to play with some of your friends? This is the only recess you get today," Jaime responded, in her patient voice that made kids feel like they were the most important person on earth. Ethan looked like he had to think about his decision. He glanced around and looked up at Laura.

"Oh, who are you? he asked with curiosity in his voice.

"Me?" Laura asked, a little startled. "Oh, I'm Miss Hanes's sister. My name is Laura."

"Yep, Ethan. This is my big sister. Do you know what? She's a doctor," Jaime said excitedly.

"Really?" the little boy squeaked out, his big blue eyes lighting up. "I want to be a doctor when I grow up. I want to save people's lives."

"Aww... that's neat," Laura stated, feeling somewhat honored.

"Uh huh. I want to be a hero," Ethan said, pausing. "Well, I guess I'll let you talk to Miss Hanes then. It was nice to meet you. I hope I see you again sometime." Ethan smiled and started to walk away.

"Aww... he's a sweet kid. He seems so polite," Laura said.

"Oh yeah," Jaime replied. "Ethan is one of my best students. He works so hard, and he's such a cute boy."

Suddenly, Ethan ran up to the two women in their low twenties. "I almost forgot. This is for you," Ethan said, quite out of breath.

He handed a picture to Jaime and blushed. She and Laura looked at the picture. It had a big heart with stick people in the middle. Above the heart, were the words, "People I Love." There was a man and a woman, labeled "Mom" and "Dad." In the middle was a small figure, with the word "Me" underneath. The stick boy was holding a leash connected to a big yellow smear. On the other side of what was supposed to be a dog, was a stick figure with blonde hair, a big red smile, and a heart on her chest. Underneath this figure were the scribbled words, Miss Hanes. Seeing this just about melted Jaime's heart.

She looked down at Ethan, and said a meek, "Thank you."

Ethan looked up with his eyes sparkling, wearing the biggest smile possible. He turned and walked away.

Jaime looked at Laura and blushed. "Ethan's so loving. He always brightens my day. I love that kid." Jaime paused, and then continued, "So, what do you need?"

Laura, still in awe from the young boy's actions, replied, "Oh, well, I was just going for a jog and thought I'd stop by. I should probably get going, though."

"Okay. Well, maybe I'll see you later on tonight at Mom and Dad's for supper."

"Bye," Laura responded, then turned to leave.

For the rest of the day, she did some odds and ends chores around her apartment. She took a nap and read some of her book. Later on, she went over to her parents' house for a late supper. In the middle of the peaceful dinner with her parents and Jaime, Laura's pager buzzed.

She left the room, and as soon as she saw the word EMERGENCY, her heart quickened. This day had been so relaxing for Laura. She briefly explained the situation to her family and left for the hospital. When she arrived, she immediately found out that there had been an accident involving a little child.

Dr. Ross ran up to Laura and explained the accident. "Apparently, the young boy ran out in the street, chasing his dog, and was struck by an oncoming car. Luckily, the dog was large enough for the car to see it ahead of time, so it had slowed down tremendously before hitting the boy. He's experienced head injuries and is presently in a coma. He's in Room 8A."

Dr. Ross walked away, leaving Laura to absorb the information. She spoke to a few more doctors, before heading towards the room.

As she walked into the room, numerous doctors surrounded the patient's bed. After observing the machines and examining the charts, some doctors cleared out enough, so that Laura could see the injured boy. She got a glance of medium brown hair, and as soon as she saw the little, scratched face, a sick feeling struck her stomach. The little face was unconscious, and no longer smiling. His bright blue eyes, sparkling with happiness, could not be seen. This was definitely not what he meant by hoping to see her again sometime.

Laura asked if she could be excused and immediately called Jaime. "Jaime, something really bad happened. I think you should come up here. Ethan's been hit by a car."

After a long and suspenseful night, there were finally some results. At 8:00 a.m., Laura uneasily explained Ethan's conditions to his parents. "Ethan has experienced some head injuries. He has a severe concussion from the impact, and as for right now, he's in a coma. He's lucky he's alive, and full recovery is expected, but it might take him awhile to pull out of it. Consequently, he will be here for a while. Dr. Ross will be out in about an hour with more detail. In the meantime, you might as well go get some coffee or get some sleep, because you won't be able to see him for a while. I'm sorry."

After a long, hard night, Laura went home to try to get some sleep, but said she'd be back that night, to stay with Ethan. She figured it'd be best for her to be the doctor to stay overnight with him, just in case he would come out of the coma and be scared.

That night, she returned to the hospital to find out that Ethan was still in the coma, but in stable condition. During Laura's night stay, there was no sign of any action. Ethan's condition continued to stay the same for several days, which was very hard on his family.

Each night, Laura stayed with Ethan and sat by his bedside. She'd look at him and sometimes even talk to him. She'd say how he was such a good boy and that he had to get better. Laura told him things about being a doctor, and said he'd be a great doctor, and that he would be good with his patients. She also talked to him about saving people's lives and said someday, he'll be a hero. Laura thought if he could hear her, maybe this would motivate him, or help him get better faster. After many long talks, she started to feel discouraged and sad. She wanted Ethan to pull out of the coma so bad.

On the eighth night after Ethan's accident, Laura was telling him a bedtime story about a prince that was trying to get home and he broke his foot. She explained that the prince's foot needed to get better so that he could go home. As she finished the story by saying that someone came along to help the prince, a little voice croaked, "You could fix his foot."

Laura stopped what she was saying, and even temporarily stopped breathing. She thought she had heard something, but reassured herself it was her imagination. She spun around to look at the little boy.

"Did you hear my Laura? I think you could fix the prince's foot."

Laura started crying and laughing at the same time. She couldn't believe it. Ethan came out of the coma!

A little voice interrupted her thoughts again. "Are you okay, Laura? Why are you crying?"

"Oh, Ethan! You're going to be okay. We've all been so worried. You've been in a coma and..." Laura rambled on.

"I know."

"You know?" she asked, confused.

"Yes, I know," answered Ethan in a calm, soothing voice. "Alyssa told me. I got hit by a car and had to go to the hospital. I was asleep for a long, long time; the longest nap I've ever taken. And it made everyone sad..."

"Who's Alyssa?" Laura question, still confused, but amazed by the young boy's understanding.

"Oh, she was the doctor that took care of me. She said she would take care of me until I got better. It made me sad to see everyone cry, but Alyssa said that it was okay, because I would come back and be with them soon." Laura stood next to Ethan's bed, in shock. She was utterly amazed. "Please don't cry Laura. I like you, and I don't want to see you cry."

She suddenly realized the tears that were streaming down her face.

"Oh yeah, I almost forgot," Ethan said. "I have to tell you something really important." Ethan lowered his voice. "Something bad is going to happen tomorrow. There's going to be a big fire. Alyssa showed me. She said that lots of people are going to Heaven tomorrow afternoon. Lots of kids are going to lose their daddies, and I don't want that to happen. Nobody should lose his daddy or mommy. If you go and stop the fire, you will save them. It starts in..." Ethan started to fade asleep. "It starts in the boiler room of a factory... the Cooper Tires Factory. You will be a hero..." Ethan faded off to sleep.

Laura, excited but still somewhat confused, informed the other doctors and Ethan's parents of his recovery. The next day, she uncomfortably went to the Cooper Tires Factory and spoke to the manager. She told him that he should have his boiler room checked, that a fire could start at any time. Reluctantly, the manager called the fire department and just as they were arriving, a spark came to life. The small fire was extinguished before it could grow any larger, and the factory was shut down until it could be checked for further fire hazards.

That night, Laura went to talk to Ethan, to tell him about the factory. He seemed so pleased that he helped. "Ethan, you really are a fantastic kid. You helped save many lives today. Once you become a doctor, you'll save even more lives."

He replied, "I want to be just like you. I want to be a hero."

Laura looked at Ethan and said, "Oh Ethan, you're already a hero."

Jessica Schroeder
Age16